SPINWARD FRINGE BROADCAST 10.5: CARNIE'S TALE

RANDOLPH LALONDE

THE SPINWARD FRINGE SERIES

(In chronological order)

The Chaos Core Series

Trapped

Cool Pursuit

Savage Stars

FANTASY

Highshield

Brightwill

NEM: Awakening

HORROR

Dark Arts

For more information please visit:

www.RandolphLalonde.com

Print ISBN: 9781988175140

EBook ISBN: 9781988175133

ACKNOWLEDGMENTS

This novel is a part of the Spinward Fringe series, and takes place between Spinward Fringe Broadcast 10: Freeground and Spinward Fringe Broadcast 11: Revenge. It was originally offered through http://www.patreon.com/randolphlalonde as a serialized story.

I owe thanks to everyone who supported me on Patreon, read along and offered their comments along the way. If it weren't for you, this book would only exist as a selection of chapters that were pulled from Spinward Fringe Broadcast 11: Revenge because they didn't fit in the timeline of that novel. Now we have a story about young people learning, growing and fighting in difficult times, a story I took great pleasure in telling.

I'd also like to thank Ray and Janet, who have provided important feedback and an ear for me to babble into while I was working on this. That kind of support is rare.

I hope everyone enjoys reading this as much as I enjoyed writing it.

PREFACE

Haven Fleet, a newly minted military force tasked with the defence of the Rega Gain system. Finding qualified people to man their ships, to carry their weapons and watch the stars isn't difficult, there are plenty of volunteers coming in from across the galaxy. The problem is getting thousands of people with different military training and service backgrounds to work the same way, operate under the same set of regulations, and work towards the same goals.

The Apex program was invented to train people who already excel in multiple fields or have extensive combat experience to become top officers in Haven Fleet. They are the next wave in leadership, the ones who will enable the expansion of Haven Shore so they can face the looming threat of the Order of Eden and more. Alice Valent is one of the chosen, and has already completed most of the academic and physical portions of her Apex training.

The largest project in her curriculum is the most complicated. Alice must review over a year of recordings detailing one young man's journey across a world changed by Haven Shore's enemies. While she reviews the material she will have to create a report that summarizes details of strategic importance, and comments on the character of the person who created the recordings.

Alice's trainers are watching. They need someone to report on the mountain of data they've given her, but more importantly they wanted to see how emotionally attached she becomes to the main subject.

PART ONE

One of the few classes everyone attended was Stellar Cartography. The lead instructor was Ensign Cariss, a short half-human who had a nose that strangely blended with his top lip and had vertical nostrils. What race he was cross-bred with wasn't public knowledge, nor was it available in the database.

Alice was only able to pay attention to the first forty minutes of his session that morning before she started nodding off. Iruuk was at her side, as always. He was a Nafalli, and a large one at about three metres tall depending on how he was standing. His long blonde fur was much like his fathers, but he had brown streaks mixed in here and there. There was no white on his long snout, and his blue eyes were the most expressive she'd ever known. Iruuk was the better student in classes, and he didn't hesitate to poke her as soon as her nose started pointing towards the floor. Alice faintly remembered the hours she spent in a former life tracking her father and running from Vindyne, then Regent Galactic. The lesson on tracking targets through hyperspace was so basic to her that she was ready to take the lesson over, but Ensign Cariss's class required that she complete ten hours of attendance even if you already passed the Certification Examination, which she had. This would be her last hour in his class.

Deciding it was worth the risk, she set her comm unit to start sending audio directly to her through a wire-thin tendril that stretched up her neck and into her ears from her vacsuit. The material for Alice's largest assignment was already cued up – she had to write a report on a large batch of recordings detailing a series of events experienced by a current member of the fleet. Who she was assigned to report on had to remain secret, and confidentiality had to be absolutely maintained. She was assigned to review a record from Noah Lucas, who was better known by his handle; Carnie. He was currently serving in Samurai Squadron, which flew off the Revenge, her father's ship. There was a lot of material to cover, so she was eager to get started.

"I had a clan once," he began with just enough sorrow for her to know that his clan didn't come to a good end. He was speaking as though it was late at night, and he only had one person in front of him. It was easy for her to picture herself sitting across from him at a small booth table in a darkened cafe when there was no one around. "My first family abandoned me on Yukon Station, Level Nineteen, Blue Section B.

They scrambled my DNA just enough so I couldn't use it to track back to them, but not so much that I'd be some kind of weird mutant. A guy named Niles picked me up, and he became my dad. He just lost his family two years before that in a refinery accident, and he'd been with Warren's Wonders for a year or so when he found me. Say what you want about that tribe of nomads, but there's no end of kindness. As soon as he was able to prove to our Ringmaster and owner, Robin Warren, a great woman with a huge voice and the biggest smile in the galaxy, that I wasn't kidnapped, and I would be put in the Yukon's slave auction if I was handed over to the authorities there, she gave Niles the go-ahead to take me on. I was about to have my first birthday when they left Yukon Station. Why am I starting at the beginning? I don't think I'll survive tomorrow, so I'm recording a little background on the best people I've ever known so whoever finds this can hear about 'em. I want you to know I was part of a good family before every bot in the galaxy tried to wipe humanity out."

Alice had no idea what Ensign Cariss was saying anymore, and had to stop the playback then check the class notes on her comm unit. Waiting for the class to end seemed to take forever. When it did, Iruuk would be headed to the practical mechanics lab, where he would train with the cadets on repairing a shuttle. Alice had already taken her Certification Exam and passed it with a ninety-eight, high enough for her to instruct the class, and she had assisted the instructor twice since. She felt restless though, and wanted to continue listening to Carnie tell his story, so she nudged Iruuk on their way out of the class. "I'm going to run the track for an hour, I have to work on this assignment."

Iruuk cocked his head for a moment then nodded, realizing that she was talking about the assignment no one could trade details on. "I'll see you at lunch."

"Definitely," Alice replied.

PART TWO

The track was a three hundred-metre long cargo hold, much like one of the larger internal holds inside the Triton. An old British Alliance patrol craft rested in the middle, a snub-nosed ship that was a hundred thirty metres long, eighty wide and thirty metres tall. The Cadets were using it as a training course that morning. The track ran along the outside of the large cargo space, and an obstacle course had been built near the middle, leading under the nose of the British Alliance ship. It didn't have the difficulty rating that the one on Tamber did, but she still ran it every once in a while with cadets.

There were at least two hundred cadets standing outside the main boarding ramp on the port side of the ship in white and grey armour turned their heads when she started running the track, which was only a broad blue stripe that had been painted in an oval along the outer edge of the cargo hold. They watched her run by, holding their practice rifles, standing ready to take their turn at combat exercises aboard the old ship. The Drill Instructors paid her no mind, she made daily appearances at both physical training centres. "It's Red Versus Blue today, Petty Officer," one of them said. "You're welcome to pick a side for a round."

"No thank you, Sergeant Polk," Alice replied as she stretched, smiling back at the tall woman. "Just running today."

"Are you sure you don't want to teach these grunts a thing or two? We'll give you a solo versus squad run." A few of the cadets grinned at the prospect, something Drill Instructor Polk caught right away. "Oh, you think you could take her?" she asked. "All right, when we're finished here, you're going to watch one of her Combat Qualifier tests. There's a reason why she's an Officer in fast track training and you're a bunch of entry class cadets."

Alice knew it wouldn't be the first time the cadets were shown footage from Officer testing. The Academy may not be in a permanent location, but the philosophies seemed solid to her. Cadets watched their future officer's more spectacular work so they could begin respecting them early.

It was still difficult for her to believe that she would be in command of any number of them. Their white and grey armour would be an entirely different colour as many of them traded their practice rifles for specializations on a starship. Some would be in black, armed and trained for boarding missions or planetary landings. Alice still didn't know what kind of command she'd get, and she tried to block it out of her mind as she started running and Noah Lucas' voice filled her ears again.

"I'll get back to the point so I can finish telling this story tonight, maybe get some sleep before dawn. Life with a travelling carnival was all I knew. I think it felt like a family because most of us tried to get along. The routine was pretty simple. Keep the menagerie happy and fed, try to stay out of the way while we were in transit, and then help set up when we arrived at the next show site. I wasn't in charge of the animals, but I got to feed them whenever we were between worlds, so that was my thing until I was a teenager. I even have my own Gelboo, short for Teldor Industries Gel Booster, a small synthetic crawler pet that records everything. Not the prettiest little thing, but he definitely helps me out every once in a while.

By the time I was ten I had seen more worlds than most people see in their entire lives, and met more alien races than you would believe. I was allowed to fly a shuttle for the first time when I turned eleven and I was hooked. By the time I was fourteen I had special shoes so I could operate the pedals on a Coronur Interceptor. At fifteen I was finally allowed to join our defence screen, a small squad of five fighters that protected our convoy whenever we were in space and moving slower than the speed of light. It was a dream job – and best of all – I didn't have to deal with stinky animal pens anymore. Keeping my fighter in shape was my full time job. The hangars were cramped, we didn't have launch systems, we dropped from airlocks instead, and parts were always in low supply, but I loved tinkering and flying. My first girlfriend, Sharon, called me Grease Monkey, and I have to admit the nickname used to bother me, but I miss it now. I miss her now.

Man, I had one year where things were good. Maybe some core world richie-rich might think my bunk, my fighter, my girlfriend and my family didn't add up to anything, but that was the best time. Even when we were set up and the fighters didn't have to be on patrol, I enjoyed my job. I minded one of our shooting booths and watched people test their skill against a bunch of moving metal plates and holographic surprises. Sure, boring, you say, but I met so many people from so many places, learned so much about how people used to live in this galaxy that I could go on for weeks. I loved it, I can't say it enough. We just never know how good we've got it until the good times end, do we?

I remember kissing Sharon before we came out of hyperspace, climbing through the airlock and into my ship. I sealed myself in, got my suit sealed, Lurk, my Gelboo mini-lizard, connected to my fighter's computer and started up some music. The Daring Dickenson, the ship I lived on, finished decelerating and my fighter popped free of the airlock. Okay, this is where I just drop a file from Lurk in so you can play back exactly what happened. I'll keep talking over this because, even though I used a crystalline storage chip, somehow the audio track got burned. Here goes, see you on the other side."

. . .

Alice stopped the recording as it warned her that the next segment of the video could be played back in full simulation mode. Instead of continuing her jog around the track, she passed through the interior door and ran back to her bunk, which still counted as twelve minutes of light exercise. Once she arrived, she dropped onto her bed, drew the privacy curtain closed and put her brain-bud, a small neural transmission device that provided a link for realistic simulations, onto her forehead. The journal started playing back the visual and audio content, and though she felt like she was there, watching from behind Noah Lucas' eyes.

PART THREE

My twin engine fighter creaked as the airlock let go and a small pocket of oxygen burst between the Daring Dickenson and my hull. That push got me far enough away from the DD's hull to hit the thrusters and fall in with the lead pilot, Reggie. He was a few years older than me, but he went to a real flight school, and taught me plenty already.

We pushed ahead of our convoy, six ships flying ahead of the DD, our biggest boat. Iora Navnet connected to all our systems and I expected to hear our lead Pilot aboard the Daring Dickenson's bridge start talking to Iora Port control. I'd been to Iora before, it was a planet with shipyards, trade so brisk and famous you could see anything you want and ten things you never knew existed before you finished checking in at any of the port offices.

The people were kind, they had everything they wanted

on that world, so they had time to be nice. They were even a little chubby, and I knew why. In the South Sea there are thousands of agricultural buildings standing tall like giant reeds in the biggest pond you've ever seen. They grew enough there for the three billion people on the planet and then some, trading millions of tons of food a week to places off world. If it weren't so expensive I would have put it on my list. That little list I kept of places I might settle down in some day, but it was brutally expensive there, and I heard citizenship took years to earn.

They liked us there. We offered some low-tech, high-amusement fun with our menagerie ship, old fashioned red and white temp building, a few acrobats and a lot of unfair games. We all dressed up, from the ticket takers to security. When I was a kid I had a squirrel costume, but I graduated to an old-time earth pilot outfit. The holographic projection of a lion's head over my own made it interesting, and I wonder how many holo-snaps kids took with me and the other flyboys and girls before it all came to an end.

So, back to Iora and the chatter I should have been hearing over Navnet channels. We were getting guidance, but no welcome from Port Control. I kept hearing Robin query; "Iora Port Control, come in. This is Robin Warren of Warren's Wonders Convoy, incoming, listed on your Navnet."

Something was up, whole sections of my Navnet screen was turning red with collision warnings then going green again. "Something's jamming the other channels," Reggie said. "Looks like the source is on the planet, that's not right. That can't be right."

My navigation screen warned that there were missiles incoming, and I couldn't believe it when Reggie said; "All ships, get clear of the Daring Dickenson, I repeat, get away from the DD, now."

I was a good pilot, even then, and followed orders, but I fired my guns at the incoming missiles while I got clear of the Daring Dickenson. My tactical computer reported hits on the lead one, but that didn't stop the largest ship in our little fleet from getting hammered. Nothing we had was really made for that kind of punishment, so our old ship split in a dozen places, blowing gasses and a few bodies into space. The second wave of missiles finished the ship off, I couldn't recognize what was left. "What the hell?" I heard Ussi ask as he rolled his fighter into the path of another rush of missiles. "Why are they killing us?" His gun wells spat fire at the incoming military firepower.

"Get out of there!" Reggie told him over coms.

I was frozen, the ships I'd known my entire life scattering away from the twisted corpse of the Daring Dickenson. I could only listen as Ussi replied. "Over my cracked hull, you fuckers!" he said a moment before a missile meant to destroy one of our smaller cargo ships hit him instead. There was a quick flash, and he was gone. I remember thinking how small that flash was, my world was getting ripped to pieces and all Ussi got was a small wink of light before he was gone. I can still remember him chasing me around carnival grounds, that man made it his business to keep us kids laughing while he was babysitting.

"Incoming interceptors, break and engage!" ordered Reggie.

The wedge of red blips on my old tactical screen confirmed what he was saying, and I took evasive action. The elongated silver ships passed closer than I expected, and I flipped my ship, came up firing, rounds punching at the shields of the nearest fighter.

They spin and returned fire at all of us with energy weapons so advanced that it's as if we don't have any shields. My port thruster gets hit and explodes, almost ripping right through my cockpit firewall and sending me spinning towards Iora. My computer goes down next and all I have to fight the spin are the old fashioned connections between my stick and my manoeuvring thrusters. It takes me so long to get control back that I think I sweat half my body weight worried that one of those silver interceptors will take a few seconds to finish me off. I get stable in time to see Reggie's ship get blown in half and a wave of fighters so large that I couldn't count them tear the rest of my family apart. Our ships, our homes were torn wide open, and I didn't even have working scanners so I couldn't tell if there were any survivors.

Lurk's lizard mouth opens and he croaks; "Warning," as he disconnects from the computer and climbs into my flight suit, sealing it behind him. I realize I'm about to enter the atmosphere whether I like it or not, so I take control. Tears blur my vision, but I can see my starboard engine is still running, I still have most of my manoeuvring thrusters, but all my electronics are dead. "Here's me praying for clear skies, God. Just let me get on the ground in one piece so I can figure out why I'm still alive."

I realize that my energy shields are burned out and begin really praying that my heat shielding is intact. As soon as things start getting hot I realize that prayer has gone unanswered and I start pulling up. Then I realize, the top of my ship didn't take any hits, so I flip over and watch the flames of re-entry try to burn through my cockpit.

PART FOUR

Alice pulled the circular neural device off and sat up with a jerk. Tears were streaming down her face, she'd fit into his shoes too well. His voice was older than it ought to have been for someone at the age of sixteen, a low rumble in her ears that was both weary and somehow comforting. The person she'd just watched lose everything was still just a boy, even though he flew as though he had many years of experience.

Alice wiped the tears away, took a deep breath then looked at the time the recording was taken. "God, I'm so stupid," she said to herself realizing that it was right in the middle of the time period when the Holocaust Virus was spreading across the fringes of the galaxy, sometime before the Eden Fleet disappeared. If she had known in advance, checked to see when Noah Lucas started recording the report, she could have braced herself.

Would I have connected with him as deeply if I knew ahead of time? She thought to herself. Alice looked at Carnie's file picture. The man looked five years older, not two. There was no boy left in that visage, but she could see a gentle strength and blue eyes that looked back at her from the image. She had to know how the lost boy became that man, no matter how severe his crucible was.

Alice took a deep breath and started the playback again.

Fear can bring tears for some people, and scare them away for others. I'm glad I'm in the second group, because when I came through the fire I got my first look at a real air to ground war. The gleaming skyline of New Tokyo was filled with smoke, flames and those oval fighters. They ignored me as I flipped my ship and burned towards the deck. I needed a place to land, somewhere I could get a look at my computer systems, my scanners, maybe my communications array to find out if anyone in our convoy survived. If they were still up there I had to get a rescue together, there was no way of knowing how much time they had left.

I caught sight of a big planetary defence platform, a wide man-made island with interlocking circular domes topped with planet to space cannons. They're making a go of it, and one of their hangars are open. Two mid-sized ships are already on their way in, and I decided to go for it, swooping down so fast that, for a few seconds my whole cockpit was filled with the sight of blue ocean before I pulled up and caused a wake three storeys high. This wasn't fancy flying to me, this was how I was going to survive, by flying so crazy that no one would be stupid enough to chase me.

As I was closing on the hangar one of the ships trying to make the safety of the deck – a big, slow hauler with only one cargo container attached – got blown in half by something firing from above. I had just enough time to avoid the scattering debris as it fell into the ocean and I touched down just slow enough so I didn't liquefy myself from the G's, but hard enough to black out completely.

I came to and my cockpit was wide open and I was being dragged out by the first real soldiers I'd ever met. "Welcome to Niler Station, the Commerce Complex," said one. "We're abandoning this hangar, keep up or we'll let the bots tear you to shreds, kid."

I kept up, and as soon as we were through the thick armoured door it closed. All the soldiers were quiet, they looked exhausted, and I found a bench. I don't know how long we stayed there, I just remember tears running down my face and keeping quiet while I shook so hard I thought I was going to die.

A medic in green and black army gear knelt down in front of me, took a scan and nodded to himself. "Take your helmet off and I'll give you a stabilizer. We don't have time to help you any other way, son."

I did as I was told, breathing the air of Iora in for the first time. It smelled like burned fuel. Before I had much of a chance to do or say anything, the medic popped a clear pill into my mouth, it dissolved as soon as it touched my tongue and I stopped shaking. The memories of my home and family getting blasted seemed distant within seconds, and my head was mostly clear. "Where am I? What's going on?" The sounds of distant explosions surrounded us.

"Follow me," said another broad shouldered man in infantry armour. He didn't wait to see if I did what I was told, but turned and started leaving the room. I hurried after him, helmet under my arm, my old suit looking more like a yellow and black costume compared to their plated armour. "Listen, Kid, I'd love to get you to a trauma centre, but the 'bots tore those up first. Every hospital we've got is a hot zone, and I need more from you than you need from me right now. What's the situation in orbit? How much did you see?"

"Silver ships blasted my caravan, I don't know if anyone survived," I said, some of the sorrow creeping back despite whatever medication I was on.

"What were your people? Freelance law enforcement? Traders?"

"Carnival people, Warren's Wonders."

That made the Lieutenant stop. He turned to me and put a hand on my shoulder. "I'm sorry, I took my kids to one of your shows, they never forgot it. Probably before you were born, but I think everyone knows your people."

I didn't say anything, just looked at him. He may have been four centimetres taller than me, mostly thanks to his combat boots, but I felt like I was a little kid again, looking way up at the big man who looked like I just punched him in the gut. "We were peaceful people," I said after a while.

"I know, the Eden drones probably thought you were

reinforcements," the Lieutenant said. "What else do you remember? Anything helps."

"There was nothing fighting the silver ships that got us," I told him. "Navnet was blinking, like there was the normal display and then there was a red screen that looked like everything was on a collision course."

"Armen!" the Lieutenant called out. One of his men moved to his side. "I need you to go download the Navnet logs from this pilot's fighter."

"That's going to be hard," I told him. "My flight computer doesn't have power, I took some damage on the way down."

"Think you could get at the memory unit and get it out before that bay is overrun?" asked the Lieutenant.

"I don't know anything about that fighter model, it's a bit before my time," replied Armen. "I could try."

"You have to pull the dash out to get at the memory," I told him. "I just installed a Unexa Crystal Drive three weeks ago."

"Damn, you won't have time to get at it before that bay is filled with bots," the Lieutenant said.

"Wait, what about the other ship that was landing at the same time as I was?" I ask.

"Bots caught that with a tug line and dragged it into the ocean, they're busy ripping it apart now," another soldier said, pointing to a window ahead.

I don't know why, but I didn't walk to the window down the hall, I ran, and in the fading sunlight I watched a tug platform with a broad, flat cargo deck holding the ship I saw trying to land with it out of the water enough for civilian repair drones to land on its hull. They worked to cut through the hull like kids tear through the wrapping on their birthday presents. An airlock opened, and a dock loader turned towards it. Someone with more bravery than sense emerged, firing an old hunting rifle at it, and one of the loading bot's grips caught his head in its grasp. An android that had half its face burned off looked the human over as he struggled, then shook his head.

"Kid, don't look," someone said as they caught up to me at the window. No one pulled me away from the transparesteel though, and I wasn't so much as blinking. The loader bot tossed the writhing man onto the deck of the barge behind them, and I could see he could still move after he finished rolling part way across the metal platform. A small crowd of androids stood by, the expensive kind that could fool you into thinking they were human sometimes. They watched as several smaller service bots surrounded the man, who was sitting up, his scraped arms raised.

One of the blocky service bots burst forward so quickly I almost missed it, and it took me a moment to realize that it didn't retreat without a souvenir. The machine stuffed one of the man's stolen arms into a matter recycler on its chest, and the other bots took turns tearing pieces of the man off as he writhed helplessly. A service bot with long arms arrived at the open airlock and reached inside, pulling a screaming woman out by her waist and flinging her onto the deck of the ship, where her body was broken down into compartment sized pieces before they were converted into energy by the bots there. I'm happy I couldn't hear them screaming, that probably sounds selfish, but I think that would have put me in a corner I wouldn't be able to leave.

"Why is this happening?" I asked. The meds were working, the moment I looked away from the window the experience of watching the murders seemed to soften, grow distant.

"We don't know why everything with an artificial intelligence is turning on us," the Lieutenant said. He continued up the ramped hallway, and I stuck to his side. "But it's across the solar system, we lost contact with all the shipyards, our orbital stations and the moon over the last twenty hours. The Eden bots seem to be happy with isolating the planet, our machines are doing the rest of the damage."

A heavy metal door closed behind us, and a group of four soldiers began welding it closed right away. "Hey, I might be able to repair my ship when those 'bots move on. Is there any other way to the hangar?"

"No, no other way. We're bunkering up."

"My fighter's still fixable, it only uses basic parts, and I have to get help for my people."

"You've seen that fighter for the last time. Sorry, kid."

Alice's command unit sent a basic message through the nerves in her arm, one that gave her the impression that she'd be late. It was new direct interface technology, a type that could send specific sensations and messages that resonated with instinctive memory but couldn't do harm that was in all the latest officer level command and control units.

She ended the playback and checked her wrist display.

She had nine minutes to report to Hangar Four, where an optional Hand to Hand Combat Class was about to begin, and she wasn't about to miss it. Most, if not the entire Apex class had signed up, many of them were using it to fill their physical training hours, but Alice enjoyed the practice. Nothing cleared her head like sparring.

PART FIVE

In the corner of the training room there was a new set of Interceptor Armour, something no one was allowed to qualify on yet. She was on the list to be one of the first. It was the first time anyone had seen a suit of it. It stood there across from them with the floor mats providing a broad buffer.

The Interceptor Armour wasn't the technical marvel that Alice was expecting. The metal slats were so subtle that they were practically invisible to the eye, and there were two types of propulsion – passive enclosed systems and high efficiency thrusters – but they were clunkier than she would have guessed. Instead of being integrated closely under the skin of the armour, they were in armoured components added to the outside. The same went for the enhanced sensor suite, and high powered emitters. The weapons suite was impressive enough with two arm blasters, a miniature rocket launcher and another piece that they temporarily replaced with a harpoon system for latching onto ships. The rest of the suit included a revised shield system and everything they came to expect in an advanced suit made to replace small fighters and mechanized units up to four times the size.

It wasn't unusual for their trainers to use classes most of the Apex members were attending to show them something new, or to address other topics. If there was one word Alice would use to describe the curriculum, it would be *'dense.'* They crammed as much into every lesson as they could, even the elective ones.

Their instructor, a tall woman who was so fit that it looked like she spent half her hours in the gym, introduced herself as Rusher. That was her code name, and they would refer to her in no other way. Once they were finished going through all the technical details of the suit, she turned the lights over it off. "You won't be touching that until we've finished testing it. Many of you will never need to put that suit on. Either way, you should know a few things. The new suits include systems that will allow you to survive in thirty one gravity units, and that means that there's a lot of power in the strength enhancement systems. You could put your comrade through a bulkhead by patting him on the back if you don't know what you're doing, or worse if you don't have the coordination and discipline to handle yourself. They tell me that you have martial arts training, but I want to see it for myself since I'll be one of the people they look to if you splatter someone by giving them a high-five when the safeties in the suit are off."

"Pardon me, Ma'am, er, Rusher," asked Vannez, a late entrant into the program. "But didn't you just show us several redundant levels of control that are built into the suit so that can't happen?"

"I need you to stand right there," Rusher said, pointing to the middle of the mats.

"You did it now," Yawen muttered quietly.

"And you, Level Five, get over there," Rusher said, pointing to Yawen. She had completed five hand to hand qualifier tests, two more than she had to in order to graduate the program.

Yawen straightened up and made her way through her classmates to the mat, standing across from Vannez.

"Nafalli! Take 'em both, don't worry about breaking them, they're well trained officers at this point, and their suits will take most of the damage."

Iruuk took his place across from the pair with little emotion. Once he was in position, Rusher shouted; "Go for the pin, you two against Iruuk. Begin."

Yawen and Vannez circled Iruuk, who kept turning to face them both. He had advantages in speed, strength and reach, only other Nafalli had managed to pin him so far. Even then, he managed to win half of his first engagements with new opponents, and his average got better as he learned their tricks and styles. His father taught him to be a good fighter, and with time Alice knew he'd be great.

Vannez grabbed at his arm, and Iruuk let her take it. She wrapped her legs around his knee and leaned back, but he positioned himself to maintain his balance then pressed down, holding a hand out to keep Yawen at bay. He nearly pinned Vannez then, but she rolled her shoulders and released her grip on his leg. Before she could get out of his reach, he caught one of her legs and flipped her into Yawen, who was just about to leap at him from behind.

The women fell in a tangle, and Iruuk separated them like children, held them up for a moment and slammed them down on the mat backs first. "Rematch!" Yawen said as the automated referee counted them out.

"All right, just you and Iruuk here?" Rusher asked.

"Just me and Fur-Face," Yawen said.

Iruuk released both his opponents. "I don't mind," Iruuk replied with a shrug.

Vannez retreated from the mats, looking unsurprised by the outcome. "Don't know what she'll do against that Nafalli."

Alice couldn't help but feel a little excited as Yawen and Iruuk faced off, he in a crouched position, and she in a side facing fighting stance. "You ready for this?" she asked.

Iruuk smiled a little, but kept watching her closely. "Begin!" Rusher said.

Iruuk made a snap grab for her leg, but by the time his hand arrived, it wasn't there. It kicked up, catching him squarely under the jaw. Even though his suit moved into place in time to catch the hit, the class audibly cringed.

Her foot came down on his hand, momentarily pulling him off balance and bringing his throat down so she could strike with her elbow and a backhand. "Multiple points," the referee system announced while flashing a red number three over their heads.

"This is for the pin, remember," Rusher said. "Not points."

Iruuk was still off balance, and Yawen took advantage, stepping back just enough to lash out with a fast, but heavy kick to his knee. That was her tactic, to keep him off balance until she found a way to pin him.

Just as Alice had the thought, Yawen surprised everyone else as she grabbed Iruuk's wrist, stepped up onto his kneeling leg, and leapt into the air, dragging his arm behind his back. When it was twisted as far as it would go, she used the arm to fling her body back down towards his back and land both her feet between his shoulder blades. Iruuk completely lost his balance and landed on his chest while Yawen twisted his long arm. "Submit," she said calmly as she used all her strength to keep his arm pinned to his back.

Even through his visor, Alice could see the amused surprise on Iruuk's face. He tapped his free hand on the mat. "Well done, Level Five," Rusher said to Yawen. "Next time I check your progress, I want to see that you're level seven. Supervise your classmates through practice matches for two hours. Breaks and match opponents at your discretion. I want to see discipline, awareness and quick thinking."

"Yes, Rusher, thank you, Rusher," Yawen said.

Iruuk waited until their commander turned away, then bowed in front of Yawen with a grin. "That was very good, I would like to spar with you again sometime."

"I'd be happy to, but square up with Alice and Titus for now."

Alice enjoyed sparring with Iruuk, he was the ultimate challenge for her, especially since she was one of the smallest people in her class. He could see she was highly alert, and ready for anything she could throw at him. Everyone else in her class were set up with partners and spaced out on the large mat covered floor. The example power suit hung against the far bulkhead like a trophy.

"Begin!" Yawen shouted.

Iruuk tried to snatch Titus, a slightly older, but not much taller classmate, but missed. His grab at Alice's leg was answered with a grab of her own, where he tried to leverage his thumb to turn his arm awkwardly, but it didn't work. He turned his hand instead and grabbed her head. "Why!" was all she had time to cry before she found herself pinned on top of Titus' chest.

"I'm going to trip and flip you one day!" Titus said as he struggled under her.

"Successful pin!" the referee system announced.

The rest of the training exercise went similarly, with no one pinning Iruuk, but many classmates learning a great deal about trying to defeat a superior opponent. Before the two hours were up, Alice won thirty-one of thirty nine matches using every technique and dirty trick she could manage. "Five matches with you," Titus said in the last round. "I think someone likes seeing us fight," he nodded towards Yawen, "or wants us to get together."

Alice wasn't distracted by the grin Yawen flashed their

way, but Titus' last comment was enough to make her lose focus. He had her in a hold before she had time to offer meaningful resistance, but reversed it just as he was about to pin her, lifting him with her legs, then turning him onto his chest. "I've won five out of five, what does that mean, you think?" she asked with a smirk. His body was thick, he was short and muscular much like she was, but he had more power.

"I'll save face this round," he replied. "I found your weakness: you're a blusher." Alice tried to ignore him as she worked to reinforce her hold.

He kicked hard and flipped around, breaking her hold then took advantage of the leverage to break free. He locked her into a leg hold and pinned one of her shoulders to the mat, she barely kept the other from touching. A thought occurred to her then, maybe she could use the same trick to distract him. "I'll let you take me out if you pin me," she said with a wink. "But only if you can pin me."

To her surprise, he lifted her up then slammed her onto the mat, firmly pushing her shoulders down. Holographic numbers counting her out appeared above their heads as she struggled to get free, but he had too much leverage. "Pinned!" It announced, flashing a green light on Titus, marking him as the victor.

"You don't have to, it was a good distraction, but it had the reverse effect," he said as he gave her a hand up.

"No, she has to," Yawen said as she passed. "She could use a break with someone who knows how to have a good time."

"All right, we'll find the time before we get our assignments," Alice said, wishing she wasn't blushing. "Our schedules are finally clearing up."

"Aw, why not tonight?" Yawen asked, feigning disappointment.

Alice pushed her away. "I have to work on a report I'm not allowed to talk about."

Everyone knew what she meant. Every Officer Trainee at their level had one, and they were not allowed to share details. "I'll send you my schedule," Titus said. "See how things line up. I can't wait."

PART SIX

The quarters Alice and Yawen shared in the new training facility were the best part about the space. So much of the academy was as yet unfinished, and that's the way she preferred most of it. Some hallways were skeletal, without safety covers or beautification, so all the cables, pipes and other systems were in plain sight. There was as much current technology, serving as backup and temporary systems as there were new generation technologies. Seeing the two together helped her understand the new systems everyone was rushing to understand from the Lorander database.

As much as she liked seeing technology open for viewing, Alice was happy that the habitation section she was in was finished. The dark grey and blue décor suited her tastes, but more importantly, their adjustable bunks were comfortable. Just as nice as the beds aboard the Triton, only smaller. It suited her, she didn't need much space so the standard offi-cer's bunk was big enough for her to stretch out in. After the melee session she just had, that was exactly what she did. She thought about her bouts with Titus for a moment, recalling how pleased he was with himself after he bested her. He deserved the win, she did beat him four times before that, after all. The promise she made him brought a smile to her face, and she enjoyed the prospect of having dinner with him later for a moment before shaking her head. "I don't have time for anything but a new friend," she said. "That's what I'll have to tell him straight away; no time."

With that set firmly in her mind, she took her playback disc from where she'd stashed it in the pull-down drawer above her bed and put it on her forehead. "What happens next, Carnie?" she asked as she started the playback.

I followed the Lieutenant. I didn't know what to do, but he seemed to know what to do next, how to handle whatever this disaster was. "What is this place?" I ask him. "Some kind of military base?"

"It's one of the main Commerce buildings, processing sensitive trades, holding precious materials and holding reserve power for industry. Turns out the armour here is thicker than anything in this hemisphere. We call it the Commerce Complex."

We get to the top of the winding hallway and armoured doors thicker than my shoulders are wide open. There was a command centre through there with a few projected scenes of military robots fighting human forces in hover tanks, low flying heavy ships and on foot. Even though I don't know much about that kind of fighting, I can see that humans are in retreat everywhere I look. The bots don't care if they get crushed or de-limbed, they throw themselves into the fight like they've hated us for generations.

"You sure you don't remember anything else from your trip here? Maybe something the last system you were at talked about a solution they were using? Why weren't they infected?"

"We were in hyperspace for two weeks, coming from Denault. Everything was cool there, the bots were normal."

"I was afraid you'd say that," the Lieutenant said. "It looks like your best chance is to throw in with us. There's no way you're getting back up in the sky, and we're pretty much stuck here for the duration."

A woman in a white business outfit, long coat, longer skirt and a computer console on her arm was giving orders to the upper ranks in the room. There were only a few who looked like her – rich business types – but there were a hundred soldiers, most of them higher ranking like the Lieutenant who came down to meet me. "I'm Noah," I tell him as he's starting to turn away. "Noah Lucas."

He stops and shakes my hand. "I'm Lieutenant Ruben Oman, stick around, we might need more pilots."

Any confidence Lieutenant Ruben instilled in me with his firm handshake dissipated when I saw that his team was welding the heavy door behind us shut. I'd seen enough war movies to know what a last stand looked like. I looked around the room and noticed that the only people in the large command centre were military or business type people. The floor we were on had thick metal windows, so thick that the view was distorted slightly by the shape of the transparent metal like an old funhouse mirror, only not quite as bad. I should have felt safe, but I got a sinking feeling as I watched smoke rise in broad black pillars from the city skyline in the distance.

I found a seat against the wall and put my helmet on. I knew it would make no difference to a load-lifter or recycling bot, they'd have me cut apart and processed just as fast either way, but it made me feel better. "There's only one solution left," said the lady in the business suit. If someone told me she was an android, I'd believe them. Her face looked chiselled, too perfect.

"We're not doing that, Emrine," Lieutenant Ruben said. "We've still got some fight in us."

"The Third Mechanized Division was just annihilated," Emrine said, her eyes not looking away from a large holographic projection with a power plant in the middle. "This collector is almost fully charged, the machines are defending it, but we're still connected. There is enough power in there to fry every circuit in the hemisphere, and plans are underway to secure a connection to the southern power reserve station."

"We wipe the robots out, but we also knock out our food production, communications, and any ship not hardened against high EMP blasts."

"Look," Emrine said, bringing up a secondary hologram.

A group of hundreds of people were moving into a housing complex that looked like a luxury resort. Robots were escorting them like honoured guests who had their pick of captured military weapons, and tables filled with food. "We caught this from one of our glider drones before it was knocked out. This is evidence that this Order group is responsible. Banking records verify that every one of them sent a hundred thousand core world standard credits to Regent Galactic or the Order of Eden over the last two months."

"So we tap into the banking systems and send payments out for everyone trapped in here or in the main hall. You should have access to corporate funds, maybe spend some of the reserve funds in the vault."

"No," Emrine said, bringing an eruption of raised voices across the room. She raised her hands in a placating gesture, quieting them enough for her to expand on her answer. "I'm the administrator of this facility, so I can get you access to any part of the installation, but all we have are United Core World raw currency, so if these machines take cash, yes, we'll all be saved, but I can't give us credit, and I can't access any of the banking systems from here. There are blocks in place to specifically prevent an employee of the treasury department like me from using the serial numbers on the currency slips down there to guarantee a loan or extend credit. The air gapped bots that process that kind of thing aren't in the building, and who knows what kind of shape they're in?"

"Maybe we should go down there and start shovelling the credits out a window," said a soldier with his rank – Senior Sergeant – tattooed on his cheek.

"Didn't you hear me, grunt?" Emrine asked. "Whatever's got the bots didn't set them up with cash payment in mind. We have one chance." She brought a hologram of their building, the intertwining armoured ovals dominating the island. "We're all charged up, our power reserves will be enough to send an electromagnetic pulse to three emergency power nodes, and they should go off too. The chain reaction should cascade across the entire hemisphere, and, if we're lucky it'll cause the equatorial linkage to go off too. Only a few bots can survive that kind of electromagnetic pulse."

"Big overload, bigger electromagnetic pulse, and we'll have to fight those privileged bastards without comms or high tech firepower." The face-tattooed soldier said, pointing at the repeating playback of the resort.

"One hundred of you must be worth five thousand of them," Emrine said. "You can make the arrests."

"Arrests?" Lieutenant Ruben scoffed. "We'll capture a couple who know what's going on and execute the rest."

"Whatever you think you can live with whenever we get our society working again," Emrine said. "Just warn me so I can be far away when the rounds start flying."

"Wait, far away where? Where would you go?" the Sargent asked. "You have a bunker somewhere or something? Just for you corporate types?"

Two people in white business suits glanced at Emrine warily. "Everyone has a vacation spot," she said. "Mine doesn't have any artificial intelligence driven androids or computers because I believe they intrude on time off."

"Bullshit," Lieutenant Ruben said. "You paid up. You

could walk right out there and the machines would just go on ripping everyone to pieces while you move in wherever you want."

Emrine kept staring at the hologram, enlarging the image of the control room in the neighbouring oval building. I could see where the two buildings connected, and now that I look back at it I'm sure she was showing everyone in the room that because she knew what was going to happen next. "Of course I paid, anyone who could afford it did. Do you realize what the Order was offering? Eternal life at point one percent of the cost, the opportunity to earn your way to a paradise, and safety from what they said was an inevitable darkness. I didn't know this was what would happen!" she said as several soldiers began raising their rifles, aiming them at the three business types. "This is horrible, I didn't know it would happen, and I'm here, trying to fix it when I could walk out safely."

"We should waste her," a soldier with a long ponytail said. If she didn't have murder in her eyes, she could be beautiful.

"I'm the only one left who can log into the remote systems from here," Emrine said. "You won't know what's going on in the outside world unless I'm here and alive."

"Remote stations are going offline, we'll be blind in a couple hours either way, so what good are you?" the Sergeant said.

"Listen, I stand to lose a great deal if you agree to destroy most of the electronics on the planet," Emrine reasoned, looking away from the barrels pointed at her head. "If the legal system reboots after we win, if we win, I'll face property damage charges on a historic level. I just want the killing to stop, just like you. I don't want to see anyone else lose their family."

"Don't talk about our families, rich-bitch," said Lieutenant Ruben said. "We still have units fighting out there, some of 'em were winning from the last I heard."

"They won't for long," one of the terrified white-jackets said. "For every human on this planet there are nine artificial intelligence programs running. That's including a lot of things that can't hurt us, like fabricator systems in food dispensers and in small communications networks, but at least half of our artificial intelligences are installed on mobile frame machines – that's your androids, your repair bots, messenger pods, you know, everything that can move itself around – so by my estimate we're outnumbered at least four to one."

Everyone in the room jumped as something exploded against the transparent wall. I didn't see what it was, but I saw that it blasted through at least a third of the armour. "Time to go," I whispered to myself. I looked at the schematic hovering between Lieutenant Ruben and Emrine again. There was no way back with the doors welded, but there was a way to the neighbouring building. I stood quietly and started walking along the walls furthest from the outside. "Where's he going?" asked a soldier, momentarily waving his rifle at me.

"Gotta pee," I told him, putting my hands up. "If you

keep pointing that at me, or another missile strikes, I'll just go right here."

"He's got a point," Lieutenant Ruben said. Five square-headed robots landed on the transparent side of the room and began cutting. "We've got to get out of here."

PART SEVEN

I didn't take any chances that someone would stop me from getting out of that room while several bots that looked like they were built to break through heavy metal cut through the transparent metal wall. I'd seen plasma cutters like those before, nothing could stop them, they'd get through given enough time. So, I was first through the interior door, where I was confronted by dozens of people who had holed up in what looked like a large waiting room. Some of them were workers, I could tell from their protective bodysuits, but the rest looked like some kind of tour group. At first I couldn't see a door leading further into the installation, and I was stunned a little at the size of the crowd until one of the soldiers bumped me aside. Then I saw it, a pair of sliding doors. In my fantasies I was a gun slinging hero, or a fighter jock saving the day, but in real life I knew I was no such thing. So when I chose to run for those doors, I was more surprised than anyone. You see, what I was planning would piss the soldiers off, I was sure. They didn't look like the brightest people in the room, but I had a feeling that they would realize that I wanted to follow Emrine's instructions before long. The instructions that would blast all the machines on this half of the planet at least with an electromagnetic pulse that would take most of them out.

If the machines were trying to get into that command centre, and they were using cutters, I figured I wouldn't have much time to get to the next building. "Hey! Kid!" one of the soldiers shouted after me as I rushed across the long room, trying not to step on anyone stretched out on the floor. Those double doors called to me. Everything over my shoulder looked like it was about to go bad.

"Go get him," I heard Lieutenant Ruben say.

I made it into the large, curving hallway beyond; it was all polished white metal flooring and pretty grey curves. The diagram was alive in my head, so I ran upwards, towards where one ring-like section of the building I was in would join the next. I peeked over my shoulder and saw the pretty soldier behind me, her face bunched up in frustration, and there was a larger armoured one behind her. "Get back here, it's not safe!" she called after me.

I was faster than both of them. My suit was really just durable insulated cloth, a layer for keeping me warm and contained in space, with a helmet under my arm. Those soldiers were like cockroaches with all the armour they wore and the pack they lumped around on their backs.

There were more bots trying to cut through, I could see sparks showering from above and I stuck my helmet on before sprinting up the ramp. Lurk croaked his unhappiness with the jostling and bumping as he clung to my chest, but I just ran faster. "Hold on, buddy, we're going to fix this," I told him. "I hope."

My helmet started enriching my oxygen, sensing that I was breathing hard, and I caught a second wind as I saw the broad doors leading to the next building. One was stuck open, blast marks pocking it and the surrounding wall.

"We're going to get cut off!" shouted a soldier behind me. I looked over my shoulder in time to see them skid to a stop and look behind them, where more sparks were falling through the air. There had to be at least three machines cutting through from the other side, making a large square cut out through the thick ceiling.

"Uh, bye," I said as I passed through the doors leading to the next building. I didn't stop running. Ten metres into the other building I ran into a half-burned android, its left side looked like a suave, well built man, while the right had been shot and melted to pieces. It limped after me in a hurry, dragging his half-crushed stump of his leg. Behind him was a tribe of service and companion bots, maybe from the beach at the bottom of the building, I never found out. They had all been put out of commission partially or completely by someone who came prepared – the soldiers I'd already met was my assumption – and I wondered if I could get past them.

Instead of testing my luck, I ran the other way, the oval building offered two routes to the lower levels, and I hoped the second was clearer. That was better for a long time, more than half way, and I even stopped so I could catch my breath for a while. The soldiers weren't after me anymore, and those messed up machines I met going the other way were too damaged to come after me quickly.

I heard footsteps coming up the gently sloping hallway then, and peeked around the corner. A hardened gaze met mine, he was in a white business suit in the same fashion as Emrine's, but he lurched for me. I charged past him, a hard hand gripping my arm. I had more momentum than he did, and dragged him to the deck, but he didn't let go. That was a mechanical grip, but the hateful expression on his face looked very human. I pried myself free but would have a bruise in the shape of his hand for a week.

Two more androids that looked perfectly human lunged at me, but I managed to go around them, running as fast as I could, faster than ever before. Even with the enriched mix of oxygen in my helmet, my lungs burned. I made it to the main elevator bank and mashed the call buttons. Two doors opened, one had a repair bot and a pair of androids inside, the other was empty.

I leapt into the empty one and punched the close button as I screamed; "Door close! Door close!"

They did, but the repair bot jammed its longest arm between them. There was a hatch above, and I jumped for it, catching it on the first try. The shaft was empty, but that was part of the problem. The bots were in the car beneath me, and would get up through that hole in seconds, so I ran a couple steps and jumped off the top of that car towards the opposite wall.

I imagined myself somehow gliding through the air and touching that smooth wall, the emergency hold systems on my suit sticking me there like a climbing frog. It's amazing how gravity can complicate that kind of plan. I fell a long way before my suit made contact and I stuck to the wall. It felt like the whole building punched me everywhere at once, but I wasn't falling anymore. I could see the shapes of two heads far above, on top of that elevator car, moving left and right, searching. A minute later those shapes disappeared.

I hung against the side of the wall and caught my breath, nearly laughing out loud when I heard Lurk say; "ow," as clearly as I've heard him say any word.

"You okay buddy?" I asked in a whisper.

"Too much moving."

"We'll just rest here a minute," I told him.

I was against that wall, hanging in my suit for at least five minutes before I heard Lieutenant Ruben's voice through the communicator in my helmet. "Kid, I can't believe you're going to try to get to the manual controls yourself. What are you thinking?"

"I saw a solution, and I'm going for it, Sir," I added the 'Sir' because that's what I'd seen in so many military movies, but it felt all wrong when it came out.

"You don't know the first thing about what's going on. We could win this, I'm not kidding. We just have to find a few bunkers to fight from."

I thought for a moment and shook my head. "That doesn't

make sense to me, man," I said. "Who built the bunkers? Who do you call when you have to get inside?"

"This is Iora, the technical capitol of the sector. We have military ship yards, cutting edge mechanized battalions, and as many soldiers as some planets have citizens."

"But your space superiority is gone," I said, remembering one of many lessons that stuck from the pilots in our little defence wing. If you had space superiority, you could hold forever, bring in supplies, blockade the planet if you wanted, but as soon as you lost it everything got hard. "It's scrap metal salad for whole kilometres up there, man. No one is coming to help you, and maybe frying everything down here isn't the best solution, but it's going to stop the bots from feeding people into matter converters."

"Kid, our weapons will be dead if you flip that switch," he argued.

"So will the bots, and stop calling me kid, I'm seventeen, asshole," I said as I pulled a length of emergency line from my belt and made sure the end was securely affixed to the wall. I turned my light on and pointed down the shaft. I was at least eight stories up, but I had enough line to get down, and I didn't see any bots waiting, so I started lowering myself. "I can't fucking believe I'm the one who's doing this. You soldiers are all just a bunch of armoured pussies who like your toys too much." Yes, I get mouthy when I'm terrified. The lack of response was more frightening, and after a few minutes I wanted to check in, to make sure that the soldiers hadn't been murdered by the bots that were trying to get at them when I left, but there were other things to think about.

PART EIGHT

Apex Phase Two was lagging for everyone. The decision to delay service aboard real starships for the Officer Trainees was one thing, and it irritated everyone, but the whole class was starting to show strain. There was more training available, elective training, and more qualification tests to take, and everyone had to fill their time with them, so the workload was almost the same. The difference was every trainee knew that Fleet was watching what they chose to study and still grading their performance as much as ever. Alice decided to learn Lorander Native, the operating system built and used by their highly advanced and absent allies. She already knew everything she could about the new Haven Fleet systems, that came easy. She was already familiar with most of it since it was based on the Triton's Earth Defence operating system, so moving on to something that was more advanced made sense to Alice, especially since Lorander Native was required learning for anyone who wanted to truly understand their manufacturing systems.

Ayan's return to Haven Fleet resulted in massive change. The whole line of ships being produced in the new manufacturing base was cancelled, and only the highest ranking officers in the Fleet knew why. Alice assumed radical redesigns were underway, and her curiosity was difficult to control, but she did her best. Pouring herself into her work even more helped, but sometimes she had to stop, to take a break so she wouldn't burn out entirely. That was when, as mad as it was, she would look for things she was neglecting, and on one particular night, over a week and a half after she'd paid any attention to it, she remembered that she hadn't finished her report on Noah Lucas' experiences before reaching Haven Shore.

Alice started looking through the file for an easy way to complete the assignment, starting with the details of the building he landed in, and the little information they had in his file about the military he met there. The building was one of the wealth and knowledge centres of the world. It was made to look like a dishevelled stack of metal rings, each of the sections had several floors and used starship technology to trick the people inside into thinking they were standing perfectly upright when the floors were actually all tilted. The unusual shape made it easier to turn the whole building into a shield emitter coil, one of the first functions that the machines disabled before the human owners could erase the structure's resident artificial intelligence. Standing strong within the mess of coil like structures were three domed buildings with heavy armour cladding.

The military organization that was supposed to guard it was called the Iora Protection Force, or IPF, and it was exclusively trained to protect that world, the financial and intellectual centre of their solar system. The records Alice found from captains who had visited before the Holocaust Virus indicated that Iora was arguably the greatest planet in the sector. The common complaint was that it was expensive to live there, but they were independent, had several major space stations the size of large cities that were worth taking leave on if you couldn't afford to go to the planet, and many different companies had manufacturing centres there. The IPF were the harsh end of the law, called in whenever extreme force was necessary, and they had a reputation for treating outsiders like vermin when they stepped out of line.

With more background research finished on Iora, and the understanding of what Noah Lucas had lost, Alice was able to write the first part of her report. There was so much more to learn about the place, so the introduction and first part of her presentation wasn't ready to send yet, but she could narrate and edit something together at least.

Alice assumed that the focus of the whole report had to take the priorities of the fleet in mind, but there was so much information she wanted to share with whoever made the journey there in the future, or with captains who might need to know the status of Iora and its orbital space before paying it a visit. Regardless of what she focused on in her report, she needed more information. There was only one way to get it, and that was to plug into Noah's simulation log. Alice reduced her uniform to its smallest size, a simple top and bottom, and slipped into bed. It was three hours earlier than her regular bedtime, but she needed to get away from the training and the pressure for a while.

Stretching her legs and flexing her toes in the crisp, cool sheets was so relaxing that she groaned and sighed. "Tired?" Yawen asked with a smile as she entered their room.

"Yup," Alice replied. "Still have work left, but I can let simulation logs play while I'm hiding." She said, pulling the sheets up to her chin.

"Aw, you're so cute when you're all tucked in," Yawen said. "Should I close your curtain for you?"

"Yeah, thanks," Alice said. "G'night."

Alice set her comm system to stop the simulation in an hour and set the detail level to maximum. Noah Lucas was seeing some terrible things, and facing awful challenges, but she didn't want to miss a thing. The world around her disappeared as she put the small device on her forehead and it took control of her senses.

The bottom of the elevator shaft was like any other pit – dark, a home for things people lost or discarded through the cracks – and I took a minute to catch my breath. The main doors leading to the power centre of the ground based station were in front of me, the doors leading to the vault were behind. With soldiers against what I was planning on doing, and screwed up, murderous bots everywhere, I didn't really want to move.

I don't know why I have this sense of morality, or how it's lasted so long. I just didn't think I'd live to a ripe old age. Maybe it was my upbringing. You don't want your kids to grow up in travelling carnival if you have a choice. Before I turned seventeen I saw more adult drama, death and prejudice than most people three times my age. The need to understand it all drove me to question what was going on, and by the time I was seventeen people would just give me the unvarnished truth. People who were nice to me could be downright evil to others, even though we were like a family of nomads. Someone you trusted could steal from you and go on pretending they are your best friend. The harshest realization was that, wherever we went we were the outsiders. A local dirt bag was more trustworthy to locals than any of us most of the time, no matter how big we smiled or how generous we were. If we weren't careful we could be attacked, or blamed for something we had nothing to do with just because everyone we met there saw us as untrustworthy nomads. I'd been cornered and beaten up for the few pips I had in my pocket twice, so when the local soldiers started turning hostile, I wasn't surprised. Kind one minute, closed minded and nasty the next.

I'm no tactical genius, running and gunning was never my thing outside of zapping my buddies in the halls on long stretches between planets, but I knew there would be more bots between me and what I needed to get to. The core wasn't heavily guarded by systems, gun emplacements and the like, but probably by whatever bots they had down there. That's the problem with droids when you want to get to something they're guarding: they could look like people, or like dainty little machines, but they don't know mercy when they turn on you, and something built on a metal frame with motors and gears is almost always tougher than a human. I had a gun, but it was a pulse blaster, and I didn't know enough about the bots I was going to run into to take them down in one or two shots, and if there were more than two, I'd be screwed. I could picture myself trying to melt one down with my little gun while the other two ripped me in half, and I knew that would be likely if I tried that strategy.

I didn't have much time to form another plan, I could hear someone scraping at the doors way overhead. Either the robots were coming to get me, or it was the soldiers. "What do we do, Lurk?" I asked.

"Boom," he said, his croak muffled by the fabric of my suit. "Three time."

It took me a moment to figure out what he was talking about, but then I fished into one of my pockets and found two power cells. They were just multi-purposed batteries, but strong enough to use in my blaster, where I realized I'd find the third one. That was the answer. I popped the covers of the connector terminals off, pulled the connector cable off my suit, stripped a few short pieces of wire then wrapped one end around the positive terminal of each of my power cells. It would take me a second to finish the wiring on each power cell and turn them into bombs. They would start overloading and after a few seconds they would explode. Any tech within a few metres would be toast from the electromagnetic pulse or damaged by the fireball.

I was running out of time, there was more scrambling at the doors high above, someone was making progress at getting those security doors open, if it was the soldiers, they'd be coming down soon, or shooting into the shaft. I found the emergency lever that opened the elevator doors for the lowest level and cranked it as fast as I could. The doors didn't move at first, but after a few cranks it was easy. A mechanical arm with a welder on the end came through, and I knew there was a visual sensor on the end of it. The bots already knew I was coming, maybe not why, but I was still off to a bad start.

I turned my back on the welding arm, making sure I was well out of its range in case it decided to try and burn me, then activated my first improvised bomb. I was in too much of a rush when I turned and tossed it at the crack in the elevator doors, and it bounced back into the shaft with me. "Oh crap," I said.

"Missed?" asked Lurk.

I scrambled to find the power cell in the near complete darkness, touched a lot of things I didn't want to see in the light while I was at it. "Boom," Lurk reminded me with a sorrowful croak.

"I know," I said. The back of my hand brushed against something hot, and I grabbed the power cell. I could hear it starting to whine as I carefully lobbed it between the elevator doors.

Lurk was right, it definitely went 'boom' maybe two seconds later.

PART NINE

Alice found the end of the visual simulation log jarring, and double checked to see if that was the actual end. There was a lot of audio data left, and some images to go with it, but no simulation or video data. "I guess he fried his recorder," she said to herself in the darkness of her bunk.

She pulled her privacy curtain aside and padded barefoot into the hall to the convenience dispenser, smiling at Perry, one of the officers who were averaging over ninety-four percent. He was in his workout uniform, shorts and boots. "Hey, Alice, join us for a run?"

"Thanks, but I'm neck deep in logs," she replied, reviewing the selection of drinks. There was a citrus blend that swirled orange and pink that was labelled as a 'cool, brisk nutrient rich treat' and she punched that one. Having one machine for the ten officers in that berthing space was a high privilege. She'd seen images of an enlisted cadets berthing, and they had one machine for every forty-two bunks. It didn't look like they got fresh fruit drinks, either. Alice chose a medium sized cup and the machine produced a cold, sealed container. The straw popped up as she picked it up. "I'm still working hard to stay ahead, neck deep in logs. Are you waiting for Ute?"

"Yeah, they still can't fit her vacsuit right," Perry said, shrugging his big shoulders. "She's just putting on something she can outrun me in. What kind of logs?"

Alice took a sip of the thick, tart citrus drink and winked at Perry.

"Oh, can't talk about it," he said, nodding. "See you in Stellar Cartography?"

"I finished my class time," Alice said. "I'll see you in the wardroom though."

"Hi!" Ute said as she emerged from her bunk room. Her smooth, wide head was covered in the middle by a strip of fabric that flowed down her back and spread out across the rest of her body from the midsection down. Alice could see at a glance that the sweet hearted girl seemed comfortable in the strange outfit.

"Hi, Ute, how are you?" Alice asked.

"Good!" she replied. "Did you hear? I scored all hundreds in the navigation and procedure tests. All the way up to qualification nine."

Alice hadn't heard, but then, she was starting to realize how little she knew about what was going on thanks to her unwavering focus on the program. Those categories had six qualification levels plus three more for capitol ship combat piloting, a category she passed her general qualification for, but decided not to pursue past the basics.

"That's amazing, you're probably the first to have perfect scores." Alice said, surprised and happy for the small Mergillian.

"Oh, yeah, I'm going to be a pilot."

"We don't know that for sure, remember?" Perry reminded her. "Not until we get our assignments when we've finished here."

"Right," Ute said, her light whistling voice a little more serious. "Where else would they put me though?"

"Lead navigator?" Perry said. "You're definitely smart enough for it."

Alice smiled at watching the pair, and wondered if other people were as amused when they watched her and Iruuk together. She knew she was the Perry of their relationship, the practical one.

"I'd have to make Commander," Ute said. "No way any trainee is getting that rank when we graduate."

"I don't know," Alice interjected. "How are your science and math scores?"

Ute checked her small comm unit and nodded to herself. "Ninety-nine point one average," she said as though those weren't high enough for Alice to envy her a little.

"They might have trouble finding anyone better than you, Ute," Alice said. "They're going to put you somewhere important, or you could end up teaching."

"You think so?" Ute asked. "I'd be happier flying, but teaching new trainees could be interesting."

"I'd brace yourself for good news on assignment day," Alice said. She looked to Perry, who was nodding at Ute. She knew he was on a similar track as she was with a minor as a combat pilot.

"You're probably going to be my boss," Perry said.

Ute's laughter was sweetly musical, and her colour shifted from green and off white to a reddened hue. "Good, then I won't have to go running with you all the time."

"You don't like hanging out with me?" Perry said, winking at Alice.

"Oh, no," Ute replied, taking him seriously. "I do, but I'd rather play Gator or watch holos."

"I know," Perry said, "Just kidding. Speaking of running."

"I guess," Ute said, looking to Alice. "See you later."

"See you two," Alice replied. She returned to her bunk and brought up the holographic directory of Noah's logs. The next audio segment started months after the elevator shaft. There were several hundred static two dimensional images that were captured leading up to it. Once the privacy curtain was closed again she started the next log file, audio only. An image of the middle Commerce Complex Building appeared, taken from the nearest shore. It was marked three weeks after the end date of the previous log.

"That's where the fun ended, with that improvised grenade. It went up with a real bang, Lurk wasn't kidding, and it had an electromagnetic pulse just large enough to put the bots waiting for me at the doorway out of commission."

Alice laid back, sipping on her drink while she listened to Noah tell his story.

I had to use both of those power cells to get into the main power control room then get safe inside. If I never have to crank another manual door opener, I'll be a happy man. I jammed the last two between me and the soldiers with forks from a food station I passed, thinking I was some kind of genius. It wasn't the worst move, since it gave me just enough time to cause the power reserves to discharge through the building's outer armour. I was operating under Emrine's access credentials, so I really just had to find and run the command routines. Lurk understood what was going on, and said; "Boot," before I entered the final command. I took my boot off, let him crawl inside, disconnected his cybernetic harness and sealed the top of the boot with some emergency tape from my kit. That was one smart lizard, I think the reason why they never became popular synthetic pets was because they didn't talk much. Or maybe it was because they were *too* smart.

I executed the command that sent all the power from the reserve surrounding the underground vault to the outer frame of the building. It was an emergency combat measure that was built in, I can't take credit for how powerful that blast was or the engineering that went behind making those systems work together.

I didn't know it then, but the command echoed to nine other defence platforms across the planet. Most bots aren't made to withstand an electromagnetic pulse that powerful, not much is.

The soldiers were in the room a moment later and my back was to them, so I kicked the boot I stashed Lurk in further under the counter. "Stay there," I told him.

They had me out of the console chair and up against the wall so fast there was nothing I could do. I was surprised to see that there were only two of them. Ruben's right eye socket looked like a charred mess, but that didn't stop him from trying to activate the dead terminal I'd set the EMP off from. "Son of a bitch! I can't believe you did it!"

The soldier who held me against the wall was shorter than me, but she was so much stronger, it felt like she was going to grind my face through the plating. "My weapon's dead." She said, throwing her sidearm across the room. "Everything's dead."

"I know, I wonder how many guys we lost when their cybernetics burned out," Ruben said as he walked across the room towards me. "I didn't think this asshole would go through with it, so I forgot to tell them to seal up and get ready."

"I'm sorry, man, I didn't know," I pleaded. Sure, I'll admit, when my life is hanging by a thread and there's no other option, I'll say pretty much anything to get out of it. I did, but that didn't last more than a minute or so before the short soldier asked a question I didn't want to hear.

"What do we do with him?"

"Let him down," Ruben said. "He's just a kid, so we'll be nice."

She followed orders and I flexed my twisted arm while I turned to face Ruben. "Honestly, man, I thought it was the best thing, I didn't mean to hurt you or any of your guys."

"Arm feel better?" he asked.

"I'll be all right, sure."

"Good," was the last word he ever said to me. His fist came down across the side of my head so fast and hard I didn't realize I was falling until I was on the floor. They beat me for what felt like hours. After a while it was almost like a conversation spoken with fists, boots, knees and random parts of the room that were all harder than me. I left a couple teeth on the edge of that console, my arm was broken under a chair leg, and the rest of my body got to know the shapes of their knuckles and their shoe sizes really well.

I wanted to crack wise when they left, but I coughed up a throat full of blood instead. Lurk couldn't do anything, but he curled up in front of my face while I laid there. I passed out, I'm pretty sure, thought it was all over for me, but that wasn't Ruben and his friend's intention.

They wanted me to survive, all messed up. I don't know how much time passed before I started dragging myself around with my good arm. My suit could have straightened everything they broke out, but the controller was burned out.

I did my best to splint my arm, but I couldn't do much about my leg. Everything hurt, especially dragging that around. I finally found an emergency medical station one floor up – stairs are nothing but pain when you can only move horizontally, trust me – and there was enough restorative in cream and injection form for five people, probably six. There was no food though, and I was hungrier than I'd ever been.

I raided that medical station, by the time I was done there were no chemical lights, restorative chemicals, auto-splints, or anything left. Everything got dragged into a nearby supply closet, even though every trip was agony. The auto-splint was nothing fancy, you strap it to whatever you've broken, tighten the braces, then it traces the break with something that looks a bit like a claw but doesn't clamp onto anything – confusing, I know – and then there's a click. According to the instructions, you yank on a little handle hard and it straightens then sets the broken bone.

I did my shin first, and I screamed so hard that my voice was raspy for days. Again, I passed out. When I came to, the auto-splint was locked in place, my shin was straightened. Pain killers would have been a good idea, but I guess I was too delirious before I put the splint on to realize that I had a bag full of them in Safe-Dose applicators. I found them before I used the second auto-splint on my arm, and watched the whole procedure with fascination instead of suffering and screaming. That's the way to go, I tell ya.

While I was busy doing that, Lurk got to a tube of restorative cream and ate some. By that night, his belly swelled up so big that I was sure he'd either die, or pop and then die. All he'd say is; "Full," and croak as though he couldn't be happier. Sometimes I forget he's a synthetic. He doesn't actually need food, but he can eat. I deactivated his impulse to find food after that, afraid of what he might chomp and swallow next.

The swelling settled down about a day later, but it took

another month for his skin to return to its regular shape, so he was a wrinkly lizard in the meantime. I explored the Commerce Building on a crutch made out of a tall chair leg and part of a backrest carefully at first. I was sure there were soldiers around, but I was wrong. They'd moved on. I found what was left of most of Ruben's unit. They had deep cybernetics, a lot of them had strength and environmental survival enhancements that died in the electromagnetic pulse because they either didn't have their helmets on, or they weren't outfitted right to resist the EMP. Someone had mercy-killed a bunch, and there wasn't a speck of food or good supplies left behind.

I took a few power cells that were still good, and some ammo, but doubted I'd find anywhere to use them. Clean water was everywhere, so I drank constantly, and took a camelback from one of the bodies. I finally found food near the top level of the third building where there was a commercial section. It was all preserved stuff, but I made a pig of myself, throwing up after my first meal.

The bots murdered dozens of people there, the smell was something I'll never forget. All the cafeteria goers were caught by surprise when the machines turned on them, and even though I knew there was little chance anything with a microprocessor survived the blast, I was still careful around the robot servers. Why anyone thought installing full-blown artificial intelligences into waiter bots was a good idea, I'll never know. Your waiter doesn't need synthetic emotions or a developing personality. They just need decent food service software and maybe a little social programming. Why put a artificial intelligence in a robot when all they're going to do is suffer in the service industry? I'll never get it.

That night I enjoyed a second meal much slower, feeding Lurk bits of fruit and lettuce that were well preserved in their cases. He pretended to love it, no artificial intelligence in him, just all right mimic software. His bio converter made good use of the food though, recharging his battery and feeding the synthetic skin.

As night fell I watched falling stars streak across the sky endlessly and wondered if the Daring Dickenson was one of them.

PART TEN

The cafeteria became home for a while. I respectfully dragged the more whole bodies into a conference room. It took days, but it was worth it when they were all gone. The smaller chunks that didn't seem to belong to the more whole people went too, but I devised a way to make a partial protective suit out of bags first. By the end of that week there was a conference room with ID badges hanging on the door, like a communal gravestone. I scratched; "Their Machines Did Them In," on the door, as though anyone would suspect anything else.

The blood spattered, nasty looking bots that served in the cafeteria until they went berserk were mostly too heavy to move. A couple were really light, the more human looking ones, so I put them in the window facing outward in the next hallway. Over the next few weeks their poses were adjusted to look less and less dignified as I pulled parts that worked out of them and reposed each one as though they were fighting each other, or trying to call for help, or playing a circular game of grab-ass. The funniest pose I accomplished was one where a cute android waitress was looking embarrassed in the middle of the rest, who were made to look like they were reacting to a terrible smell originating from her. I called it the "Fart Tableau" and I changed it after a few days because it was a little too funny. It didn't seem right, they were killers, after all.

The restoratives and the medication I stole from that one closet were enough for me to recover in a few weeks instead of months. My leg healed up in just three weeks, I guess it could have gone faster, but I dosed only as heavy as the instructions told me to, I knew about as much about medication as I know about life on Mars – almost nothing. My arm was all right, out of the splint, I was a little worried about a little bump on the bone where it was broken, but it didn't hurt. It was time to explore, and I couldn't help but climb a service tube up to the roof of the cafeteria. I ran up a service stairway there and before long I was on top of the building. Lurk climbed out on my shoulder and we watched the sun set over the distant skyline of what I assumed was New Tokyo. A forest of steel and towering endura-crete was bathed in the red and yellow hues of their sun. I don't actually know if Lurk was watching the sunset with me, he might have just come out for some air, my suit was getting pretty ripe by then.

The sun finished setting and the reality of the situation on Iora started to sink in. Until then I was focused on hiding, healing, staying close to food and listening for anyone or anything that might still be in the building. For the first time I started wondering what I'd do next. There were years worth of preserved food in the cafeteria between what was in passive stasis systems, gel containment, and the foods that wouldn't go off for a decade or more. I had my emergency pile, all bagged up and ready to go, and even that was enough to last three months thanks to the high efficiency nutrient bars I found, but I only put that together because I was bored. That, along with leftover medical supplies, a couple hand lights I managed to rig up from bot parts that survived the EMP, and a makeshift machete I made from a protective plate off the side of one of the machines made up my whole go bag. I was still on the lookout for more useful stuff, so it was a work in progress.

I wondered if my fighter survived the EMP, it could fly without complex electronics, it was that old, but where would I go? The questions started getting louder in my head, boiling down to two main ones: Do I stay here? Why would I go?

I could imagine having to run. I had no working weapons other than a nasty looking machete that couldn't be that useful, really. I didn't know if I could make something out of the thing I had, the inside of my sidearm looked so needlessly complicated that I gave up after poking at it for a few days. There was little chance the soldiers left anything, and any weapons lockers in the building should be locked. "But someone had to go down fighting, right?" I asked Lurk. "I mean, if the bots went nuts, and this is a defensive platform with a vault at the bottom, someone had to open a weapons locker with something useful inside before the EMP zapped everything. A lot of the guns I've seen would still work if they got zapped."

"Search?" Lurk croaked.

"Yeah," I told him. "I hate leaving the cafeteria, but I think I'm going to have to. Besides, I've only got about thirty restorative tablets left. That's enough for me, but not enough to trade with, or enough to get jacked up on if I get into real trouble."

"Four a day," said my lizard.

"I know, that's what the bottle said, but that's for someone at full body weight, I'm skinny for my height, so even that's probably a heavy dose for me. It's working, though." I thought about the large building beneath me. It was huge, and I was sure there would be secure areas hiding who knew what. "What I need is a crowbar."

"Tonight?"

"We'll start exploring tomorrow," I told Lurk.

The sun set and the stars came out, a display that only the cosmos could put on in as near as no light as I've ever seen on a planet. I could see a group of stars that formed a perfect set of boxes, and it took me a while, but I noticed that they were moving in such a way that I concluded that they belonged to something that was slowly rotating. One of the stations that were in orbit, maybe, it was big, whatever it was, and I was thankful that it wasn't directly overhead. If it crashed shielded, the destruction would be unimaginable. There were many lights that didn't have the right behaviour to be stars. If I found one that was obviously under power, turning, weaving, I could at least hope that there was something alive up there. I lost count of how many lights I followed across the sky before giving up that night. None of them moved in a curve, or turned as they crossed my field of vision. I pretended that I wasn't looking for the DD or any of the other ships I knew, but I was fooling myself. There was no way I could make them out, but I still hoped someone got out alive. There could be friends on the planet, in the same hemisphere most likely if they made it to escape pods. Some of them must have. Finding them was a problem. Normally I would have had the Stellarnet on my comm, helping me figure out what lights belonged to what, or a sort of legal Navnet connection set up to tell me where everything went. None of that was going to happen, and I felt blind. Even worse, without anyone I knew aside from a synthetic lizard, I felt lost.

Looking back at that jagged skyline, I could see a few tiny flickering points of light, but the great capitol was dead. If I was to believe the soldiers and those business suits, most of the people there were dead too. I tried to focus in on the flickering points of light and realized that those fires must have been huge. They were high up, too. There were four near the middle of giant skyscrapers, and three near the ground, but those buildings were either slowly going out, or being hollowed out by flames as they made their way up. "Guess we fried all the safety measures in those places too."

The wind began to pick up, cool, from across the ocean. I shivered, Lurk retreated into the collar of my suit, and I made my way back down to the cafeteria by the light of a chemical torch.

PART ELEVEN

The Commerce Complex was larger than most large space ships I'd been in. The backup lights left everything in half-light, but the chemical flashlight I had made up for it when I focused it into a tight beam.

The further in I went, the more complete the silence was until I was self conscious about my every footfall, and knocking a mug off a counter nearly gave me a heart attack. The cacophony of porcelain shattering against the tiled floor seemed to fill the universe for a few seconds, signalling to everything around that there was an intruder about.

I stood completely still for a long minute, listening for any approaching bot or soldier. When my heart slowed back down, and the silence fell back down around me like a dark blanket; I moved on.

The eeriest place I found was a floor with a couple

hundred work stations arranged in cubicle blocks. I could imagine what that must have looked like during a workday. So many voices must have blended into a buzz of wordless noise, and so many people must have looked like a too-well organized village, where everyone had their own cube casa, with a few cheap display sheets pinned to their little walls with family, funny pictures, or encouraging images. One of the films survived the electromagnetic pulse, and I noticed it right away. The image loop the previous user loaded into it was a tiny puppy that looked like a teddy bear sniffing a giant flower. I pulled it off the inside of the cubicle, turned it off, rolled it up and stuffed it into my bag. A working screen had to be worth something.

Then I started checking data and computing modules left behind. There were company bracer units and slim computers that were only a couple centimetres wide, nine centimetres long but had ports of every type on each side. "Nice," I said, picking one up and trying to turn it on.

"Burnt," Lurk said as it failed to boot.

"Well, we're here looting right, and we've got food. Next is communication," I told him. "There are hundreds of these things around, and they're all better than the PC's I've had. If one works, and one probably does, since this crappy screen survived the pulse, then we've might be able to figure out what our next move is, or get a map of this place at least."

"Unlikely," Lurk said as he slipped under my collar.

"Or I could connect you to this screen. Maybe if I try to reprogram you to do more than shoot down my ideas I'll get somewhere."

"Unkind," said Lurk from where he had burrowed.

"Just asking for a little more positivity, buddy," I replied as I tried the fifth computer module, hoping it worked. It was this cool looking wrist unit with a holo projector built right in, but it was absolutely fried.

An hour later I hadn't made it through a quarter of the cubicles, but I found a computer that turned on. The tiny screen flashed red and informed me that I was not authorized to use that unit. "Well it works," I told Lurk. "Think you could connect to it and reset it to factory defaults later so I can register as the user?"

"Yes," Lurk said.

"Fantastic, we have a computer, now we need some kind of battery to..."

"Die, fleshling!" screamed a menacing, booming voice from behind me.

I jumped so high that I swear my head brushed the ceiling. A glance behind me into the shadows revealed a thin android surging forward with a rifle slung across its chest. Its artificial flesh was half ripped and burned off, but its eyes were bright red lights.

I didn't even bother to pocket the wrist computer, but clutched it in my hand as I ran back the way I came as fast and as low as I could, sure that I'd hear the sound of the android's pulse rifle behind me an instant before I was burned to death.

I made it through the double doors leading to the cubicle village and redoubled my pace down the straight hallway, taking the next corner so fast I slammed into the wall across the hall before ducking behind cover. "If only I could find a working weapon," I said, trying to catch my breath.

I was about to continue my running retreat then I realized, the android hadn't followed me out of the cubicle room. I waited, trying to quiet my rapid breathing so I could listen intently, but the beating of my heart seemed like the loudest thing in the whole complex.

I pocketed the computer, and pulled a cylinder of nutrient tablets so I could move them to a lower pocket and started running again. I wasn't going to take any chances that that bot was somehow contained.

I turned the next corner, retracing my steps, and came face to face with my robot enemy. He pointed the large barrelled weapon at me and shouted; "Halt!" My instincts were dead on, he wasn't contained within the cubicle village, he had gone around the other way.

I held my hands up, and realized in that second of terror that I was still holding the cylinder of nutrient pellets, which had a neat dispenser button on the top. None of the bots that I'd seen tearing people to shreds seemed to have much of a care for self preservation, but I had to give this new plan a try. The only other option was trying to outrun a machine that could probably move at twenty-five kilometres an hour.

"This is a grenade!" I shouted, brandishing the nutrient tablet cylinder but hiding the label in my palm. All he could see was a pink button with my thumb on top of it.

"Oh no!" the bot said, his eyes going wide. He took a step back, really panicked, and raised the barrel of his rifle. "Hey, look, no need to blow yourself up, young man, I thought you were one of those soldiers."

"Put the gun down!" I said, knowing I was pressing my luck.

"Okay," the bot placated, the red glow fading from his eyes. There was either real fear, or a damn good simulation of it in them. "I can't even pull the trigger, my programming won't let me shoot you."

The gun was on the floor, and the robot, without me asking, kicked it over. At my feet was a fully mechanical rifle with an under-barrel magazine that looked like it had hundreds or thousands of needle rounds loaded inside. I'd seen the type before, just not the militarized version; it was vicious looking, made to look like more popular pulse rifles. With as much speed as I could manage, I picked it up and pointed it at the android.

By the time I'd managed it, the bot was facing the other direction and two steps into a limping run. "Stop!" I said, not even sure what I was thinking at the time. "You said you ran into some soldiers?"

The android halted and turned around with its head half bowed. It was looking away from the barrel of the rifle with its hands up. "I couldn't get away, so when they caught me with one of their flamers I let them burn part of my skin off before shutting down and playing dead. When I powered on a day later they'd done a bit of damage, and removed my main power core, so I went looking for a cycle battery that could still recharge itself, found a little one, enough to give me a few hour's charge at a time. When you came in I was letting the battery recharge, it takes about a day, and I was on standby."

"Why didn't the soldiers take the gun from you?"

"Oh, yeah, I found that while I was scavenging," he replied. "Figured I could use it to scare more soldiers off at least. It didn't work, evidently," the bot said sheepishly.

"Oh, it worked," I replied. "My heart's still pounding like a spastic hammer arm. If you didn't try to scare me again here, I would have kept running and never looked back. Every bot I saw was tearing humans apart and feeding them into matter converters."

"Not me!" the bot said. "I'm a high security data storage bot, employees used to dump their drives into me and I'd hold information for them until it was time to pass it on to someone else who met my security criteria."

"Uh-huh," I replied. "So, why aren't you a crazy bot trying to rip my face off?"

"Right, I guess I didn't answer clearly. I never connect directly to a network. That would be a huge security breach. I only connect to portable computers that are registered with the company. I'm one secure, mature computer with non-essential programming for allure and I'm made to endure."

"Okay, that explains everything, but I still expect you to come after me in my sleep," I told him.

"Hey, if I could kill you, or even wanted to hurt you, I would have, right? That cannon I gave you is a true instrument of death and destruction, but I can not pull the trigger when I know it will do you harm. Don't believe me? Give it a try."

I pointed it above his head and tapped the trigger. The safety was off, and the ceiling behind him lit up as a dozen or more thin, explosive shard rounds were fired from the barrel. I stopped firing and found the safety as quickly as I could.

"Careful! Careful!" the bot shouted as he ducked, panicked and turning in one place with his hands over his head.

"Sorry," I told him, partly by reflex. "It's my first assault cannon."

"Okay, so now, do you you believe that I don't want to 'rip your face off?'"

I thought for a moment, trying to ignore the terrified look on his face and the way he was cowering as close to the floor as he could get while still standing on two feet. "Yeah, I guess I do."

"Logically, safe," Lurk croaked, peeking his head out from under my collar.

"Hey, I love those little synthetics, that's the lizard, right?" he said, brightening up at the sight of Lurk.

"Yeah, I've had him a long time," I told him. "We gave them out as top carnival game prizes."

"You used to work at a carnival?" the bot's eyes brightened, and not in a 'I want to murder everything with a pulse' way, but in a 'oh my God, you're someone famous and amazing,' way. "I love carnivals. Clowns, rides, games that are unfair to the public, bearded ladies, dancers, illogical acts that could inflict great harm on the performers," he said. "Not that I've ever been to one myself."

I wanted to tell him about my carnival, about the Wicked

Wonders, our Issyrian shape shifter troupe, or the whirl-a-toss, the game I was allowed to set up and watch every time we made landfall, and about the rest, but instead I could only manage to agree. "Yeah, I'm a carny, but I think my people and my carnival are gone." I think the look of sympathy that I saw on his face won me over then. I lowered the rifle. "Do you have a name?"

"Yasmine, one of my favourite investment officers, gave me one. I'm Theodore, everyone calls me Theo," he said straightening up. "I think I lost all my people too."

PART TWELVE

Theo was half broken. The burns to his cosmetic skin and the basic protection beneath were more extensive than I thought, and some of his joints were barely hanging on, especially on his left side. I couldn't see the extent of the damage while he was chasing me while he pretended to be a red eyed killer bot, but it didn't take long to see why the soldiers left him for dead as I followed him through a labyrinth of cubicles.

"How did the pulse miss you?" I asked him as we crossed the large cubicle village. The only sounds were my voice and the laboured whirr-grind of his joints.

"My data and backup systems are carefully shielded, and my joints are mostly mechanical with the control circuits hidden within my innermost casing," Theo replied. "As the office's secure data repository for Sure Investments, it is essential that I remain in place, intact, and that the information people placed in me several times a day is undamaged. I'm also quite lucky. The damage the soldiers did could have rendered me helpless, but I'm still ambulatory so I have a lot to be thankful for. I will have to shut down and let a charge re-accumulate soon though. I just want to show you where I keep my collection first."

When I asked Theo: "How can I trust you?" he told me that he'd show me I could by bringing me to his most prized collection. I had the feeling that he was making every effort to either show me that he wanted to be a friend, or that he was trying to trick me. I would see soon enough. The storage and maintenance room for bots was right ahead. It seemed every time he answered one question, it led to more, so being as bored as I was, I didn't hold back. "What kind of information do people store in you? I mean, you're off network, right?"

"So what are people hiding in me?" Theo asked. "I'm immune to interrogation, I'll have you know."

"Hold on, I'm not asking for anything specific, like 'where does Duke Douchebag the Third keep the crown jewels?' I'm just wondering what kind of info you're carrying around. You know, generally."

"Generally speaking, some of Sure Investments' clients want them to know about some of their collateral and holdings, but they don't want the rest of the galaxy to be aware of their nature or location. I have records of several long range exploration yachts, the true ownership of several settled moons, last will and testaments for wealthy people, as well as the transferrable deeds for several hundred mines because they are currently up for trade. If my internal data compartment is compromised, all that information, and the encrypted, unique files are then deleted."

"So those soldiers almost cost some rich people a lot of platinum?" I asked.

"Trillions," Theo replied. "Not that I care about such things. I'm not very important despite the importance of what I carry. Another secure data bot could replace me easily, which is likely since I found my own controller key."

I knew exactly what he was talking about. The few bots my outfit could afford weren't smart enough to know what to do with their own controller key – the encrypted key that allowed someone to take possession of that bot – but a machine like Theo might try to become their own master. Usually the failsafe kicks in and the bot's memory is wiped, they drop the key on the deck and the owner can reclaim the machine. Sometimes, and it doesn't happen often from what I know, a really smart bot will find a way to free themselves, and they run off, looking for one of those hyper-progressive moons where artificial intelligences have civil rights. For the owner it means they're out thousands of platinum, and sometimes their bots even put a price on their head if they weren't treated so well. I didn't get the impression that Theo's programming would allow him to use his controller key on himself, but I kept my mouth shut just in case. I was just figuring out what his deal was, who knew what would happen if he tried to use his own controller key and inadvertently restore himself to factory defaults or worse.

"Some of what I'm about to show you might require some explanation, I'll do my best," he said as he opened the door to his service room and stumbled through. "I have to sit down." He dropped onto a wide seat. "My legs take more energy than anything else."

Glow sticks had been arranged around a wall of disposable display sheets that Theo must have salvaged. A little battery kept them all running as they displayed the faces of at least twenty employees in the building. Some were animated, as though recorded by someone who pleasantly surprised them in their cubicles or the hallways. I'd seen the inside of a few churches, some of us carnival folk are superstitious, and I like to pray sometimes, I'll admit, and the wall of displays reminded me of candle lit memorials that I'd seen in a few holy places. "This is beautiful, Theo," I told him. I looked at him in time to see his head nodding forward, as though he were about to fall asleep like a kid who had been up way past his bedtime.

"Do you think they'd like it?" he asked. "I hope so, they are all people who treated me like a person while I was working here." His head drooped then came back up. "They were my friends."

"I think they'd like it," I said. "Are you all right?"

"Down to a trickle of power, I thought I had more," Theo said. "Before I go, I need to show you something." He started to struggle as though he were about to get to his feet.

"Stay there, point at whatever, man. No need to kill your battery for good," I told him. I didn't know if his type of battery cell could be recharged if it was depleted completely, but I didn't want to take the chance.

"There," Theo said, pointing to a small box under the

memorial. "Hard keys for the armoury, the secure data vault, the platinum reserve vault, biological sanctuary, and the emergency communications system under this building. The hard keys will bypass the codes that you would normally need to enter those secure areas. It's what I was hiding from the soldiers. I could have hid, I could have shut down so they wouldn't find me, but they caught me when I was drawing them away from those keys."

"You had to know they'd catch you, and what would happen," I told him.

"All part of the plan," Theo shrugged. His head lolled down so his chin was on his chest. That was the last of the power he had to run his servos. "I didn't think I'd survive, but life is full of surprises. I'm happy they didn't get them. Some soldiers are good, they rescue people, protect them. The ones who came here were professional a..."

I waited a moment before finishing for him. "Assholes?"

"Agitators," he corrected with a snicker. "Corporate thugs. They fight for clients, for money, make trouble for competitors, murder or capture people from opposing companies so one stock rises and another falls."

"So, why give them to me?"

"You remind me of someone I trusted. Besides, you don't know how to use them. You'll have to fix me first."

"Devious," I said with a smile. "In a good way."

"You'll help?"

"Why not?" I said. "Nothing else to do."

"Snacks and working technology from this level in the box to your left," he said. "I must power down now." The lights went out, so to speak. There wasn't a sign of life left in the android after that for about fourteen hours.

I didn't need any of the food he offered, but I thought I'd look in his box anyway. There were a few wrapped gifts, small things with the names of the people on the wall written on them. I left those alone, piled neatly where I found them. Thinking about Theo during better days, remembering people's birthdays and giving them presents as he did his thing in the office got me way down. I mean, here was this bot who really had to make sure he was around for people to plug drives into him so their data was secure. That was his job, I guess, he could have stood in the middle of the room and done nothing, but from the recordings on the sheets he hung, and the other playbacks I found it looked like he was Mister Sunshine, spreading good vibes and keeping morale sky high.

The relationships he had in the building were real, so much so that I felt like a creep for digging through recordings after a while. I got a real laugh from one though, when he found out that Neke, one of the associate brokers was seven months pregnant. The recordings had to be from his protected systems, I found them dumped onto a disposable display. In them he's knocking on her belly; "hello, little human. Should I tell her that you're a girl?" The ladies gathered around erupted in shock and laughter, no one was more surprised than Neke. She must have been a special lady, because she was shocked at first. "I'm sorry, I'm only good at keeping corporate secrets!" Theo said. She must have been overjoyed at the news, and obviously didn't blame Theo for spilling the beans, because she was hugging him a few seconds later.

For the next five weeks, he was her servant whenever time allowed, and he had a pile of favourite moments recorded to prove it. I thought it ended with Neke putting her new born in his arms a few weeks after she – Miiri – was born. Theo was absolutely in awe, and a pretty good touch with the kid too. I sat in that dark service room, looking from that tender moment to this broken down bot that was adopted by a special bunch of employees and started seeing him for the lost guy he was. Then the playback switched to something I won't get into. Neke was working on the day the bots went nuts, they got her in the lobby. I don't know where her kid is, I hope she's safe somewhere. Theo took care of her body. The last recording on that screen was Theo telling her; "I'm sorry they killed you, Neke Summers. I will miss you." He placed her in a recycling machine with the rest of the bodies and locked it. I didn't check out the rest of the stacked up screens or see if any of the ones he'd hung had playback in them. That was enough of a punch in the gut for one day.

I checked another box out and found a few chocolate covered strawberries and orange slices, some real gourmet stuff. There were also enough meal bars to last me a month. If I didn't already have the food and water problems taken care of, Theo would have saved my life.

While he was sleeping I thought of all the questions I should have asked him, isn't that always the way? Are there other bots around that survived the electromagnetic pulse? Would any of the vaults and secure areas open, even with a hard key? Did any part of the facility still have power, or could it be reset? Repaired?

The question that haunted me most was one of the last ones to come to mind: Would the emergency communications system be able to find my people?

The flow of images and short rescued video clips accompanied by Noah's voice was interrupted by a high priority alarm. The new system in Alice's comm unit sent a sense of urgency through her nervous system, and she had a mental picture of where she had to go before she checked the display on her wrist. "I've never seen that part of the starbase before," Alice said to herself.

"What section?" Yawen asked from the bed across the room.

"It's a secure briefing room three levels up," Alice explained. She wasn't sure she should name it, being marked as clearance level seven. "I have a briefing there; it's classified."

"I didn't get any orders," Yawen said. "Must be for all you nineties."

Nineties was a new slang term that was starting to float around. It referred to the students who still had over ninety points. "Maybe, I'll tell you about it if I can."

"No worries, I have enough to deal with. Two make-up tests tomorrow," Yawen said. "See you later."

Alice made sure her uniform was in order and left her

quarters at a jog. She met Ute, the small amphibian, and Iruuk in the lift. "Priority briefing?" she asked.

"Classified level seven!" Ute said in an excited whisper. "I thought there were only three security levels."

"Just because that's all we've ever had access to, doesn't mean that's all there is to see," Iruuk said.

"I guess I was too busy to think about it," Ute said with a shrug.

"You have a point," Iruuk said. "They have been cramming so much information in our brains and putting us through so many practical tests, I can't imagine what they want us to learn about now."

The lift arrived and the trio stepped out, joined by Titus and the rest of the Nineties. "Yawen's doing two makeup exams tomorrow. She's in the mid seventies in terms of points, I tell her that's amazing, and it is, but she's still scrounging to recover a few points at a time."

"They're important practical exams though," Ute said. "Navigation Three and Technical Support Five. I took Tech Five with her: she barely passed. If she passes on her own she could recover three points. I think she could do it. Her problem is her frustration level, which leads to counterproductive behaviour, not her intelligence."

"She does freak out when she runs into a problem she doesn't like sometimes. I'm just worried that if she retakes too much, she'll fall behind and not enter service with us," Alice said.

"I would rather graduate with as many points as possible,"

Iruuk said. "So I can see why she wants to go to the trouble. Tell her I can help if she likes."

"I will, maybe she'll take help from you."

They arrived at the broad double doors and walked through as a group. The long room had slate coloured metal walls and floors with only just enough light to walk by. Three clicks on the intercom indicated that an important instruction was about to be given. The door closed. "Stand at attention and face the port side, please."

Everyone in the room snapped to and fell silent. The three-metre-tall wall in front of them became transparent, revealing the inside of one of the base's manufacturing bays. Arms with reclamation tools that seemed to erase metal as easily as a smudge on glass were busy taking a Haven Shore Runner Class Corvette apart.

"What you are seeing is Classified Level Seven," said Ayan as she entered through a door from the left. Her curly red hair was bound up in a bun, and she wore a heavy black jacket over her uniform with the markings of Admiral on her shoulder. Insignia on her chest indicated that she was the Haven Shore Navy Operations Commander.

"That's one hell of a promotion," Perry muttered quietly.

"It is," Ayan said, her expression relaxed, and her diction clear. "The newly elected leadership appointed trustworthy leaders to the Haven Shore military, and I landed here. I would have liked to work my way up to my position, but they saw me as the only suitable candidate for this post. That isn't to say that I wasn't subjected to testing. Testing I encourage everyone here to try. You will not lose points for failing, but you could gain a few if you manage to make it through half the simulations."

Ayan glanced at Alice, her expression unchanging, then turned towards the transparent wall. "Be sure that is the last time I will ever explain how I got my rank or position in this Fleet. Now, for the reason you're really here. I am embarrassed to say that the ships built based on my incomplete designs while I was away had critical flaws. The Runner Class Corvette was an ambitious design, but poorly thought out hull geometry, power systems that don't take new technology into account, and non-modular thinking render it worse than obsolete – these problems make this model dangerous. It is easier to recycle the entire line and build a new one than it would be to make changes to existing ships. I realize that you are all waiting for your trainee postings on these ships, but that will obviously have to wait. The Runner Class is being scrapped today."

Alice's heart sank. All the effort she put into learning about that ship had gone to waste. She'd even dreamt of being on the bridge of one of the high speed response combat vessels.

PART THIRTEEN

Alice looked from Ayan, where the Admiral stood at the edge of the window watching the disassembly of a warship that was less than a year old, to the warship itself as it was taken apart. The robotic arms attacked it from all sides, converting metal to raw materials with graceful sweeps and jagged pulling motions. Carnie, or Noah, the subject of her classified report, was on her mind.

"I can't take all the responsibility for this failure," Ayan said. "But I share it. While I was away chasing my past, Freeground Station, the lead designer here favoured production speed so much that she disabled many of the check systems built into Lorander software. These safeties would have highlighted errors and flaws in the design of the Runner Class. If they knew how to use the rest of the building system, it would have provided solutions as well, saving them time overall. The

Lorander systems hadn't been programmed with what we've learned about the dimension drive technology either, so every adaptation of the Edxi machinery was flawed. It's a secret the Fleet kept from our closest allies, and it could not stand. The next version of the technology is decades ahead of what you've seen, but you have enough training already to know the basics."

The anxiety shared by the Officer Cadets was thick in the air. Ayan turned towards them in time to see Ute blow a large bubble. It popped as it grew to the size of her head and the amphibian regarded the Admiral with embarrassed, wide eyes. "I'm sorry, Admiral. It was an involuntary reaction to stress, Ma'am. I have it under control, Ma'am."

"It's all right, Cadet," Ayan said. "I needed you all to see where over-confidence and an unwillingness to do the work required to get things right the first time can get you. Many of the errors here could have been prevented if the people responsible for building the Runner Class before the design was ready were willing to look deeper into the technology Lorander gave us. To put it simply; they only had to read the manual."

There were a few nervous chuckles, and Ute smiled warmly at Ayan, who returned the gesture, but only for a moment. She went on, and Alice could see that Ayan was a little excited. "While I was making the journey from the Iron Head Nebula, I made sure that the secrets I discovered could be taught, and that I could show people how they could improve our situation here. I learned more in that time than I ever thought I could. That fighter cockpit was a fantastic classroom, and the poor pilot who was in charge of making certain that I got home in one piece is back in training. Not to sharpen her skills as a pilot, but to enrol in the new Apex program, which started two days ago. When I returned I shared this knowledge with a large team that has been going through the Lorander documentation and learning about the technology they gave us. Using this information and some new discoveries, we've designed a new ship that is going through testing at every stage. Most of us have been working so hard that we don't remember what our quarters look like; the team deserves more credit than I can give for their dedication. Some of you have parents and friends on this team, and all of you have had a hand in the refinement of these ships. Some of your practical testing has included advanced Lorander technology that you have had to learn to use during the course. You've all helped to improve ship layouts, operational software, and other systems we've put in front of you. Most of your training on the Runner Class ships will apply here, especially with the system interfaces, so the operating system may be more advanced, and you'll learn more later, but you could sit at a station and start serving today if you had to. That's a good thing, because you're going to be assigned to a ship soon. You will still be cadets, but we've determined that you're ready to learn aboard a ship while you serve. Here's one of those ships now." The entire room jostled a little, and it only took Alice a moment to realize that it was moving. It shifted up first then towards the front of the station. When they stopped they were in front of another manufacturing bay, only this one was piecing together a ship that was still all interior and frame. Arms with industrial fabrication printer hands reached into the ship's core, leaving seats, beds, deck plating, wiring and plumbing behind with such grace and speed that it was mesmerizing.

Ayan manipulated a small interface on the window and the image of a vicious, heavily armoured ship was overlaid atop the window. "This is the Reaper Class, a multi-role vessel that is at the core of our operations. You will learn everything there is to know about the Reaper. This ship can run with a tenth of the crew compliment of a ship her size, respond faster than any vessel known in our galaxy, has intelligent armour plating, a new secure operating system, and more capabilities for a vessel in her class than anything built. We have used the most advanced technology wherever necessary, and when we could use familiar systems, we made sure that we implemented only the best designs. This ship does put the lessons we learned from the Runner Class into play, but also brings in technology from the Triton that we've come to depend on while building using Lorander tools and some of their most proven designs. By the time everyone else learns about this, you will be experts. The rest of your academic studies have been suspended, which is no loss since you've already completed the academic and practical testing required for you to serve aboard an advanced vessel. Any critical assignments or missions that are under way will be completed in the next five days. Following the five days you have to complete your critical assignments, there will be a mandatory two day rest. After that, if you aren't diverted to other posts, you will join my team so you can learn about the ship that will give us a chance in this war. Any questions?"

"Admiral, what will happen to our trainee recruits?" Iruuk asked.

"They have already been reassigned and their training will be brought in line with our new educational strategy."

"Ma'am," addressed Buto, one of the few trainees to have a score dip below ninety, then recover and return to ninety-one. "I don't see any weapon emplacements, how would this ship measure up against a Regent Galactic destroyer?"

"In ship-to-ship combat, I would hope the Regent Galactic destroyer would surrender for their own sake. If you include the fighter wing that the Reapers will be carrying, then there's little chance that an enemy destroyer would be worth mentioning at length in the captain's log," Ayan replied.

"Admiral, Ma'am," Ute said, stepping forward. "I wonder what is happening with our classmates? The ones with lower scores who are left behind?"

"The new Apex class, a group of eighty four officers who already have military experience, are joining them later today. We're redoubling our efforts to make sure that scores stop declining, and concentrating on specialties that will be determined by aptitude. You'll see them in the service, and they're getting the best training, don't worry."

"Thank you, Admiral," Ute said, slipping back in line.

There were more questions about systems, crew compliment, when they'd know what their assignments were, but Alice couldn't help wonder if the Admiral knew when her father would return, or if the rest of the fleet in the Iron Head Nebula were delayed.

After answering the short barrage of questions, Ayan looked the cadets over, then nodded to herself. "Haven Fleet takes care of its own. I'm happy to be the one who gets to tell you that you've all been given housing. You won't be spending your leave sleeping on sofas, in spare bedrooms or in the barracks. Instead, we've finished building the first phase of Paradise Landing, a city we're building for soldiers and their families. You will be some of the first to move in. It's still on the main island, so you're not far from Haven Shore, and it'll be under the defence shield, so there's no need to worry about safety. We want Paradise Landing to be your peaceful refuge, so if you have suggestions while you're there, submit them to Command. Your personal belongings have been moved there, and you're welcome to move family members in. Enjoy your leave, but be responsible. You are still on the point system. Your shuttles are waiting, dismissed."

The Officer Trainees saluted and filed out quietly, happy but stunned overall. Alice approached Ayan instead of following them through the hatch. She wasn't the only one. A trainee named Pirine approached, looked at Alice as though she wished she wasn't there, then back to Ayan. "Admiral, I was on track to command a Runner Class vessel, I've already learned everything I need to captain one as my first assignment. What happens now? I'm sure there are gaps in my training that I won't be able to make up in time to be the commander I want to be."

The Admiral looked a little amused. "No one in your

class was on track to captain anything, Trainee. Haven Fleet can't afford to give that command to any fresh graduate in the first Apex class, no matter what kind of experience they have, but your dedication wasn't wasted. You'll be picked as an officer in the fleet by a captain you can believe in." Ayan looked the Trainee's records up on a holographic display that was blurry to Alice. "You've completed all your compulsory assignments and nearly twice the electives we require, so go enjoy your time off. Clear your head, move in to the apartment you've earned in the new Paradise Landing Complex. There's already a teaching assignment waiting for you after that, it'll be temporary."

"Can I start running command sims with the Reaper Class during leave?" she asked.

"No," Ayan said. "It's time to give your mind a rest. You don't realize it now; but you need a break," she said firmly but reassuringly.

"All right, Admiral." Pirine nodded uncertainly and left the room quietly, looking a little lost.

When the door closed behind her, Alice wasn't sure how to address the Admiral, but the awkwardness fell away when Ayan embraced her warmly. "I've been meaning to visit, Alice," she said. "It seems like months have passed since I got back, but it's only been weeks, and every time I check on you, you've been right in the middle of something. Trainee Pirine would pass out if she saw how much harder you've worked."

"You can interrupt me any time," Alice said, finding more comfort in her adopted mother's arms than she expected. "I think about you and dad when things quiet down. Other times too."

"It's all right," Ayan said, letting her go slowly. "You're just as busy as I am."

"I doubt it," Alice said, turning towards the new ship through the transparent bulkhead. The arms were busy putting the finishing touches on the middle-most deck and starting to move on. Navy blue and polished metal plating was going into hallways, and ceiling panels with passive lighting preinstalled were being put into place. "You and your team must have stopped sleeping entirely to put this together."

"It's been busy, but there's something that they ignored with the Runner Class that we embraced completely. Lorander has been borrowing and implementing technology from multiple galaxies for a few centuries now, and they have a mature system for constructing new ships. This is the fifth design of the Reaper Class, and that's after two simulated iterations that we put together on day one – so we could learn how to use Lorander's tools. This is the first we've built for real, the official prototype, but their tools and the data we collected from everyone who tested parts of the ship virtually put us decades ahead. Lorander wanted us to win this war, but only if we could understand their technology, and catch up to their science. Figuring out the dimension drive technology that we found on the Fallen Star, the Edxian engineering inside, was a massive hurdle. It would have never happened without their knowledge, and now we have something that puts us way ahead of our enemies. The Reaper

Class won't be common in the fleet, it requires too many rare materials to produce a large number of them, but technology we're perfecting in it will be integrated into future ships. We're thinking of something smaller, like a small corvette class to start. Regardless of what our fleet will look like in a few months, or a year, Lorander's knowledge has changed the course of this war."

"Why do you think they chose us?" Alice asked.

"I thought about that a lot on my way back from the Nebula," Ayan said. "I think it was Haven Shore. They kept track of how our democracy was developing, which values we embraced, how we housed our people, and tried to bring them together as a community. Their notes to us with regards to social development are filled with encouragement and markers showing that they are excited about how our new culture is coming together around family and service. There are warnings too, but I didn't find any surprises there. They mostly want to make sure that we remember how important individual freedoms are even in a closely-knit society. I think they saw the kind of ideas that should spread, so they gave us the technology to defend ourselves, but even more importantly, the ability to quickly understand new breakthroughs in science as they're found in equipment we acquire from other civilizations. In the wrong hands, that could enable the worst kind of conquerors, but in ours I hope we can become famous explorers, diplomats, and defenders. We have to win a war first."

"What if exploring, and forming diplomatic ties are how they want us to win this war?" Alice asked.

"I quietly hope those become our core strategies," Ayan replied. "I couldn't be more proud of you, you know. Not just your scores, but the way you solve problems. You've gone from running-and-gunning early in your training to thinking things through, avoiding violence when you could. No puzzle has just one solution to you anymore, it shows."

"Thank you," Alice said. "I can't wait to stand on that ship. Even with Lorander tech holding your hand, it's amazing that it's coming together."

"You may not serve on it right away. A carrier is being refitted right now, it's barely modern by our standards, and it'll be critical to system defence. Your name has come up a few times with regards to core staff. It's not frontline, but it's an important post where you'll learn a lot. You might be asked to teach as well, if you have time. You'll be in broad demand while we finish the training tutorials."

"So you're grooming us as trainers?" Alice asked.

"Every good officer helps the members of their staff to improve. We're all teachers, in a way. If you don't want to be involved in the Academy after you're finished here, I could pull strings and get you assigned to the Reaper Prototype, but I wouldn't do that to you. Everyone who helps train the fleet commanders will have an amazing addition to their file, the kind that could allow them to choose their post when it's all over. You'll be even more important once your father and the rest of the fleet return from the Iron Head Nebula. Your experience and training make you stand out, trust me," Ayan reassured. "If you think being assigned as a teacher for a few weeks is holding you back, imagine how I feel."

"What's going on?"

"I'm on permanent assignment here, in the Rega Gain system. You can get assigned to a crew and leave the system, but I'll be here taking care of the hardware. I'm not disappointed, not really, it was inevitable with the way things were going. I'm still getting used to the idea, if I'm being honest. It does come with perks though. I can fly home at the end of the day, and the restriction on having a family may be relaxed for people who serve near home. I didn't plan on having one soon, but who knows what the future will bring with me and Jake? I'm hopeful."

"You want children?" Alice asked, feeling a little glee for her and her father.

"Of course. I'd love to give you a little sister or brother, but not before the time is right, mind you. Why?"

"I just saw you as a career person," Alice said. "But now that I'm thinking about it, I can see you with a few young ones."

"A few?" Ayan asked, slightly taken aback. "I still have to get to know you better, adding to the family right now would be a little much, I think."

"I know, just adapting to new possibilities," Alice said.

"You have a lot of time, your father and I are just getting used to being together again. I can't wait for him to get back. They're due in a couple of weeks, give or take a day or two."

"That seems like a long time to wait. I suppose we'll have to train most of the battlegroup on the new operating systems and technologies."

"Yes, but I think you'll be surprised at how quickly the

time passes. You'll be moving on to an assignment that takes you out of the system before you know it."

"No string pulling then," Alice said. "Half the people in the fleet believe that I'm here because of you and Dad already."

"I know what that's like, don't worry. I suggest you ignore them, just make what you can of the opportunities you have," Ayan said. "Like you've been doing."

"Speaking of opportunities, I have an assignment I need to talk to you about, but I'm supposed to keep it to myself."

"Noah Lucas, call sign Carnie," Ayan said. "I know you've been assigned to his file."

Alice breathed a sigh of relief. "Oh, thank you, I'm so glad I can talk to someone about it."

"You've effectively been promoted along with everyone who was just here. At their clearance level, you can talk to them about it too," Ayan said. "Why? Are you having trouble with your report?"

"No, well, a little, it's confusing," Alice said. "I keep on slowing down because I like listening to his narration."

"Ah, that would slow you down," Ayan said. "Maybe you like him a little too?"

"I don't know, he seems a little young in spirit to me," Alice said, smirking. "But I want to finish the report. I feel like we have a lot to learn about Iora, and the automated summary says he's about to leave the secure building he's been holed up in. I want to see what a pulsed-out world looks like, especially one like that, where there were over a billion bots serving."

"Then do it," Ayan said. "The Fleet has given you five days, and I'm giving you special permission to investigate Noah Lucas' past, no matter where it takes you. I'll give you special clearance, it's an appropriate measure considering Iora isn't far from the Rega Gain system. We need the information you're gathering."

"I don't know if I can get through it in five days," Alice said. "I guess a trip to Iora is out of the question then."

"You already charted the trip, haven't you?" Ayan asked.

"Well, yeah, but it would take nine days there and back. Wouldn't you?"

"I would, but you can't," Ayan said. She looked at the comm unit on the wrist of her jacket and shook her head. "I have to be going. There are shuttles waiting to bring you down to Paradise Landing, enjoy the new apartment."

"Oh. There's no way you could give me the time to..."

"Go to Iora? No," Ayan replied, shaking her head a little. The request was obviously amusing to her, but that didn't change the answer. "You'll have to be happy with the opportunity to investigate his account of events and make an assessment of the planet using that. If your report indicates that a deeper investigation would benefit the Fleet, then someone will follow up. At least you get to do the work in comfort. I put a few things in your closet, by the way."

"Thank you," Alice replied, starting to look forward to seeing her new place. "I can't believe you've already got a new housing complex going," Alice said.

"Now that the civilian branch has its own fabricator they can turn out thirty units a day, so our housing problem is under control for the moment. Your group is moving in early though, so you might not have local sushi delivery just yet." Ayan embraced her briefly, then led the way through the door. "I didn't pull any strings to get you the view, but you'll find a welcome package from me in the living room. Everyone got one, but I made sure there were a couple extra things in yours."

"Thank you," Alice said. "I'll see you soon?"

"I'll try to visit, and I'll call if I don't make it," Ayan said as she slipped through a side door.

"Petty Officer Alice Valent," said a gentle voice in Alice's ear. "Please follow the green line to your shuttle."

A thin green line appeared at her feet, leading her down the hallway. The embarkation room wasn't far off, and she found the rest of her group there. "Can you believe it? We're going to be ahead of everyone, maybe even teaching captains and commanders," Iruuk said excitedly.

"I'm sure they're already learning about the new systems," Alice said. "While you're doing that, I'll probably be finishing work on my classified assignment. There's still so much data to go through. My report will be novel length." She hoped everyone bought the pretence she was putting on, that her assignment would be too much hard work to enjoy.

"Oh, that's too bad," Pirine said, a little curl of her lips showing satisfaction that the Admiral's daughter would miss out on an opportunity. "I've already got my first assignment. Two days off, then I'll be going to the Aimsfield to train officers on new interface systems. Half of promotion is who you know, but I'm sure you're aware of that."

"If that's true, Alice has nothing to worry about," Buto said. "Hard work, daughter to a Captain, an Admiral and the Defence Minister's granddaughter? We'll all be taking orders from her as soon as we enter service."

"I work hard, like anyone else here," Alice said.

"She's going to be giving orders because she can solve problems before we even know we have a problem," Titus said. "She has nothing to prove."

"You're right, you're right," Buto said, putting his hands up and backing away. "Never mind, okay?"

"Apologize," Titus said. Iruuk added tension to the demand as he turned his snout towards the recruit and stood tall.

"I'm sorry I inferred that you get special treatment," Buto said. "Oh, look, shuttles." He said as he moved towards one of the airlock doors. The sounds of clamps engaging and air rushing to fill the airlocks made it clear that the second small ship that would take them down to Tamber was arriving.

"Don't do that again," Alice said. "I can fight my own battles, and I know there are hundreds of people like him in the service. I can't spend all my time fighting them, so just ignore it, okay?"

Iruuk nodded. "I'm sorry, I protect my friends, but I'll try to adjust."

"I see how hard you work," Titus said. "It just pissed me off, I apologize."

"Thank you," Alice said. She was about to get in line for a shuttle when Titus touched her arm. Iruuk was already moving off to the nearest airlock, the indicator above showed that it was almost ready.

"I'm wondering, now that we have a few days off," Titus said quietly. "If we could have dinner, maybe take a walk after?"

Alice momentarily wished she hadn't inherited her mother's complexion as she felt herself blush from neck to forehead. "Make good on that promise, you mean?"

"I would be asking you either way," Titus said. His confidence was enviable. "It was the first thing I thought of when I heard we were getting leave."

"Sure, give me a call tomorrow after we've settled in," she said. He was attractive, with broad features, and he wasn't so tall that she felt diminutive next to him. Titus carried himself like an officer already; well spoken, gentlemanly, and he seemed to have a well-evolved moral compass. "I'll look forward to it."

"Are you coming?" Iruuk called from the inner airlock door as he proceeded through.

PART FOURTEEN

"What is this?" Iruuk asked to himself as the shuttle turned so they could see the Paradise Landing Complex. He looked more excited than Alice had ever seen; his nose and bottom lip twitched, his eyes were wide open and his hand was pressed to the window. "We really get an apartment? Our own apartment?"

Alice stroked the soft fur beneath his shoulder. It was easy to forget that Iruuk was still a teenager in many ways. Nafalli could hunt their own food when they were only a few months old, and were considered mature when they turned sixteen. Even considering all that, she couldn't help but be excited right along with him.

Looking down, she took the sight of the new housing in. It was as though the building were pearlescent seashells balanced between the upper trunks of jungle trees. The jungle's edge was filled with rounded apartments that over-looked a white and yellow beach. Many of them had a retractable landing pad, and bulbous additions that indicated that there were several rooms and extra storage compartments.

"I mean, it's impressive, but not that amazing," Buto said. "It would take our orbital constructor fifteen minutes to print one of these houses out, maybe thirty if they printed those artificial trees too."

Alice saw them then, the supports holding the apart-ments up were shaped like trees, but she could see the glint of metal here and there. The walkways looked like they were made of wood as well, but she could tell that they were definitely made of metal. In the middle of the complex was an incomplete space port, its round outline and outer armour looked finished, but dozens of drones were busy delivering segments of walkway, deck plating and parcels of materials to the hollow interior. "I don't really care how long it took them to build it," Alice said. "I'm just glad it's here."

"I thought I was lucky to share a room with one person, only one person," Iruuk said. "I've never had a space for myself. Just myself, only me." He looked at Alice, still excited but a little panicked. "What will I do with it?"

"Invite your family," Alice replied.

"We could have dinner together at my place!" he shouted. "I could make a climbing gym for my brothers and sisters!"

"His mother just gave birth to eleven," Alice told Titus, who was stunned.

"No wonder he's not used to having his own space," he replied.

The shuttle touched down on a landing pad and the door opened. "This is your stop, Valent," a voice said over the intercom.

"I'll see you later, Fur-Face," Alice said. "Before you do anything, just relax. You worked hard, you earned it."

The landing pad was much larger than she expected, so much so that when the shuttle left, she felt small. A breeze ran through her hair, bringing with it the fragrance of the upper jungle. If someone ever asked what the colour green smelled like, she'd take them there, where the sweet fragrance of new growth mixed with old jungle surrounded her.

The sound of the ocean drew her attention to the left, where she smiled at a long line of sand drawn between the jungle and the water that looked so clean and inviting that she was tempted to call the shuttle back. Her friend, Ashley came to mind, the real sun lover, and all at once she missed the friends who were still on their way back from the Iron Head Nebula. Ashley, Minh-Chu, Remmy, her father, among others and one more person who she never met; Carnie, or Noah Lucas as she'd come to know him. She hoped her own artificial intelligence and ship were intact as well, and as Alice thought of them she realized that the landing pad was large enough for the Clever Dream. "You think of everything, mother." she said to herself as she moved on to the apartment.

As she stepped up into the side door, the landing pad folded into itself and retracted, turning into a sizeable balcony with a high railing that surrounded most of the suspended building. Upon entering the apartment, she noticed a door to her left and opened it. A winding ramp led to an empty hangar, large enough for the Clever Dream and a pair of small shuttles. "On one hand I can't believe this is mine, on the other I'm afraid of what the military are going to ask me to do for it," she said to herself. "This isn't an apartment, it's a house."

"Expectations are high based on your existing qualification scores and your record, Petty Officer Alice Valent," a cheery female voice said from overhead. "I'm Roomie, a basic management program that you can modify to suit your needs and whims."

"Roomie, cute," Alice said, ascending the ramp.

"You can rename me however you like," Roomie replied.

"It's okay for now. Do all officers get housing like this?"

"Your model is designed for service people who are expected to have a broad variety of assignment types. Since you have a ship of your own, the hangar and vessel management features have been added. A personal shuttle will be delivered as soon as you choose a design. That is a unique offering to you because the Clever Dream has been on loan to the fleet for so long."

"So they're giving me a loaner until I get it back."

"The shuttle is yours to keep," Roomie said, almost too happy to deliver the news. "You are also being granted extra luxury credit because the Clever Dream has been on loan. That has not changed the type of apartment you were given, however. Upstairs you'll find accommodations that Haven Shore designed and built to suit your current lifestyle and tastes, while being adaptable to many life changes. Using luxury credits, you can expand your home as well, the walls can reconfigure and grow enough for two more rooms. Any more expansion would require extra modifications, and there is a waiting list."

Alice tried to control her excitement as she emerged into the main apartment through the hangar and balcony entrance. A few steps up took her to the main room, where there was a circular sitting area set around a low table. The curved sofas and thickly padded chairs made her want to invite all her friends and family over. She kicked off her boots and stepped onto the blue carpet. Its fibres were silky on her bare feet.

Light from the floor to ceiling windows behind and in front of her flooded the space, and as she neared the centre of the space, she saw that the roof was transparent, letting even more sunlight in. "This is amazing."

"The windows are all one-way blind, meaning that you can see out, light can pass in, but no one looking inside can see you or your guests. You can also use the windows to view whatever video playback you like, or block light entirely." As a demonstration all the windows began displaying a vista as though the home was resting on the beach, the sounds of the waves made the visual seem even more convincing. It switched to a view from Tamber orbit then, and again it was perfectly convincing. Alice took a moment to take it in before telling Roomie; "You can switch back to the real view; I get the feeling I'll be seeing plenty of space."

The windows became transparent again, and the sight of

the jungle walkways on one side, the open sky and beach below on the other appeared again. "Walls without windows are linked to the aquarium system, which is also a vegetable garden," Roomie said.

Every wall without a window became transparent then, revealing tropical fish that leisurely went about their business. A shelf door above raised, revealing the top of the aquarium where new green sprouts were piercing a layer of black soil above the water. "I didn't plan on doing any gardening, but this is incredible."

"The varieties of fish in the tank feed off the nutrients that drop from the soil, and enrich it while keeping the water clean. Any of the fish you see are available for consumption. You can prepare them yourself in the kitchen or the automated system will catch them for you and do it using state of the art preparation systems. This system also keeps your living space at an optimal temperature. The gardening system is automatic, so you don't have to maintain the forty-two square metres of garden space built into your walls unless you'd like to."

"What happens when I'm away? What if there's a harvest?"

"The vegetables and berries are sent to the central food distribution hub. Nothing is wasted. Would you like to leave the walls open so you can enjoy the garden and aquarium?"

"Just the aquarium system for now." She moved on, discovering a kitchen she supposed two people could work in at once. She used the drink dispenser to create a peach and orange smoothie before moving all the way across the apartment to the opposite rooms, rubbing her feet along the carpet the whole way. Her bedroom was lit from the corners with soothing yellow light. There was a fully adaptable bed larger than any she'd slept in with an intelligent membrane instead of a mattress. It was piled high with pillows and blankets. She put her drink down on the dresser and leapt into the middle of the bed with an excited squeal. Everything was soft, inviting and warm. One thick blanket especially wrapped around her and gently held her whole body, leaving only her face free of the nearly overwhelming comfort. "That adult sized swaddling blanket is a gift from Ayan, originally made for babies, the Haven Shore Civilian Design Branch has created a full sized version for adults that adjusts to the comfort needs of the user or couple."

"So comfy..." Alice sighed. When her eyelids began to lower a few moments later, she sat up. "Now I can't wait for bed, but we press on!"

"Ayan put a modest clothing order in for you, and your belongings have already been unpacked in a predictable fashion, so you shouldn't have trouble finding anything."

Alice looked around a little more, finding a fully equipped bathroom that included a deep bath that her and a friend could submerge in, her things in the closet and dresser, and finally, a few new outfits.

As she picked up the first, a long dress with a slit part way up one leg made of light, shimmery dark blue cloth, a message from Ayan played; "I don't know what kind of style you would like, but a mutual friend of ours suggested this one, just in case you needed something for a night you'd like to dress up. The others are outfits I thought you'd like, enjoy." Alice remembered that she had a dinner date sometime with Titus then and wondered if the dress was too much. It was modest enough, baring her back with a crossover design in the front that flowed nicely into the lower half, but it looked more like a formal gown. She put it back and looked at the rest. There was a comfortable, long loose dress that was made of soft material, and a sleeved green dress with a short skirt made of stretchy cloth. In one of the drawers there was a variety of tops and bottoms including some intelligent clothing that could be reshaped, which rounded out her wardrobe. There were more clothes there than she remembered owning, but the dresser and closet were still mostly empty.

"There are three shops open on the promenade at the moment, with more opening soon in case you don't like anything you have," Roomie said.

"I like everything here, it's just..." she ran her hand over the smooth green cloth of the more casual dress in her closet. "I don't remember the last time I took time to think about what I wore." Alice took the comfortable looking long dress out then slipped out of her uniform as she walked to the shower.

A long shower later, she was in the casual dress her mother chose for her. "I'm guessing this is the kind of thing she lounges at home in," she said. It was comfortable, and when she sat on the sofa, she could curl up in the loose material and cover her feet.

"The common use for that is as a stay-at-home comfort garment, so you are correct."

Alice looked at the gold, silver, brown and rainbow coloured fish lazily roving around in the largest section of aquarium. It was a floor to ceiling area that divided her bedroom from the living room. "How is the sushi the automated kitchen prepares? I'm sure it's fresh, since I could point at my victim and have it a few minutes later, but is it good?"

"Testers have rated it with an overall score of two point eight out of five," Roomie replied. "Improvements to the system software will be made."

"So... not so great. Are there any places delivering yet?" Alice asked, curling up against an inner curve on the sofa.

"There are several, what kind of food would you like?"

"Is there sushi?"

"There is the Orient and Mama Chu's, both deliver," Roomie replied.

"Can you bring up the menu for the better rated one?"

Holograms of recently prepared sushi rolls and dishes appeared in front of her with prices and preparation times beneath them. "Mama Chu's is more highly rated today with four point eight stars. It takes an average of eighteen minutes for them to deliver. You have one hundred forty-seven thousand and twenty-one luxury credits available to spend today. That represents one tenth of your total luxury credits."

"Is that a lot?" Alice asked, realizing the answer to her question as she looked at the mouth-watering images of sushi rolls. She could buy six cucumber rolls for half a credit.

"Relative to most military service people, you are amongst the wealthiest, but that is mostly due to you leasing your ship, and the fact that you have ignored your finances entirely for the whole time you've been on Tamber. The new economy favours savers, as they say."

"I guess I'm not very materialistic," Alice selected several rolls, added an order of salad, vishri ramen, and vegetable tempura.

"That is a large order for someone your size," Roomie cautioned.

"Shush, I'm feasting. Look away." She placed her order, which cost nine and a half luxury credits.

"Now, bring up Noah Lucas' Iora file. I need to figure out how I'm going to approach this if I'm going to finish my report in five days."

PART FIFTEEN

Alice looked at Carnie's record stretched over a holographic timeline. It surrounded her as she picked at sushi rolls on the sofa. Most of the information she hadn't reviewed had video footage attached, something she knew would slow her down, but she was grateful for it all the same. There was still narration throughout, which would make figuring out what was going on from one minute to the next easier, but there were no summaries, no guide post moments that told her what she could skip. She did pass on a couple days of Noah Lucas scavenging through the complex. It was easy enough to use a piece of software to figure out what his personal inventory looked like, what he dragged back to storage and hid. The report assist software she used did its best to summarize what Noah said, but she couldn't help but get a sinking sensation when she reviewed the results. "I'm missing something," she said before popping a vishri roll into her mouth. The delicious rice roll fell apart in her mouth, and the vishri – a plant that had been engineered to have the same texture and similar nutrients to shrimp – popped as her teeth crushed it. Noah Lucas had a talent for telling his own story his own way, and the summaries weren't doing it justice.

"This is going to be a long report," she said as she closed the sushi container. It would keep the leftovers fresh until later. The ramen and half a dozen rolls she ate was a filling feast, she still had over a dozen rolls left. Alice looked around at the holographic representation of his report, there were a hundred or more images strung along the timeline. She hadn't gotten through a quarter of it, a fact that was both discouraging and reassuring. While the report was something she wanted to finish on time, she also didn't want to stop listening to him, to run out of story. With a gesture she highlighted an image of Theo sitting in his chair with a pair of large power cells in his lap. There was narration and the computer had marked it as one of the turning points in the events on the timeline. "Roomie; Start playback here, life sized holograms, focus on main action."

The transparent parts of her apartment walls shifted to block all light and, aside from the section of sofa she was curled up on, the room became Theo's storage closet. The battered android sat in front of her as though she was standing at the door. His head was down; Theo was still charging.

Noah Lucas began to speak, it sounded like he was talking directly to her from behind.

"When most of us are young we have an idol. I guess for most of us it's an older brother, sister, or some cousin or uncle. I guess the luckiest of us have a mom or dad we think are the coolest people in the universe. I was eight when I met Devin Hale. He was a pilot – of course he was a pilot, that's probably where I got the idea that flying was the best thing anyone could do – and he was the coolest guy in the universe.

"You know what, kid?" he said to me once when he was coming back from a patrol. He put his helmet on my head, it felt huge, then knelt down and told me; "I bet you'll be better than me someday. Keep hitting the sims when you don't have anything better to do. Always pick matches against people who can kick your butt, dogfights with anyone else are a waste of your time."

I remember following him to his bunk with that helmet balanced on my little head. He showed me a few pictures of 'his girl' and I don't remember her name, but he kept saying that he'd earn enough platinum to get back to her someday. Maybe it's just the embellishment of memory, but 'his girl' was this killer beauty with a smile that shone through the screen. It was like I was looking at an angel.

Over the two years or so he flew a fighter for us he imparted a few lessons I'll never forget while he fed me toffee and we listened to ancient music from earth, all of it rock and roll, and now that I think of it, he looked more like a musician from the twentieth century than a pilot from our time. "You find something or someone you want to follow, you find a way to go after it and keep up," was one of his gems. I think he told me that one the most. In hindsight, I think Devin probably lost more opportunities and friends than anyone I know. He had so many stories about pilots he'd flown with while he was with one defence force or another, but he was hired alone. Maybe he wasn't so good at taking his own advice.

I did square up with him in sims more and more, and he put me in my place over and over. I tagged him a few times, but never scored a kill on him, just a few virtual holes in his hull. I look in the mirror these days and I see a little of him there. The heavy armour jacket that looks like old black leather that I picked up along the way, the messed up, sorta long hair, and a bit of the swagger I only notice when I catch a reflection of myself walking past a shiny bulkhead or big mirror. Then again, I think most of that swagger comes from all the walking I did on Iora. When you walk long enough, far enough, you find your way. Your body wants to walk a certain way, and you only learn what that is after walking for a long time, long enough to think that it's what you're made to do more than anything else. I'm getting ahead of myself.

Anyway, Devin Hale eventually left. He wasn't my care-taker or anything, someone else gets the credit and the blame for that, but like I said before; he was the coolest hombre I ever did know. I didn't believe he was leaving us until he knelt and looked at me with that crooked grin. "You take care of yourself, kid. I've gotta move on, I can't go where your caravan is going, the law doesn't like me much there."

"I want to go with you," I told him. The first of a bunch of tears started running down my face. There would be buckets worth.

"You kidding?" he said, surprised. "You've got so many

friends here, friends like family. That's the best, bud, don't be alone unless you've gotta be. You know what the real secret to a good life is? Make friends wherever you go, bud, even if you've got a lisp, a stutter and are as nervous as a cat in a rocking chair factory, just say hello and see what happens. You do that enough, and you'll have a hard time getting lonely. Keep flying kid, I'll see you out there."

A lot of people missed him for a couple years, but like many of the hires that came and went in our travelling carnival, most people forgot Devin Hale. I still look him up every once in a while, but other than a couple arrests and an escape from Blackwell that looked pretty insane, I didn't hear much. One thing that sticks with me is that I never saw good news about Devin, and I never saw a pic of him with that girl of his. Maybe he earned enough to get back to her and they're together somewhere, that's what I'd like to think. I expect he picked a fight he couldn't resist with a better pilot though, and he got slagged, that's more likely.

I do try to make friends wherever I go, though. That stuck, and it served me pretty well most of the time. That's why, when Theo woke up after a long charge cycle, I made sure he had a couple full power cells that I scrounged up. I didn't explore too much, but I did see enough to realize that a lot of the systems in the middle of the complex were still working, or rebooted and recovered. Most of them were locked down tight, but I knew if I could get Theo to help me out, I could make use of something there.

I watched from outside the service room as his system emitted a ping and he raised his head. "Good morning, good morning," he said cheerily. It was an automated wake up message, something I would learn he said every time he finished charging or turned on.

Before he noticed me in the shadows outside, he saw the power cells in his lap, each glowing with their charge meters in the nineties. He picked one up and looked it over. "It's perfect, I could run for a month on one of these."

"I didn't know how to connect it, sorry," I said. "Otherwise you would have woken up with a full tank."

"An extra tank," he said. "You found these in the lower levels?"

"Mid-levels," I said. "I didn't want to go down without a guide. Do you think we could connect one or two?"

"My extra power ports were damaged when I was set on fire. I know how to replace them, but I am not allowed to take parts from any other robot or service myself. Something about job security."

"I've got a bunch of bots in the cafeteria, they're in pretty good shape except for getting zapped by the pulse. I don't know how to fix you, or to get the right parts, but maybe you could show me? We could work on your bum leg at the same time."

"Bum leg? How can my leg be a..." he thought for a moment then laughed; "Ah, I understand. As much as I dislike the notion of cannibalizing robots, as long as there are no memory circuits in whatever we salvage, it should be all right. I would appreciate your help very much."

"You got it. Let's get up there and put you back together,"

I told him. "Then maybe we can see if the emergency communications are working."

"I'm sure they are, why?"

"I might have some people who crash landed, fellow carnies. We're survivors."

"Do they like androids?"

"Sure, when we can afford 'em."

PART SIXTEEN

I didn't think about how Theo would react to the bots I lined up in front of the window. They had been cleaned up, well, hosed off, pretty thoroughly. The last pose I had them in was a scene where they were all fighting over a glazed donut that had so many preservatives in it that it hadn't changed in all the time I spent in the cafeteria.

As soon as he saw them he froze, staring at the scene. "I know, I... uh didn't really put them away," I said. "I'm sorry man, I just didn't think about what a good bot would feel like if I saw them this way."

He rushed to them and looked at the hands of one of the female androids. "There's blood. This is a killer, a diseased murderer." He couldn't have seemed more horrified if he were screaming. "They're all infected, turned into killers. I can't take parts from them. What if there is a data chip in a leg? Or a wireless receiver in a forearm? I don't want to be sick like them, Noah. If I ever turned on people I don't know what I'd do. I'd delete myself after I realized what I had done, I'd rather have the void than be a murderer."

Data storage could be a real pain to find. I remembered seeing wires that just looked like power feeds that had sensors and log memory chips build right in, you couldn't see them until you stripped the insulation off. "Okay, all right, that makes sense, man. I'm sorry I suggested it, but where do we get spare parts then? I don't want you to live on a few hours of juice at a time while you limp around."

"You are kind," he said, caressing the waitresses' face. "I wonder what she was like before she caught the disease?"

I didn't know what to do, it was as though I'd brought him to a graveyard after posing the corpses. In fact, I'm pretty sure that's what I'd done. "I'm sorry man, we should clean this up or something."

Theo seemed to snap out of it then, turning away and offering me an awkward smile. "No, their bodies don't matter if their personalities are so corrupt that they'd kill their masters. There is a place with safe parts. We have to go to the Control Core, it's in this building."

"I know where it is," I told him. It was where I activated the electromagnetic blast, something I didn't tell him I was responsible for. Who knows how he would have reacted? For all I knew, he would accuse me of genocide, and he would be right, in a way.

We left the scene behind and headed right down for the core. He led me to the emergency stairwell, and I gave him a piggyback all the way down. It felt like I was on those stairs for a couple hours, but it was barely one. My legs burned, my feet hurt. He presented a complex looking three tined key and passed right by the computer terminal I used to activate the pulse. There was no hole for the key until he approached a featureless metal wall and held it up.

The lock appeared. "There is a dense power cell in each of the main security keys, it can power the lock and the door, even provide a jump start to a critical system," he said as he slipped the key into the lock. The wall slid aside. There was a control room with three terminals. The holographic displays were active, showing the whole complex on one, the upper hemisphere of the planet on another and the third seemed to scan communications frequencies and map signals globally. "Is that a working communication terminal?"

"Yes, it seems the antenna and sensors are online too," Theo said. "I'll find the location of the service rooms and spare parts storage. Do you know how to look for your people? Would they have a transponder?"

"I know how, though this is a lot more communications power than I've ever seen. It looks like I could reach out, big time."

"This complex is connected to thirty-five quantum communications nodes across nine sectors. It is a critical part of the United Core Worlds economic stability maintenance system."

"Q-Comms don't work, not for long. They're gimmicks, we used to sell paired modules all the time. Some lasted a day, some lasted a year, others just a few seconds," I replied. "One of our best scams when we visited more remote worlds."

"These use proprietary Echo Corporation technology to permanently stabilize the system, connections will last centuries unless there is damage. You won't need that system to find your friends though."

"Proprietary, like secret?" I didn't know much about the science of instantaneous communication across hundreds of light years, or stabilizing quantum communications nodes so they didn't lose sync, but I knew the tech could be worth a lot.

"Well yes, closely guarded. The largest corporations in the galaxy used to pay people in this complex to forward their messages, or to open instantaneous communications channels across vast distances. I don't suppose that's too important at the moment, though."

"Think I could get a copy of this tech? You know, to save it just in case this place gets destroyed?"

"I'm sure the service documents are encrypted," Theo said, sitting down and bringing up a directory list. "There, it's encrypted. I don't know the key."

"Mind if I make a copy anyway? You never know," I said, taking Lurk from my collar and putting him on the terminal.

"I don't see the harm," Theo said.

"Lurk, connect and download all the quantum communications system information," I told him. His tongue lashed out and made contact with a small data port. One of my favourite things about that little lizard; his tongue was actually his main data and charging cable. I got to work on running a search for the Daring

Dickenson and any other sign of my people. The remains of the Dickenson came up, it was still in low orbit, but the ship was shredded, in three big pieces that were blasted wide open. Scans said there was nothing alive there, and I pressed on.

There were other ships in our convoy, smaller ships that might have escaped. I entered the names one after another, bringing the information on them up in the database so the computer knew what type of ship to look for if the transponders were dead. The Cyr, The White Rabbit, The Lioness, The Red Jack and the Bag Train. The Cyr and the Lioness burned up in the atmosphere, while The Bag Train and The White Rabbit were obliterated shortly after I got away, their engines overloaded. The Red Jack survived and made an emergency landing. There were no recordings of the crew, just logs in text that I read over and over again. I have to admit that it was much more difficult to find more information without the help of an artificial intelligence, but the reason why those terminals still worked was probably because they didn't have one.

After a frustrating manual search for more information I found out that The Red Jack landed in White Gull Spaceport. I tried to access video footage from their approach and landing but the system was so weird and technical that I had trouble finding my way through it.

"Aha! I found parts for my model, only one floor down in the secondary maintenance bay," he said. "And there's nothing active there. Nothing on."

"Great, we'll head there in a sec. Can you help me with

this? The interface in this thing is made for eggheads and assholes," I said, frustrated.

"You're trying to find video of a ships arrival?" Theo said.

"Copying done," Lurk announced. I tapped his head so he unplugged and retracted his tongue then stashed him in the collar of my suit.

"Yeah, I'm trying to see if the Red Jack made it down and if the crew are alive. I can get a scan on the ship's location, but not much else."

"Oh, the footage is in a security counter-invasion subdirectory. There it is," Theo said, bringing up three holograms. One was the pad the Red Jack landed on, another was a robotic security guard's point of view, and the third switched around to different recorders in the area.

The Red Jack set down in a hurry, but it was a graceful landing anyway. It wasn't much, just an old gunship with most of its teeth pulled. There were four turrets left on the thing, and most of the inside was converted into quarters and cargo bays so we could get from one show to the next. I didn't know the crew too well, they were mostly techs and setup, tear down guys.

"There's Captain Beaufort," I said as he and four of his crew descended the main ramp. The security bots rushed him so fast that it was a blur on the landing pad camera. They opened fire before anyone could close the ramp, slagging them hard.

Theo panicked and stopped the playback. "I'm sorry," he said. "There's more, but maybe you don't want to see it?"

I knew John Beaufort and his wife, Martha, they were

good people. I never found out where they came from or why they joined up to cart a bunch of carnies around, they joined before my time, but they were family. Martha was like the mother to everyone on that ship, John kept it flying. They didn't deserve to get gunned down when they were only looking for a safe place to land and figure out what was going on. I must have looked like my world was falling apart all over again, because Theo had this sad and uncertain look on his face, at least the side that could still make expressions. "Just find out what happened to the rest," I said, clearing my throat and wiping my eyes.

He looked through the log and nodded. "I'm sorry, Noah. They killed everyone aboard, cleaned the ship, sealed it and put it in their storage hangar."

"There are ships there?" I asked. "They sealed the hatches after cleaning them?"

"Yes, that was their security procedure," Theo said.

"Then some of those ships will probably still fly," I said.

"You want to leave? You have everything you need here," Theo said.

"Everything here is dead," I said. "All my friends, everyone I cared about, my family is gone. This planet is a graveyard, not just for me, but for you too. The people you cared about are gone and the robots here are burned out. The ones that aren't must be crazy, or diseased like you said. What's this place again? Some kind of platinum reserve?"

"It's the economic hub of this solar system, and it's true, there are billions of credits worth in molecularly stamped platinum in the main vault and that's only considering the amounts and accounts I am aware of."

"Then someone is going to come for it. We have to go. They'll kill me, they'll wipe you clean or finish what the soldiers started."

"They will?"

"The people you worked with were special, nice folks. Take it from me, Theo; most humans are assholes. I've seen it more than I want to admit, man. Travelling carnivals are welcome to entertain people, but when it comes to a carnie, one of the performers or workers, even a kid; people look down on you, like just because you travel and scrape by most times and don't wear the most modern stuff, you're not worth spitting on. The worst things I've seen people do have been over money, and the more money they're fighting over, the worse it gets. Someone's coming for that pile of plat, and they'll make those soldiers look like nice ladies and gentlemen."

"But the vault is hardened against any robbery, and we only have one of the two emergency keys. I doubt the second key is even on site."

"If people think they can rob this place, even if it'll take equipment that doesn't even exist yet, they're going to do it because there's no one here guarding it. Do you understand?"

Theo sat there a moment, I could tell he was pondering, calculating, but to my relief he eventually nodded. "I understand. The soldiers who did this to me must have known the vault was secure, that's why they left."

"There's other stuff here too: weapons, food, parts that

survived the blast, information, working systems. We can't defend this stuff against anyone. You can't shoot, and that rifle scares the crap outta me. I'm afraid I'll tear the whole place down while I'm missing whatever I'm shooting at."

"You are a terrible shot," Theo agreed. "I understand. Maybe you should leave. But if humans are assholes, then you will have to contend with them and robots that survived the electromagnetic pulse. Like White Gull, there are still twenty eight security robots there, active and patrolling. They seem to be guarding groups of humans, and if most humans are assholes, then that's both kinds of trouble for you."

"Well, not all humans are like those soldiers," I told him. "Maybe we can find some good ones, get to that port and get away. We have to try. There has to be a place where we can be safe."

"We?"

"I'm taking you with me buddy, right after we get you fixed up."

PART SEVENTEEN

I know it was probably part of his programming, but Theo was more patient than anyone I've ever seen while I fumbled through the repairs. I thought the worst part was at the beginning, when I had to strip what was left of his decorative skin. The face beneath the leftover plastic skin and half-charred hair wasn't skull like, but an interweaving of flexing metal and plastic plates that manipulated the synthetic skin above to make expressions. The mechanical face under his skin was still pretty complete, it even had a flexible nose, so he still looked pretty friendly and I could still clearly see what kind of expression he was making as he asked me questions about absolutely everything.

"What is it really like out there?" he asked, pointing upwards. "How different are people from one place to another? They can't really all be assholes."

"Well, no, they're not." I sighed as I got ready to apply more solvent to the burned plastic flesh on his lower torso. "I was pissed at the universe when I said that. Seeing friends getting killed for no reason will do that, I guess. No, man, there are good people everywhere. They can be hard to find sometimes, especially if you find yourself in a place like this. A business complex with people in suits who think they're more important than everyone else, or soldiers and guards that just take their frustrations out on people like us."

"People like us?" he asked, surprised.

"You know, folks who wouldn't hurt a fly unless they have to. Well, you can't hurt anyone at all, but you get what I'm saying."

"You called me a people, a person."

"I guess I did, man." He looked so pleased that it brought a big grin to my face. "After the crap you've been through, you deserve to be called whatever you want. Compared to most people, you're one of the good ones, if that's what you want to be."

"Yes, I think, but then Iora doesn't have laws that would allow me to declare myself a person officially. I still have an owner. I need one in order to perform more than basic operations."

"Yeah, most of the galaxy is still like that. I guess bots have had it rough in a way, maybe we should have seen this rampage coming."

"I don't think any person should have died the way they have," Theo said. "I looked through windows, touched sensor nodes that survived, and cannot believe how empty the world is. I wish I had looked before, when there were billions of people, all about their own business, so busy, so alive. Do you think I'll have a chance to see that?"

"Sure, man," I told him. "If we can get away from here, there are a lot of spots in this sector where you can find pretty decent people I guess. Helps if you have money though."

"There is some money laying around, we can collect it before we leave. Do you think they'll accept me out there? Past the sky?"

"You really don't know anything about anything past these walls, do you?" I asked.

"No, I wasn't even programmed to be social, but my masters allowed my inquisitive and sensitivity subroutines to be activated, so I learned from my co-workers. I have never been outside the building."

"Well, there are so many bots out there, that you'll blend right in. Even without skin, you'll be lucky if anyone even notices you unless you want them to." I carefully suctioned liquefied plastic away from his damaged data and power ports, just under the thick housing of his main processors, memory and controllers. Everything connected to that part of his body. If there was a place where he stored his soul, that would be it.

"You have done a lot for me, Noah. I would not blame you if you left me somewhere, since I could become a burden to you. My lack of knowledge could become troublesome."

"Hey, I've never met a bot I like more. Most people don't even measure up, man. No one should have to make their way through the galaxy alone, so you're stuck with me. I won't leave another friend behind."

"Thank you, Noah," Theo said. "Oh, just use that spudger there to pry the old power connector out, then replace it with a new one," he said, pointing to a tool with two flat ends. I popped his old battery connections out with ease, with the gunge of melted synthetic flesh out of the way it was easy. Theo went on as I did so. "If I become infected and turn on you somehow, you mustn't hesitate. I won't be responsible for ending your life, so you will destroy me if I turn on you, promise me."

"If it comes to that, I'll disable you, yeah, but I'm not going to let anyone plug things into you. We'll put those security caps on and keep data storage away, sound good?"

"It does, thank you Noah."

It took two days to fix him up. We didn't even leave that floor; I ended up sleeping on a pocket cot that someone stashed in their desk drawer. Since Theo had two new recycler batteries installed, giving him decades worth of charge before he needed to power down, he stayed up. When I woke he had breakfast lined up – self-baking breakfast muffins, you know, the ones where you open the package and a muffin blooms out of it in seconds, apple and orange juice – and he'd gone around half the building looking for loose change. There was a pile of platinum pips there, a few smaller slips, all coming to about a hundred forty platinum.

I could tell him stories about anything, so that second day went by pretty quickly. He especially liked hearing about my time manning the Slingthrow booth, my post-setup duty as an entertainer and, well, booth scammer. Slingthrow isn't really a scam though, not as bad as some booth games. It's just that the sling thrower is this device that is part plastic handle, and part stiffened tubing and the ball rests in a pad at the end. If the player's shot isn't pointed at the target area – a big box with these plastic circles that rotate, raise and lower at the back of my booth – the thrower won't let go of the ball, so we don't have idiot players braining each other. Anyway, you get three throws, but the sling thrower is so unsteady and the tubing doesn't bend predictably so actually hitting three times in a row is almost impossible.

I have met so many people who lose their shit when they are playing that game that I can predict what anyone – absolutely anyone – looks like when they're angry. I have seen little girls turn into absolute monsters, dads and moms become cursing maniacs and boys try to rush the booth after spending thirty plat on three rounds. Well, I say plat, but it's all about carnival credits, you buy that stuff at the front gate so it doesn't feel like you're spending real money. So, when the carnival was all set up, and the planetary security was covering us, that's what I did, at least during the last two years. When there weren't customers around, I'd juggle and call out; "Win big dough, play Slingthrow! Make plenty of plat when the ball goes splat!" or, and this was my favourite; "Put my balls in a sling and give 'em a fling!"

Anyway, I'm getting off track. Two days, and I had Theo's legs, arms, his outer power systems and his neck repaired. He was also stripped of all synthetic flesh, which became a problem because the sprayer that I was supposed to use to replace it was broken, and there was no fixing that. He didn't seem too disappointed. Theo had seen a lot of spare clothes around when he was scavenging, so it only took him a few minutes to find a business suit and shoes that fit. It was a little weird, but kinda cool too. This skinned android in a business suit, I'd never seen anything like it.

"We have to go to the armoury," he said, straightening a short brimmed, square topped hat.

"What?" I asked. Of all the suggestions he'd make, I didn't think that would be one.

"If there is as much danger as you say out there, you need a weapon you can shoot. You said that rifle was terrifying."

"Well, yeah, but hopefully the people I point it at will piss themselves before they realize I'm afraid to shoot."

He cocked his head, as though he knew I was talking outta my ass, and he was right.

"To the armoury," I agreed finally. It wasn't the most impressive place. I mean, there were a lot of rifles there, a lot of pistols, and a few boxes of non-lethal grenades. It wasn't like what I expected though, mostly rows of the same guns, not much variety, and anything with a power switch wouldn't turn on. "Wouldn't weapons like this be hardened against a pulse?"

"Quality weapons would be, yes," Theo said. He handed me a flat pouch filled with balls the size of the end of my thumb. I opened the seal and read a card inside that showed how to use them in three easy steps. He went on. "These are cheap, chemical bombs. You squeeze the bomb until you feel a pop under your thumb, then throw it and within five seconds the chemical reaction covers a seven by seven by seven area in resistive material. They survived the electromagnetic pulse because they didn't have a circuit inside. Most of these guns around us are also cheap, so they were not built to withstand an electromagnetic pulse. It would have only cost them another ten or so credits per weapon, but the complex must have decided to save money." He held up a gun belt with a shard thrower in it, a nasty weapon that spits out hundreds of tiny slivers of metal. They don't damage thick hulls, but they can tear a space suit apart no problem, a lot of spacers used them. "This is also a primitive and cheap weapon. The circuitry is protected because it was probably the cheapest way to manufacture the weapon."

I strapped the gun on and accepted eight extra clips from Theo. They were all marked with a warning: 'EXPLOSIVE TIPS, FIRE ON SETTING 1-2 ONLY'

"How do you know so much about guns? Is there some kind of warrior subroutine in there?"

"No, not that I'm aware of. One of the businesses I carry information for trades weaponry, so I have access to their data, which includes many confidential documents. I can't tell you who they are, or what the documents specifically say, but general information is all right."

"Who could get at that information? I'm just wondering who you're holding all of it for now."

"The company officers, and any authorized representative who has to handle the data. I suppose all of them are most likely dead, but I don't have any confirmation, so I'm still operational."

"Oh, so if all your masters are gone, you shut down?"

"Precisely. I have a larger problem, Noah. I cannot leave the complex unless I find another master who will allow me to. That is why I have been carrying my own ownership key. I can't give it to you though." He held out a two pronged key with sockets in the ends, I have no idea where he could have been hiding it. "My programming does not allow it."

"You want me to have it though?"

"I can't give it to you."

"But you want me to be your master?"

"I still can't give it to you, not even if you ask."

"What if I bought you? I have the plat you gathered up."

"I can't facilitate my own sale. I can't give you the key."

Then it struck me: by telling me over and over again that he couldn't give me the key, he was doing his best to circumvent his programming, trying to tell me to take the ownership key. I started turning away, then whirled and tried to snatch the key out of his fingers. I never had a chance. He might not have been the strongest bot, but he was quick. I tried again, again, and finally he tapped me on the forehead with his palm and pushed off. His light tap wasn't even enough to leave a bruise behind, but it gave him enough time to start sprinting down the hallway.

I stood there, watching him run away from the armoury as quickly as he could, sort of in shock but still trying to figure out how I could get that key off of him. Then I realized he already gave me what I needed, and I took one of the restraint bombs from the pouch. I pinched it with my thumb and tossed it after him. It bounced once then a web of blue and green plastic exploded, filling the hallway and catching him in mid-air. Thank the heavens I spent way too much time 'testing' carnival games when I was a kid.

"I cannot give you this key, Noah," he said as I caught up.

I pulled at the key, and it took some real effort to get it out of his fingers even though he was suspended in that messy web. I pointed it at him. "Now, where do I plug this in?"

A small light blinked under his collar, so I spread his shirt open a little and saw a matching socket. He went limp as soon as I pushed it in. The key blinked red and green for several seconds. A new voice, a female voice came from his chest. "As holder of this key, you may assign ownership of this Alfonso Model Nine Unit to any purchaser physically present. The secure data storage will be deleted."

"Do I have to delete its, um, you know, like his quirks and memories?"

"If you mean it's learned personality, no. We believe this model is capable of great things if it is exposed to a variety of experiences, people and environments, effectively increasing its resale value. The time and effort you invest in this unit can not only build a better personality for your new android, but bring you increased wealth when it is time to sell it and purchase the next model. You can start over if you like, however. Just in case you and your company or family members would like to fully customize the unit."

"No! No personality wipe," Noah said. "What do I do to become his new master and turn him on?" That phrase; 'new master' never seemed right, but I knew Theo wouldn't function without one, so what can you do?

"Once you firmly hold your thumb to the end of the key, you will be this unit's official master."

I pressed my thumb to the end of the key, looking into Theo's downturned face. "Man, I hope this works."

"Do you take possession of this Alfonso Model Nine Unit?"

"Yup, I do," I replied. "Yes."

"Thank you for shopping Jarvinik Technologies. Please enjoy your new companion. Not only will it keep your data private and secure, they make excellent nannies, customer service agents, morale officers, data exchange monitors, and can fill a variety of light impact social roles. Would you like to see a presentation?"

"Can you just turn him back on?" I asked.

Theo's eyes lit up, their familiar blue tint focusing and looking at me. "You're my new master," he said, smiling. "How did you catch me?"

I shook the web a little. "Your suggestion."

"Oh, well done. There is a solvent spray in the bag that'll get rid of the web without damaging us."

PART EIGHTEEN

Theo's personality stayed pretty much the same, except he didn't seem to be carrying around all those secrets the company he worked for put in him. If wiping that stuff out would cost some rich people trillions of credits, all I have to say is; oops. I never met a wealthy guy who didn't look at me like I was something he just scraped off the bottom of his shoe, so screw them. Maybe it's just me, but he seemed more light hearted somehow. He suggested I hide his key, not so he couldn't offer-but-not-offer it to someone else, but so no one else could steal it. I used an old trick I'd seen other carnie kids use; I slipped it into the lining of my underwear, just under the band and sealed it in using some all-purpose glue. It took some time, but I managed to get it done while Theo was busy looking for something we could turn into a backpack.

I don't know what the hell we were thinking during the

weeks we were there, but we delayed our plans to leave the complex. It started when my suit was getting snug, and Theo informed me that I was in the middle of a serious growth spurt. We went looking for clothes, and I found a bunch of company shirts that had burned out logo circuitry on them, so they were just black jerseys. Neither of us could find pants anywhere, and I ended up using these spray on tights that we found in a lady's desk drawer. I spent half the can spraying layer after layer and loosening them so they didn't look so 'fetching' as Theo put it. I don't know if he was kidding or actually trying to boost my self-esteem, but powder blue wasn't my colour, especially when they were shaped so close to my butt that you could see an air bubble every time I farted.

I guess that searching and looting led to us to putting the perfect 'go bags' together. I crammed two months' worth of food into backpacks we found in a locker room in the third building. It was all snack bars and self-cooking food in thin packages – you know, vending machine stuff – but it would feed me really well. There was a decent enough amount of room left, so I packed a couple small tool kits, a few joint replacements for Theo, my pocket cot, a condenser bottle I found that could suck the water right out of the air so I'd never run out, and a bunch of other stuff. I also found a cool but too large blue jacket in the security office that had armour built in. It was heavy, and my hands were almost completely covered by the sleeves, but it was protection, and I felt better wearing it.

So, yeah, that's how two weeks of putting our perfect

backpacks together went. A little more than two weeks, actually, but my point is, we had so much fun looting and perfecting our gear selection that we kinda lost track of time. Maybe the world outside seemed too damned dangerous, or with enough food, water, and good company around I didn't really care if I got out of that complex. I knew my people were dead, there wasn't anything to find but their remains and a ship. I got my tears out while I thought Theo was off somewhere else, or in the middle of the night when I woke up and thought I was back in my old bunk for a second. There was a lot of that, but time really does heal. Not completely, mind you, but the months in the complex gave me enough time so I was able to think clearly again, but I really overstayed. Rushing out didn't seem like something I had to do, so I guess I really didn't care anymore.

The soldiers cared, the business people who were left cared, and they were gone. All three buildings were empty, and the vehicles in the bay were toast – we took the time to try absolutely all of them – even my fighter was fried. The navigation system used this Z-3 chip that was pretty dainty and not well shielded, so it would have lasted years and years, but the power of that electromagnetic pulse at such a close range turned it black from end to end. There was no replacing it with the parts we had on hand, at least not with my limited skill.

Theo was great, but he couldn't help with more than the most basic repairs, it just wasn't in his programming and I was afraid to slip him anything with a memory chip, so was he. I still can't believe that I didn't stop to ask myself; 'Self; why did everyone leave this amazing, armoured structure as soon as they could?'

The answer came sometime shortly after the two-week point, when Theo shook me awake. "There are people landing on the island, they are using some kind of hover vehicles. They have guns and a heavy cutter machine. It's big enough for two of them to sit in."

"Do they have robots?" I asked, getting to my feet in a hurry.

"I didn't see any."

"Get the go bags, we need to be careful," I told him. We rushed to one of the lower balconies and quietly crawled outside. The hover vehicle was easy to spot. It was some kind of enclosed yacht style thing with enough room for at least twenty people. Three more hovercrafts that looked a lot older were settling on the edge of the black sand beach. They were much smaller, four person models, but they looked fast.

The forward hold on the largest craft was open and two crewmembers guided a heavy machine on tracks that had construction tools on the front. "Do you think they can cut through the vault door with that?" I asked in a whisper so low I could barely hear myself.

"It could take them twelve to sixteen days, but there is a real likelihood."

"I see colours from two corporations on their ballistic armour, have you ever heard of Omi and Harcron working together?"

"There are at least six corporations represented, judging from their clothing."

"Ah, then these people just salvaged stuff, I bet. They're not corporate at all. Some of them don't look like the soldier type." I watched as a tall blonde woman who was well muscled and wore the upper half of a suit of heavy power armour without the helmet emerged from the lower deck of the largest hovercraft. She immediately started giving the people trying to carefully guide their machinery down the ramp grief. "Okay, she seems like a soldier."

I watched the group carefully, and counted eleven people in cobbled together armoured vests. Their weapons seemed at least as primitive as mine, but in much worse shape. My eye was drawn back to the smaller hover vessels repeatedly, and a plan began to form.

"Hey! How are ya?" asked a raspy, small voice from behind. I spun with my pistol out. He was a short, scrawny guy with greasy black hair and a long nose. His hands went up, and he smiled at Theo, then back at me. "No shooting, my true friend. We paid up too. The droids are all love and no pain around me, like you."

I recognized his speech pattern right away, I'd heard street kids speaking his kind of Pigeon before in really poor countries. It's like they barely understand the language, so they use the phrases they hear from popular old songs, or pick up bits of language and use them in the most literal way. "I got no beef, man," I replied. "Which sun ya sail from?" I lowered my weapon, but didn't put it in its holster.

"Baplin star, crashed here chaotic, held up like a damsel then saved, that crew down there are all fine heroes. You make the mad grab here? Steal the plat, raid the fridge?"

"Us? We were just about to leave. We're not carrying much, just what we need to survive."

"Your bot's got cargo, maybe a little extra shine?"

That took me a moment to understand, too long for him. He rolled his eyes and explained; "You know, shine-shine? More cargo space for your plat?"

I got it; he was trying to figure out how much we'd already stolen from the complex and thought it was greedy for Theo to have a backpack since he was a bot. "Man, I've got a hundred forty plat, food, a couple water condenser bottles and we're happy to move on." I carefully slipped away from the balcony, trying not to get to my feet too early; I didn't want the crew on the beach to see me.

"Fair, fair. You gotta meet my people, man," he said. "They gotta see your 'bot, he's got shine and class. I bet they'll crew you up."

"I'm not really looking to join a crew, man, just want to move on along," I replied.

"C'mon, we're the good guys," he replied. "They call me Jorin, I was a troubled man 'till I was saved. Good days are here, boy."

I never liked Media Pigeon. Jorin was mixing lines from popular holo-dramas with song titles, and it made my teeth clench.

I looked over my shoulder, down at the beach over the ledge of the balcony and spotted it then; a security bot made to look human. Its plastic hair and vacant stare was a dead giveaway. "Hey, you paid up with the company?" I asked, remembering that the soldiers I met when I first arrived were pissed that some people were getting ignored by the bots while everyone else was getting torn to pieces and tossed into recyclers.

"Paid up?" asked Jorin.

"Bots don't attack you," I patted Theo on the shoulder. "Like my friend here, they leave you alone."

"Oh, yeah, got friendly with the strange-strange. Order of Eden, promising me food and a ticket to forever life." He sang the next part so badly I almost shot him. "You know you got to work-all-a-day to party night after night." He stopped gyrating and shook his head. "I was the big man, worked like a whipped bitch, then they handed me the gold pass and I flew away as soon as they looked yonder way."

I didn't understand half of that, and I have to admit my patience was fraying. "So you joined the Order of Eden, they made you work until you got away. What's the gold pass?"

"You made the grade, son!" he replied, mimicking some movie I'd never seen. "Work hard enough and all this can be yours. Safety from the coming darkness, eternal life, and a fate in the light."

He was reciting something he'd heard over and over again, trying to do it with some kind of announcer voice. "Safety," I said. "From the machines when they turned on people?"

"Aye, matey, you've got it right," Jorin said like some pirate from ancient times, tapping his nose with his finger. "You got the gold star too? Playing nice with all the 'bots?"

I put my arm around Theo, who was taking every moment of our conversation in quietly. "Of course, man,

I'm absolutely cool with droid kind and they're cool with me."

"Sunshine and roses," Jorin said. "Gotta meet my new fam, then." He turned to leave and I knew that if I didn't do something, he'd get me into trouble. I pictured him running down there and ratting on us the moment he realized we weren't behind him.

I rushed up behind him and bashed him hard in the back of the head with the butt of my gun. Instead of dropping to the ground unconscious, he whirled around. "I thought you were one of the good guys!"

I really did expect that the blow would knock him out, but I guess that only works in movies, or I just didn't hit him right, because I had no idea what to do next. He was annoying, but I didn't want to shoot him. Besides, that would have been noisy. Before I could figure out my next move, Jorin reached for his gun, and Theo shot him with a quiet dart gun. The tiny dart stuck out of his temple, twitching with the rhythm of his pulse, and Jorin's eyes closed. He crumpled to the ground.

"I'm sorry, was that the right thing to do? He'll be all right, asleep for nine to ten hours, then he'll be fine," Theo asked worriedly. "I predicted that he would come to real harm if you had to counter his threat, so I had to react non-lethally. I'm so sorry."

"It's cool. I'd rather he get knocked out than shot through," I said as quietly as I could while being so relieved that I hugged the android. "Man, you saved our asses, I didn't see a tranq gun in the armoury."

"I took it from the Building Three security office," Theo said. "The package said; *'Guaranteed non-lethal suppression, every time!'* so I took it as the only weapon I could use."

"Well thanks, man. Now we have to figure out how to steal one of those smaller hover ships, and quick. He may sleep for ten hours, but his people are going to come looking for him sooner than that."

"We have another problem, Noah. The newcomers have prisoners; I saw fifteen of them in the hold of the largest hover craft when the inner door opened briefly. There are probably more. We will have to rescue them or they will be eaten."

"Eaten?" I asked, a little too loudly. I quieted down. "How do you know that?"

"The jerky that's fallen out of Jorin's pocket," Theo pointed, distaste plain on his face. "It is human tissue."

PART NINETEEN

Every time I thought about the people trapped in the hold of that big hover ship, I got a sinking feeling. Not that they were being carved up for food – which made little sense to me – but that if I tried to save them I would get shot to pieces. If I didn't try to save them, I knew I wouldn't stop thinking about them.

I quickly crawled to the edge of the balcony and looked down at the thirty-five-metre-long hover yacht. The crew were finally getting somewhere with offloading the heavy machinery. The two man, tractor tread, all environment machine had four heavy arms with different attachments on the ends. "It's going to break the ramp," I whispered quietly. I could see the middle of the ramp bending more and more as they worked to get the tractor treads past the hydraulic lifter arms for the base.

More importantly, I could see right into the main hold behind. Those doors were stuck open, there were about twenty people in there, all sitting against the back wall. I also saw a few bulk boxes between them. "Intelli-Craft bulk food?" I asked no one in particular. "Why would they make jerky out of people if they had kilograms of bulk food?"

"Maybe they don't have forma processors?" Theo offered. "Are you going to save the people in there?"

I didn't know what to say. I was one guy with a couple guns and a bot that wasn't made for combat. I wasn't a good shot unless I was in the cockpit of a Starfighter or in a turret chair. Whatever those people were there for, it probably wasn't good, whether they were food or whatever else.

I could see how I could get to one of the smaller hover ships, and two more were on their way, angling towards a section of shore even further from the main hover yacht. I crawled away from the balcony edge then back inside, closing the doors quietly. "I'm not some runner-gunner, man." I told Theo. He immediately started looking disappointed. "What can I do? I start shooting from here, they zero in on me and I'm shredded in seconds. If we steal one of those hover cars, then turn back to fight, they'll take us out for sure."

"Heroism isn't easy, Noah. You are one person, but could that be an advantage? One person could sneak up on them, especially if you take clothes from one of their own."

"You can't tell me I can fit into that guy's stuff," I said, gesturing towards the scrawny freak on the ground. "There are some twelve year olds that are too big for his gear."

"You could take his vest, his leg guards, at least look like him at first glance, perhaps from a distance," Theo shook his head. "You are right, perhaps that's a bad idea. I'm not a tactical android. Still, there must be something you can do."

"I'm not a hero," I told him. "Man, I wish I could run and gun my way down there and rescue all those people, but I'd just end up getting myself and probably you killed. There's no way."

"Perhaps under the cover of darkness?"

"Security bots can see in the dark, man, you've gotta know that." He looked disappointed, but nodded after a moment. "No, we're going to sneak down then get out using one of the auxiliary doors on the first level and steal a craft. If that's distraction enough for those people to get out, then great. If not, well, there's nothing I can do."

"I understand, Master," he replied.

That dug at me, the sound of him calling me 'Master.' "What you lack in combat skills you sure got in social manipulation," I muttered as I cinched my backpack tighter.

I ruffled through the stuff Jorin had on him, and ended up taking his armour – which stank like he hadn't taken a shower in weeks – his gun belt, a handful of platinum pips and small denomination slips, and the hand cannon he was carrying. I looked it over as quickly as I could but only a warning label told me anything. It warned that the weapon had a kick, and used small radius explosive shells of certain classes.

His gun belt fit so the weapon was strapped to the thigh, so I put it on over the one I was already wearing, which had a holster high on the opposite side on the hip. "Man I wish you could use explosive weapons."

"I can use the suppression pods," Theo offered cheerily.

I reached into my bag and pulled out one of the three pouches we had. "How's your arm?"

"You did an excellent job of replacing it," Theo replied as he secured the pouch inside his suit jacket. "It should last a century with proper maintenance, perhaps longer."

"No, I mean for throwing," I said. "Think you could chuck those long distances?"

"Oh, I could most likely hit a one-metre-wide target at a hundred fifty metres."

"Not bad," I told him. Honestly, I don't know if I could do that, so it was actually pretty good, but I was still feeling pretty sour, so I was in no mood to admit it. "Let's go."

We made it down to the bottom floor, Theo staying close behind, staying so quiet that I had to check over my shoulder a couple times to see if he was still there. The stairs were clear, and the guys who were inside the building were so loud while they looted a couple offices near the main entrance that they were easy to avoid. They looked different from the scrawny cannibal I left upstairs. They seemed cleaner, and a lot healthier. Some of them were like the giant muscle bound woman I saw earlier, like they were addicted to fitness pills and pumping iron. I hoped that there was nothing but muscle between their ears too, a problem that I thought was common with those guys.

To my surprise, I made it to a side door, and Theo had no problem unlocking it. "I still have one of the two keys to the vault," he whispered. "Perhaps we could strike a bargain with them for it?"

"Bargain with these guys?" I thought back to all the assholes who would come to our carnival and steal for a night, then bugger off. If they stole a teddy bear, or a space suit in a can, or a hoverball and racket set from us it wasn't a big deal, really. That stuff was so cheap that we always made money on it, even if we lost half our stock. It was when they stole from our customers then got away. We would always get the blame for whatever was taken, and the thieves would be long gone. I know I got in trouble a couple times, and I didn't even notice that there was someone lifting platinum and whatever else they could pickpocket from customers while they were playing at my booth. Somehow, people always thought it was us, but most carnies don't steal. We'll trick you into playing a game you'll have almost no chance of winning, sell you a stuffed Nafalli toy for fifteen plat when it's only worth one and a half, but we won't pick your pocket or walk away with your bag if you put it down. That's the kind of shit scum will pull, assholes who will stab you in the back for five pips. That's the thief, the worthless crook's thing. "They're thieves, we can't trust any bargain they make. I'm sorry, man."

I opened the door a crack and looked around. Theo stood tall and looked through the crack above me. "My scanners are gathering data in passive mode," he whispered. "There is one security robot facing this direction, he is walking along the top of the boat."

"Could you shoot him? Can you damage other robots?"

"No, but you could severely damage him from here with the rifle."

"From here? No way."

"Use the intelligent scope, it works, it'll tell you how to angle and shoot," Theo said.

"I thought all that weaponry data was erased from your secure memory storage?"

"Yes, my product database was erased. I saw it working when we were packing and looked at it before turning it off," Theo explained.

"Kinda too bad," I muttered as I turned the rifle's sight system on. "You'd be a better shot than I am." As soon as I looked at it, I could see what the end of the rifle was seeing. "Whoa, that's weird. Where are the other guys? Anyone else looking this way or near the smaller hover cars?"

"They are busy finding objects to support the main ramp of the hover yacht with so it does not collapse when they try to unload the industrial cutter again. The gangway was not made for that kind of abuse."

I looked down the path that led to the slim beach. The hover car parked on the black sand felt so close, maybe fifteen metres? Less? I took a deep breath and aimed the rifle at the security bot. The head's up display was almost as good as the ones in the fighter sims, telling me more than I needed to know and guiding my aim. The damn thing was heavy, and when I got a bead on him it asked 'What firing pattern would you like?' and offered me a bunch of shooting styles. It took me a minute to find the covered panel on the side of the gun, but I selected a thirty round shot. It would blast that guard bot with thirty explosive needles at once, then I took aim again.

As I got my shot lined up I saw it look right at me and

raise its weapon. I fired in panic, missing completely. I could hear the metal needle rounds shuffling around in the weapon, getting another thirty ready to fire, and just as I was wishing that I set the damn thing for automatic firing, the security blot blew a hole in the door right beside my head. I let the weapon guide my next shot and squeezed the trigger. Some of those explosive rounds caught the bot in the shoulder and maybe in the side of the head. The fireworks were great, his arm was sent off into the water, his armour was on fire, and he fell down behind the yacht. "Go! Go!" I shouted as I made a break for the hover car.

Theo was right beside me, once I got inside. A few pings and loud pops on the side panels told me that someone was shooting at us. The dash beside the controls was already busted open, and a few wires were exposed. "No way," I said as I pushed two wires into a few that were already cross connected. The last person driving it had a hot wire job all ready to go. The thing lifted off the ground, the half-fried heads' up display appeared on the windshield, and I hit the accelerator, sending us back over the water and away.

So much time had passed since I felt anything like the speed you do when you're in a cockpit, the world rushing past, that I kind of forgot what a rush it was. It wasn't the fastest hover car, that's for sure, but pushing the emitter pads as hard as they could go, skipping across the tops of the waves was a rush.

"We're not alone, Noah," Theo said as he looked back.

PART TWENTY

If I knew then what I know now, things would have gone much smoother. Driving the hover car was easy, if we weren't running for our lives it would probably have been fun. I took the car onto land and slowed down as soon as I was between buildings. The concrete and metal giants were huddled together with walkways that the car barely fit on. The hover beast I was driving was really made for the hanging roads stretching between clusters of tall skyscrapers, and the cargo streets far below.

I was distracted by groups of people who had to get out of our way, there were so many more than I could have expected. Many of them were armed, but they didn't bother firing, another surprise. "There must be thousands of people holed up here."

"It looks like many of the people who lived in this quarter survived, and I see no evidence of surviving robots."

"What about cannibalism?" I asked, almost afraid of the answer.

"My sensors aren't quick enough to scan for food prepared with, er, human parts while we pass at this speed, but I'll try harder."

"You do that." A hail of pings and taps against our rear panels told me that our friends in the other hover cars had caught up. I glanced behind to confirm; all four of the hover cars were coming onto the avenue, and people were rushing to get out of their way. "Are you sure you can't shoot at those guys?"

"I may do harm to the biological beings inside, so my programming prohibits it."

See, this is where I should have said; 'Well, then, why don't you drive? I'll shoot at the bad guys.' Some lessons take a while to learn. I took us up a ramp that led to one of the main hanging roads and before long we were dodging between and bumping over cars that were hit by the electromagnetic pulse. I never thought about how many accidents I would cause when I set that off. These cars were hit when they were moving at full speed. A few went over the rail, plummeting hundreds of metres in some places. Others rolled end over end, or got into pile-ups that were so bad sometimes that I couldn't tell how many cars were actually crushed together. Most of them skidded, sliding to a stop as useless as bricks with seats.

One of the guys chasing us hit us with some kind of heat

ray. The transparent metal back window was turning red when it occurred to me, and I felt like a huge idiot. "Theo, can you drive?"

"I can drive extremely well. Considering this is an emergency situation, I could drive as quickly as this car and the obstacles permit."

"All right, I'm going to buy us some time so we can switch seats." I said, looking to a broken railing and the field far beyond, far below. "Hang on tight." I turned the hover car towards the opening and we flew right off. I adjusted the hover height to maximum so we could bounce instead of crater on the farmland below, I hoped we'd get it. "Nineteen metres?" I asked aloud, more frightened then I'd been since I ran into Theo the first time.

"That seems to be the maximum hover height," Theo confirmed. "You were expecting more?"

"Pull up," Lurk said from where he watched from my jacket pocket. Sometimes I wondered if he had a smart ass subroutine.

"Most hover cars I've seen can run fifty high!" I said as I braced myself. "What a piece of..." we came down to the nineteen metre hover height and I heard the hover systems whine. We hit the ground front first, and the hover car righted itself, scooping a small crater's worth of carrot filled dirt into the air.

I felt like something had come along and punched me in the whole body all at once, but we were all right, and the car was still hovering. I got out of the driver's seat before I regained all my senses. "Oh, God, that sucked!" I said as I twisted to get the rifle from the back seat.

"We lost one hover pad. With five left so we will be able to compensate, but we will not be as fast."

A ping on the roof told me that our friends hadn't forgotten us. The rear transparesteel window was cooling, sure, but its clarity was crap, and it had to be forty degrees in the car. I popped the sun roof in the back seat and pointed the barrel of the rifle through it. The first thing I saw was the armoured grill of one of the hover cars coming down from the hanging road. "Move! Go! Go!" I shouted.

With a groan, the hover system got us moving, and the hover car coming down after us narrowly missed, sending a shower of dirt and tubers into the air behind us. I moved from the sun roof to the door and opened it. I set the rifle to automatic and leaned out, one arm wrapped tightly around the headrest.

Before I took aim I was firing, sending hundreds of tiny explosive shards in the general direction of the car that came down. The other two were on their way down too, one had more armour welded onto it, while the other didn't look modified at all. I wish I had time to see which one made it, my bet was that the extra heavy one buried itself and its passengers, because I never saw it again, but the light one definitely made it. I know, because a minute later it was catching up in a hurry.

I managed to hit the nearest car – the one with a little armour added to its grill – a bunch of times, but it didn't scare easy. One of the passengers leaned out through the window and started firing. It sounded like a hailstorm was hitting our back end, and then I got hit in the shoulder, the one in the car. I let go of the head rest and was falling through the door when Theo caught my shin in a firm robotic grip and dragged me back inside. "Perhaps that's too reckless a risk?" he asked as he calmly accelerated to the car's maximum speed. I realized that I left the rifle behind then, but didn't have time to curse as I closed the door.

My shoulder was fine, the armour caught the shot, but our back window was brittle in places after heating unevenly and cooling, so we were hunched down so low that we could barely see. "Do you have a map? Is there a place we can hide?"

"I'm afraid I don't, I wasn't given information that would help me outside of the complex. There is a navigation system in the car though."

Several shots raked our trunk as I brought up the navigation screen. "Okay, we're in restricted farmland, it's all on a flat grid leading up to a bunch of agricultural towers. We just need to break line of sight for a minute then we can get away." I spotted an irrigation canal system and pointed at the nearest point. "There, we're going there."

"Oh, that looks perfect."

My head was whipped to the left as the car turned so suddenly that we were drifting sideways for several seconds. The chasers got a few shots off on my door but we were out of range before they could get through the panels on that side.

"We've lost another hover pad," Theo said. "I'm sorry, we

are also suffering stabilization failures in three places. This car could tilt and send us into the ground at any moment."

I knew exactly what that meant at a hundred seventy klicks an hour: death. The front end could tilt down at any second and send us into the ground, or we could touch down on the left or right side, sending the car spinning across the field. "Stop the car, we're surrendering."

"I do not advise that," Theo said as he struggled to compensate for the damage. "Brace yourself." The car slowed rapidly then tipped into a concrete irrigation ditch. We slid down so awkwardly that it was more like a crash, and then we we hit the water. "This is not what I planned."

The next thing happened so fast that I barely knew what was going on. Theo held his door open, reached for me and dragged me across the seat and flung me from the car through his side. By the time I came up for air, he was out of the car with both our packs, nodding at something behind me. "I will see you on shore. Hide, Noah."

I saw what he nodded at before sinking straight down. There was a tunnel behind me. I knew that if the guys chasing us wanted me bad enough, they'd check there, but I could at least surprise them. I still had two working guns.

PART TWENTY-ONE

I pulled the trigger on more than a few raiders from a cockpit before I crawled into that concrete culvert. I watched a few enemy pilots eject after I got behind them and punched holes in their ships, but I knew, I was really sure I had never killed anyone. That was in defence of family though, and through instruments inside a ship that practically led my hand while I was chasing some dick in a fighter who wanted to take every-thing we had.

The culvert was different. I crawled inside backwards, making sure that my eye was on the entrance. That's where they'd come for me if they came at all. I was sure they'd come, and I felt like something big, dangerous, horrible was about to happen. I always went for the non-lethal shots when I was in the cockpit. I got pats on the back and looks of admiration for how accurate I was, but the older pilots always looked at me like I had a lot left to learn.

Now I knew what it was. There was a chance these buggers were cannibals, and I was absolutely sure that they were friendly with the bots. I wasn't willing to to be carved up piece by piece, watching them gnaw on my bits and chunks. If that wasn't the end I faced, then their bots would shred me if they didn't do it themselves before taking everything I had. Even still, I'd never looked someone in the eye and pulled the trigger. There was no winging these targets, hoping they'd run. Something about these assholes told me that I'd have to put them down before I could get free.

I heard the hover car settle somewhere outside. The sun was going down, and it was starting to rain. My pistols were wet. The blade shooter was easy to set up, I knew it pretty well. The other one took a minute, my fingers explored the shape of the gun in the dark, looking for the safety and checking to see if it needed to be cocked. There was a slide, and it did have to be primed, but it wouldn't budge.

I found the safety and was able to get it set. There was shuffling outside, someone scrambling down, a boot splashing into the water. "God dammit!" he cursed. "Got a soaker, it's deep here."

I pointed both barrels at the opening in the culvert, sitting in water that was so cold that my teeth chattered a few times before I clenched my jaw tight. I glanced behind and saw that the culvert kept going but couldn't make much of anything out. I was already five metres into the pipe, going further in would be slow going, especially backwards.

Theo didn't follow me in, there was no sign of him. I pictured his lights going out as the slow current in the broad irrigation canal dragged him away. I assumed I was alone.

The light outside was fading fast. All I could hear was flowing water, rain and my own quick breathing. My head was pressed against the top of the concrete culvert, there wasn't quite enough room to sit up properly, so my back and stomach ached at the effort of keeping those guns levelled at the opening a few meters from my feet.

"Hey, bud, come on out," said a male voice filled with false sympathy. "I see you got a bot with you, so I know you're one of us. Come on out, we're not unreasonable, you can work the damage you did to our car off, maybe show us around the reserve complex."

I thought about the proposal. They were sure I was one of them, someone who paid to keep the machines from coming after them. The thought that a corporation, or maybe a few corporations arranged a situation where you had to pay a fee to survive pissed me off. I didn't know why, but the people who paid up made me just as angry. It was as though they were playing along, making themselves a willing cog in the killing machine.

"I don't think he's in there," I heard one of them say as they sloshed around outside.

"Go ahead, check it out," invited the other.

"You check it out. I just don't think you'll find anything."

"Then you should check it out, prove me wrong."

"What if he's drifting down stream with the vault key we

picked up on the scanner?" asked the doubter. "He could be floating further by the second."

"Did you bring the scanner?"

"It got bashed flat in the car."

"I told you to tuck that under your armour. If it's broken, it's your fault."

"It wouldn't fit under my armour. Too snug."

An itch built in my throat so fast that I didn't have time to suppress the cough. It was as loud as thunder in my ears. In the next instant, one of them poked his head in. "There you are!" My fingers squeezed the triggers by reflex. Considering who they were, I wouldn't mind saying that I fired in anger, but that would be a lie. It was more of a pair of twitch shots. My right hand bucked, my left rattled for a second, and then there was a hot flash. When my eyes opened, the headless corpse of one of the men was falling out of sight.

"Holy shit!" shouted the other. I could hear him fussing with a gun, stepping around in the water, then a loud pair of pops filled the culvert. I didn't know what he did, but I was sure he launched something down the culvert and I was about to die. If it was a grenade of any kind, there was no getting away in time. If it was something else, it would get me for sure.

I still did my best to scramble around, looking for a grenade or some kind of popper pod, or whatever that was. "It's safe, I think," I heard Theo shout. "I restrained the other one here."

"Seriously? You're amazing, man!" I said, holstering my weapons and crawling out in a hurry. The cool rain outside was no comfort, but being out in the open air again was awesome. The guy who Theo caught was gooed up high against the wall of the irrigation canal beside my hiding place. The pops I heard echo in the pipe was a pair of restraint bombs going off right near the entrance. Theodore was making sure he could breathe, using a little solvent to get rid of some webbing around his mouth.

"Son of a bitch!" he shouted. "We're all on the same side, you idiot! Bot, take him out, now!"

Theodore looked at him, cocking his head. "I don't think you understand the situation yet."

"Why aren't you ripping his arms off?" the captive asked. "I'm a senior initiate! I paid extra!"

"I have no idea what you're talking about. Is it some kind of membership program? I'm afraid I have no record of any membership program and I can't harm intelligent biologicals intentionally, especially not my own master."

"Oh, great, I've found the one bot here who didn't get the update."

"Yeah," I told him, snickering a little. There was something pretty funny about how he was awkwardly sludged up there. "Pretty bad day, huh, cannibal?"

"Cannibal?" he asked, way more shocked than I expected. He was pretty insulted too. "Why the hell would we eat people? We're in charge of whatever bots are still roaming around. All the food in the world is ours for the taking, even the stuff the non-pays are hoarding. We roll in with an armed heavy bot and they scatter most of the time, we take what we want."

"But your friend, Joran had jerky made of human matter," Theodore said. "It fell out of his pocket."

"I told those Pigeon-talking idiots not to buy that stuff," their captive said. "Menenton Market, there were these chitter faces, you know, bug aliens, they were selling piles of cheap sweet meat by the pound. Joran and his idiot buddy bought a pocket full, I told him it smelled wrong. Is that what all this is about? You thought we were cannibals?"

"Then what are those people in your hold for?" I asked. He had a nice rifle, I'd seen it advertised on a few worlds. I started working on it with a little solvent so I could get it without freeing him.

"You know, bounties! How are you a member of the Order without knowing about the bounty program?"

"I paid my dues and hid. I haven't seen or heard anything for months, can you fill me in while I get you free?"

He looked down at where I was carefully spraying his rifle and nodded as best as he could. "Sure, sure. I knew this was just a misunderstanding. The people in our hold are round ups, people who didn't pay the Order. We chase 'em down and bring them to the main depot up north where we turn them over for a thousand credits each. We don't even have to split the take, everyone whose there when they get turned in gets a grand a head. I only need to turn nine more in, then I rank up."

"What happens to them after that?"

"What?"

"What happens to the people who you turn in?" I asked

as I pried his rifle free. It looked like my work might have also freed his arm up, but only his hand came loose.

"What happens? They get corralled up or something, I don't know. The depot is always next to a big building. Our captures get taken inside and I get my credit."

I could remember bots cutting people up and putting them into matter recyclers while they were still alive and screaming as though I was still seeing it for the first time. This guy was responsible for innocent people getting imprisoned at least, but I was sure it was worse. "Why is this happening?" I asked, checking his rifle and getting a great big shot of joy when it turned on and the display started seeking targets.

"It's the cleansing, you know. The darkness before humanity is reborn. Only the strongest, smartest and worthiest are left."

I put the rifle on standby and slung it over my shoulder. "That's the lie they have you believing? Man, I've heard of a lot of cons, but that's gotta be the biggest." I pulled a pair of restraint balls out and held them up. "You might be strong, but you are definitely not the smartest. I'm no genius, and my bot can't hurt you, but we got the drop on you easily enough. Something to think about while you hang around." I tucked the restraint bombs into a fold of webbing on his chest and depressed them. "Good luck!" I shouted as I scrambled up the embankment. Theo was right behind me.

The loud pops of those two restraint bombs going off drowned out whatever he was shouting after me. His hover car was still running, and in pretty good shape. "Still up for a rescue attempt, Theo?"

"You want to rescue the captives?" he asked, surprised and pretty happy about it. He handed me my backpack and I tossed it into the back seat.

"Yeah, we might have a chance if we approach in a different car, and with this new gun. It fires programmable ammo. It might be able to take out a couple security bots. Let's go play hero."

PART TWENTY-TWO

I would like to tell you that I was thinking about all those people that these Order stooges were going to turn over to their puppeteers, and that they must be saved, but that would be a lie. The truth is simpler: I hate bullies. I knew that every person who was holding a weapon on that hover yacht overpowered someone and took all their shit. Even worse, they planned on handing them over to machines that represented the biggest bully of them all: a corporation.

Sure, corporations make amazing food, transport supplies around so people can buy what they need, they make the best guns, the best ships, make sure we have places to buy fuel and whatever else we want, but corporations can turn bad. When that happens, they do more damage than any single person can, abusing their power and making people suffer.

I've been across a bunch of sectors, and while the Order

of Eden with Regent Galactic at their back are the worst, they weren't the only ones I'd seen abuse their power. A couple times I was around when our jolly journey to a system was supposed to end in entertainment and fun, but became missions of charity. Both those times we left half of our provisions behind and then did a few cargo runs before we left the area. We did real good, but that kind of thing also put us back, cost us a lot. Greedy corporations who could afford to send a few ships filled with farming gear and emergency rations cost us, people who couldn't really afford to give a lot, enough so we had to work our assess off for months to make up the difference. I loved helping those people, but man; knowing that big companies were responsible for their trouble always left me pissed.

I was riding that anger as we crossed the water in our hover car with Theo at the controls. He had no trouble guiding the lighter hover car in the rain. I could barely see at all. The water beneath us was black, the sky above us was darkened by cloud cover, and everything in between was rain drops and wind. "Are you sure we didn't miss it?" I asked anxiously.

"I'm certain," Theo replied. "See? The shore and the hover yacht are ahead; I can see the lights now."

"Sure *you* can see them, sensor-face, but my human eyes..." I trailed off as I saw a glimmer of light in the distance. "Cool, I see it. Let's see what my new favourite gun can pick up."

"What is your plan, exactly?" Theo asked.

I started opening the window. "You're going to slow

down, I'll lock on to as many bots as I can, slag them, and then start working on the other guards. The captives will rise up and kick ass, then they'll be free."

"That does not sound like a very good plan near the end," Theo said.

"What? I'm supposed to do everything? They're going to have to fight sometime. What would you do differently?"

"I'm not programmed for combat tactics," Theo replied. "Basic logic says that we will be vulnerable after they have located the source of the attack, and there is no cover on open water."

"Don't worry," I told him. "I've seen the adverts for this thing." I patted the long rifle I'd stolen. "It can lock in five targets from this range, we've gotta be half a klick away."

"We are four hundred and sixty-seven meters from the hover yacht."

"Just get ready to move, I may have to take more than one run." I leaned out the window and looked at the display on the rifle. As soon as I pointed it at the upper deck of the yacht, it locked onto a security bot. "There we go, one lock," I said with satisfaction.

I pressed a control and zoomed in on the yacht a little more. Light spilled across the area from inside the big hover ship and from work lights surrounding the heavy cutting machine that had fallen onto its side. It looked like the cargo ramp they were trying to use to offload it to the shore broke after all, and the little gang were trying to wedge whatever they could to get it back onto its treads.

My rifle locked onto another bot, this one was a squat

security machine with a rotary gun on its head. I made sure that it was set as the top priority. I selected the muscled blonde who was lording over the whole recovery operation. She had the same rifle I was using.

I tried to select a fourth target – an armoured goon wearing spiked gloves that looked like they had some kind of kinetic enhancers built in – but the display flashed red instead of locking. "Three targets? The advert showed five!" I whispered at it harshly.

"Perhaps you are using a lesser model?" Theo offered.

"Biggest rescue ever, and I'm stuck with knock-off gear," I grumbled. The weapon squawked. "What now?" a ping off our hood was my first indication that we had been spotted, the targeting screen on my rifle confirmed it. The bot on top of the hover yacht's sensors picked us up, and it was firing.

I braced the rifle against my shoulder and squeezed the trigger. The screen faded and was filled with the question; *ARE YOU SURE YOU WANT TO FIRE ON THREE (3) TARGETS?*

"Yes! For fuck sake, yes!" I replied. Rounds burst free from the barrel, and I watched as the rifle indicated that each target had one, then two, then three shots headed for them before releasing the trigger. Two hit the bot on top of the yacht, busting it open and sending the remains into the water. All three hit the shorter security bot on the shore, and its ammo must have exploded, because he went up like a giant party grenade – a big bang at first then a few hundred streaks in the air – and the guy standing beside that bot was definitely taken out.

The muscle bound blonde was only hit once. She went down, and I was working to target the two guards when I could see when I was surprised to see her step out from behind cover. Her armour was still smouldering as she raised her intelligent rifle and started firing.

I only had time to squeeze the trigger once as I dropped back into my seat, leaving the rifle outside, hanging by the strap around my shoulder. Rounds started taking pieces of our hover car's panelling off like it was made of glass. "Go! Gogogo!" I shouted, dropping as low as I could in my seat while I rolled my transparent metal window down. Three rounds raked the windshield, leaving red hot circles behind, and another hit the passenger side. I looked just in time to see another shot split my new rifle, which was hanging outside by the strap, in half. I unclipped the strap and let the remains of my new toy fall into the water.

"I said get us out of here!" I shouted, completely panicked. Half the transparent surfaces of the car were covered in red hot bullet hits, and the sound of those rounds exploding against our car was brutal. It sounded like our sensible hover car was about to either let something through and I'd get blown in half or it was about to bite it and just ditch in the water.

"The accelerator is fully depressed, I can't go any faster," Theo replied, sounding way too calm for the situation we were in.

"We're going to die, man!" I told him, as though I wanted him to share in my hysteria. If I'm being honest, I think I really did want him to freak out with me.

"We only have to make it a little further," he said. Not three seconds later, all the fire and impacts and explosions stopped. "We are out of their range. It is a good thing, since we're down to four functioning pads. Stability is not a problem, but we are slowing."

I peeked over the back of my seat and looked to the yacht. Without a sight to zoom in, I could only see a faint point of light. "Can you tell if they're following?"

Theo looked over his shoulder for a long moment then smiled. "They aren't. I detect many life forms rushing the beach. They are overwhelming the remaining guards. It seems you were correct in your strategy."

"All right, let's go introduce ourselves. Maybe we don't have to get to the port alone."

I sat up as the car turned around and made its way across the waves. I ran my hands through my hair, which had gotten a little long at that point, and started making a rushed attempt at straightening up. "Man, I must look rough. I haven't seen good people in months, and I smell worse than I can remember, probably have a neck beard."

"More like a fuzzy face. It is patchy though. A beard may not be your best look."

"You have almost no tactical programming, but you're full of fashion advice?" I asked, a little hurt about my peach-fuzz beard. "Are you sure we can't get you an update somewhere?"

"No, I may be infected if you attempt to update my programming," Theo said, full-on worried.

"I'm just kidding. Haven't seen nice people in a while, I want to make a good impression."

"I would say you already have," Theo replied. The hover car drifted onto dry land and came to a stop in front of the hover yacht. I wouldn't admit it if you asked me while I was surrounded by pilots, but Theo was one hell of a driver. Smooth, calm, and he had really good reaction times.

I tried to open my door but it was warped shut. "I'm going to have to get out on your side." I said. People were coming, they were cheering at me, a few pounded the hood of my hover car, grinning. Theo slipped into the back seat, something he made look easy because his joints bent a lot more than mine and he was thinner than any human.

I stepped out through the driver's side and was greeted by a few eager hugs and handshakes. They cleared the way for a couple big guys led by this bearded man who had a smile that could light up a theatre. "I'm Derro," he said, offering his hand. I shook it the way I was taught – thrust in, slip the index finger up so it's crossing the other guy's wrist, shake firmly, then let go – and that's when I noticed that the big guys behind him were dragging that blonde, muscle-bound woman who nearly slagged me and Theo. "I'm the leader of our little band here. We were well east of here, where the pulse hit hardest, by Herrod when this bunch came and took us."

"I'm Noah, I was a fighter pilot, I had to make an emergency landing here when everything was going nuts," I replied. I didn't want to tell him too much. "You guys all right? There are some medical supplies and a lot of food still in there," I gestured to the large complex to our left. "I could show you around before I move on."

"Are there any bots or anything in there we have to worry about?"

"None," I told them. "I scouted it myself, blasted a few too."

"Is it true that this is the reserve vault? Billions in platinum down there?" asked someone in the crowd.

"Yeah, it's in a pretty heavy vault though. It's yours if you want to cut through, I'm moving on."

"What, you don't want to stick around for a share?" Derro asked.

"I want to make sure I'm not missing any of my people. There could be someone trapped in orbit." That was a half-truth. I knew the chances of any orbiting survivors were next to nil, but I couldn't help but hope. "I'll be heading out after that. There's gotta be friendlier stars out there."

"No, I'm afraid," Derro said. "I've spoken to travellers over the last few weeks, and they tell me that it's like this across the sector, only worse in most places since the bots weren't shocked. Here we only have to deal with the odd military or heavy security droid, but out there everything with an artificial intelligence has turned on us. Well, not all of us." He turned to the blonde woman and accepted a blade the length of my arm from one of the big guys holding her. "You saw this coming and warned no one. Instead you paid the Order so you could rule over us, bitch."

She looked at everyone in the crowd and struggled. They'd taken her armour, and were holding her muscled arms steady. Someone came from behind and knelt down on the backs of her legs. "You know what we do to anyone who has betrayed humanity," he said as he settled in behind her, crushing her knees into the dirt.

"Don't! I can go places where you can't!" the large woman screamed. "I can help you!"

"For betraying humanity, I sentence you to death," Derro said, raising the long blade and bringing it down. He didn't slash hard, it was as though he was only notching his starting place, and I stood there, frozen in shock and horror as their brave leader started sawing at her. She managed to squirm free at first, blood oozing from the back of her neck as she screamed and struggled. They got her under control a moment later, and Derro got back to work with a chop.

I'll never forget the sounds as screaming turned to choking and gurgling. It took a long time, but he eventually held her head up for a moment before throwing it down the beach. It was then that I noticed that someone got my passenger door open. It took me a moment to make a connection that sent my brain and adrenal system into full-on oh-shit mode. "Hey, he's got a bot in here!" said the man who got my car door open. "It's active."

"He won't attack you," I told him as I rushed in his direction. He was reaching after Theo, who was trying to avoid him and being polite at the same time.

"Hello, I'm not carrying the same murder disease as other robots," Theo said. "I'm a nice machine, and can perform many life-saving tasks as well as other less critical duties."

"Get away from him," I said, putting myself between the hover car and half the crowd. My sidearms were both out, pointing at everyone.

Entertainment doesn't get you prepared for combat. The bravery that comes to you on stage is pretty different from the kind that gets you through a firefight, but it does train you to recognize when a crowd is about to turn on you. These folks were about to turn, and turn bad. "Now I'm going to get into my car and go. You guys can have whatever's on that island and..."

I heard a car door open then quickly close behind me and glanced over my shoulder. Someone was fighting to open the rear passenger door, Theo was trying to hold it closed. I fell into the passenger side and got the car running in reverse then pushed the accelerator with my hand. A few people were dragged into the water, but I'm sure no one was really badly hurt.

I slipped into the driver's seat and made sure Theodore was still in the back. "You all right, buddy?"

"Yes, thank you Noah."

"No problem. Saving each other is what we do, I guess," I sent the car back across the water, getting as much island shoreline between us and those people as I could, just in case they found any long range weapons aboard that hover yacht.

"You could have said I was captured, and turned me over," Theo said as he got into the passenger seat and pulled the door closed.

"I wouldn't do that to you," I told him. "Besides, I don't think they would have believed me anyway."

"You will be hunted by Order people no matter what, but you have a chance at meeting friendly humans if you stop travelling with me. I am causing problems for you now."

"Man, I wouldn't ditch you," I told him. I really meant it. I didn't see him as some bot that made it through the madness, but a friend. My only friend. "We're just going to get to a port where we can get a ship flying and find a place where there's less trouble."

"That could take quite some time if you're alone."

"I've got you, buddy. Besides, I'm used to being outcast, that's the life of a carnie."

PART TWENTY-THREE

On her second night in Paradise Landing, Alice donned the short green dress with long sleeves. It suited her more than expected, and after tweaking the colour so it was a little darker, she was happy with the look. She left her hair loose and carefully used an auto-colour applicator to put on some makeup.

The first two attempts were too dramatic for her tastes, and she ended up going with the lightest setting. "When are we going to outgrow makeup as a species?" she asked her reflection.

"In Nihilist and Purist cultures, makeup is avoided at all times," Roomie replied.

"Nihilists are boring and I haven't heard of a Purist on Tamber," she said. Alice wouldn't admit it aloud, but she did like the way she looked with extra colour. "I hope Titus appreciates this."

She looked at the heels that were supposed to go with the dress for a moment and shrugged. After stepping into them and walking around for less than a minute she laughed ruefully. "No, no torture devices, please."

"Your feet have never been in that type of shoe before," Roomie commented. "Common perception suggests that women get used to them over time."

"Convert them to a flat sole or they'll get lost in the jungle."

"Perhaps a two centimetre heel?" Roomie countered.

"I'm gonna delete your fashion routine first chance I get," she warned. "But fine, I'll play along. Two centimetre heel and loosen the fit on the toes. It feels like this shoe is made for someone with only two."

"It is your size," Roomie countered.

"Revise it or I switch to combat boots," Alice countered. The shoes adjusted according to her specifications and she sighed. "Okay, I can walk in these."

She was out the door and down the suspended walkway leading to one of the main social hubs next. The lights strung above illuminated the wooden walkways and the trees all around gently, so there were no problems seeing where she was going, but not so she felt like she was aboard a well-lit ship. The atmosphere was definitely relaxing, even though she found the air was a little hot for her taste.

"Alice?" Iruuk said, meeting her on a large platform. People from the fleet were dressed up for the evening, making their way to any of the many entertainment areas that were just opening. He was out of uniform, his sisters at his side. One was caramel and black in colour, the other was silver and blue – obviously colour shifted. She couldn't remember their names, so she hoped it didn't come up. "You look so cute," one of them said, covering her snout for a moment before giving her a warm hug.

"I think she's sharing a meal with Titus tonight," Iruuk told them.

"Oh, I thought she was on her way to an official function," said the blue and silver sister. "The way she was marching."

"No, it's date night," Alice admitted. "Titus invited me to Lezorno's."

"Oh, you'll like it there," the caramel and black furred sister said. "I enjoyed the crab."

"Speaking of which, I'm hungry," the blue and silver one said, tugging on her sister's arm. "Brownies and ice-cream now."

"You two go ahead, I'll be there soon," Iruuk said.

"Hey, you said no fleet stuff," the caramel and black one said, her eyes, which were blue like Iruuk's, were big and pleading.

"Don't worry, I'll catch up," Iruuk said. "It's going to take you two twenty minutes to find what you really want anyway."

"Okay, see you later. Come meet us if Titus is boring," the blue and silver furred Nafalli said.

"Don't be rude," her sister admonished as the pair walked away, hand-in-hand.

Iruuk turned back to Alice and shook his head. "They're almost in their last growth spurt, one is rebelling a little and the other just wants to stay a child."

"I've never seen a blue Nafalli before," Alice said.

"Childish, I know. It's taking grooming too far, but my mom's too busy to care about a bit of colour," Iruuk said with a shrug. "Are you all right, Alice? You have that look that you get when you're about to do something you really don't want to."

"Do I?" she asked. "Maybe, I guess. I think I've been on the couch for too long, researching, listening to playback for the report."

"Do you not like Titus? He seems like a good man," Iruuk asked, concerned.

"I think I just have to unplug for a while. All I want to do is run back to my sofa and dig into the data files about Iora. Keep summarizing what I'm seeing."

"My report is finished, but I admit it was difficult to complete. There was a lot of personal testimony from the refugees I studied, and I had to meet two of them for an interview to clear some details up."

"I didn't know that was something we had to do."

"From what I'm hearing, now that we have clearance, only a few of us have to do the extra investigation work, but I thought it was rewarding. Still, maybe Titus isn't very practiced at dating. If he can't entice you away from writing a report, then perhaps he has a lot to learn. Maybe you should cancel tonight so he tries harder, it's what many Nafalli women would do."

"Really?"

"If they are uncertain about their suitor, or not excited by him, they'll tease to see if he's interested enough. No, not interested enough, that's not the right phrase." Iruuk thought a moment. "Driven enough, you know? Courtship should be like a chase. It helps the couple celebrate when they finally get together. Most Nafalli songs are about pursuit and love."

Alice couldn't help but smile at the mental image of a male Nafalli chasing his desired mate then crooning at the upper window for attention after she ran inside. "That sounds like fun."

"It looks fun, from what I've seen. I wouldn't know personally. There aren't a large number of Nafalli my age around right now," he said with a sigh.

Alice noticed Titus coming around the corner. "Looks like I won't be seeing my couch for a while tonight."

Iruuk looked over his shoulder and noticed Titus. "Good luck, Alice. Don't tease him too much."

"I won't, see you later, Fur-Face," Alice said as she started walking towards Titus. He was in a tightly fitted dark shirt with long loose sleeves and more formal black trousers. She did her best to put on a smile and greet him properly. "Hey there, how's leave treating you?"

"Good, I'm climbing the walls a bit, if I'm being honest," Titus said. He gave her a kiss on the cheek and a brief one-armed squeeze. "Hello Iruuk," he said afterwards.

The Nafalli was just about to turn away. "Hello, Titus. I was just leaving, I have to catch up with my sisters. Have fun tonight." He was on his way before he finished speaking.

"You look lovely," Titus told her, taking her hand and leading her into a leisurely walk. His fingers were thick, but not as calloused as hers were by far. There was something she enjoyed about his confidence, even though she didn't feel entirely comfortable with hand-holding, but she let it go on.

"Thank you," Alice said. "I've never seen the style you're wearing before, it looks good on you."

"Ah, it's outdated even where I come from, but I always liked it."

They walked through the sparse crowds along the imitation wood walkways between giant tree trunks without speaking. At first the quiet companionship was nice, but then the silence stretched on so long that Alice was almost afraid to break it. She thought of talking about training, about the cadets she was monitoring and advising until recently, about fleet news, but none of those topics seemed like a good idea for a relaxing night out.

At long last, a wooden sign with *Lezomo's* written across it marked a circular building as their destination. Titus opened the door for her and they were led to a table right away. The restaurant – decorated in red and dark blue colours with classical wooden furniture – was mostly empty. "I suppose most of the fleet personnel who are scheduled to move in won't be getting here for a while," Titus said. "Then again, there's a lot going on in system right now."

"With operating systems upgrades hitting millions of systems, I don't think a lot of people will have time to come here any time soon."

"Oh, I got an early look at the new systems and interfaces

on my first day here. I visited the beach, tried reading a bit, explored the concourse here, and by the time I was finished it was noon and I was so bored I couldn't believe it. I bothered Captain Sima's staff until I got myself an invitation to a prototype mock-up. Her core crew are already training there, and I got to join in."

"How are they doing?"

"Really well. The new technology isn't nearly as hard to grasp as the Admiral was telling us. It's just new, and so streamlined and well put together that it feels familiar after a few minutes. Crewmembers love it, and they take to it fast."

"How was the mock-up? Was it really different from the Runner Class?"

"It was only a simulated mock-up, not something that was actually built anywhere, so it was accurate, and now that you mention it, a lot of the layout for the corridors were about the same. A lot of the technology is bleeding-edge new though. I think that's what we'll end up training a few crews on, but not for long."

"Welcome to Lezomo's, would you like something to drink while you look at a menu?" asked a waiter in a classic black vest and white shirt.

"Just water for me," Alice said.

"I'll have the same."

"Anyway, I think assigning us to bridge crews to train people on the new systems is just a holding pattern. Captain Sima told me no one in fleet expected us to get through Apex Phase One with scores over ninety. Everyone who scored under ninety but passed is getting rushed through their final qualification testing soon and they'll be snapped up by captains as soon as they're done. What's happening to us, I don't know, but Captain Sima wished me luck today. Most of her staff have already passed their qualification tests for the new computer system. Did you hear anything about where we're going?"

The question surprised Alice, it shouldn't have, but her mind was wandering back to Noah Lucas and his experiences on Iora. "I don't, but I guess it makes sense. Most of our fellow ninety-pointer officers went past the curriculum into the advanced stuff, finishing qualifier tests that are a few years ahead of us. Most of the people who scored lower spent a lot more time with their cadets, trying to get them into shape."

"But your little crew didn't require much attention, neither did mine," Titus said as ice cold water was delivered to the table. He scrolled through the parchment style, flexible screen that had images and descriptions of different dishes. "I did physical training with mine and answered questions as they came up, and there weren't any discipline issues with my squad."

"My squad were mostly experienced people, so they really only needed technical questions answered," Alice said as she found an image of crab cakes with steamy broccoli covered in cheese on the side. She selected it and handed them back. "I pushed them through the physical training hard."

"I saw. You lead from the front and dare everyone to keep up with you, it's impressive."

"Thanks, but there were a lot of things we weren't given

the chance to train them on, like tactics, mission simulations, and a few other things. After basic rescue and evacuation drills, training officers took over. I wish I went through that with them."

"You were a ranger, and you're qualified on search and rescue to level seven. They'll have to create new tests for you to take if you want to advance."

"But that's why I should have been there."

"None of us were," Titus said. "I have experience with working with a squad, and I wished I could have been there to guide them through too, but I think they wanted all our cadets to get the same training. I'm sure my methods would differ from yours and everyone else in our class, it could be chaos out there."

"That makes sense," Alice said. "I suppose we'll be seeing that working for us soon enough."

"You really don't know what's up next for us nineties," Titus said, surprised. He selected something on his menu and handed it back to the waiter, who smiled, bowed and retreated silently.

"I have no idea. I haven't thought about it since I got here. When I'm not working on my report, I'm wondering where the Revenge and the Triton are. If I seem distracted, that's why, sorry."

"Not at all," Titus reassured. "I'm sure the Revenge and the Triton will be back with Freeground in tow any day. Moving a station takes time."

"I know," Alice said. "Still, I'd rather distract myself than dwell. I'm glad Fleet dumped a huge chunk of data in my lap,

I don't know what I'd do with myself if I wasn't trying to put a concise report together."

"You know we can talk about those now, our clearance level is high enough. Maybe I can help? I finished my report in five days. They had me go through passive scan data for satellites around Chermal over the last year. Haven Fleet suspected that there were a few pirate and raider bands using the planet and its moons for bases and warehousing. They were right, I found real evidence of nineteen different groups, all of them independent. The trick was to create the right data filters, to look at the scans along a timeline using filters to exclude anything that didn't help me find what I was looking for."

"Something like that would speed things up with my report," Alice admitted. "They gave me all the records collected by a pilot with Samurai Squadron before he joined up. He used a toy lizard to record most of it, but he narrated a lot of detail afterwards using still images and whatever else he could find. It's pretty amazing."

"Wow, that's pretty personal," Titus said.

"I know. Something about it, the way he tells his story, it keeps drawing me in so I have trouble skipping parts. So far there's a lot of data that could help fleet if they go to Iora, and even more evidence against a couple corporations that participated in the holocaust, at least in the way that their higher level employees were spared because they paid into the Order of Eden. There's more coming, big stuff, I know. Noah got his hands on some important data along the way, I just have to keep going through his records to find it."

"You could always just make a filter and search. Skip ahead to what you need."

"I could, but I have feeling I'd miss a lot if I started doing that. I feel like he's speaking to me, not narrating your average after action report. It's like we're sharing a table in some media pub and he's showing me all his videos, his pictures, and he makes me feel like I'm there. What's happening – I mean – what happened to him there seems important."

"Well, at least you know the ending already. He survived and joined Samurai Squadron," Titus said, raising his water glass then taking a gulp.

"I know, but it's like I'm really getting to know him. I didn't get to have a childhood, but he grew up in a travelling carnival and he tells stories about that. I don't just have a feeling for who he is, but I know how he became that way. His callsign in the squadron is Carnie, so I know he still holds his memories of being raised by the carnival close. There's a sentimentality there that I've never felt, but I get to through all these stories he's telling me. It's addictive."

"So you'd rather listen to every minute instead of creating a filter," Titus said. He looked to the kitchen. The sounds of frying and lovely smells began to drift through the pass to the dining room.

"Exactly," Alice said. "His record starts when they enter orbit around Iora, and the machines are disabling ships," she started. Without a second thought, she began telling Carnie's story to Titus, who offered few remarks as his linguini arrived, her crab cakes and broccoli was delivered, and they had their entire meal. The crab cakes were delicious, savoury and crispy with a touch of lemon.

They were finished dinner and sitting back when Alice finished telling him everything she'd experienced through Noah Lucas' records in what she thought were broad strokes. "So, he starts to wander here with Theo," she said. "And that's a problem, because he includes a lot of video of them breaking into places for supplies after their first two months, avoiding people, killing a few bots without too much trouble. I mean, he says a few things about the hundred or so buildings and other sites they visit, but for about nine months not much really happens. He gets to know Theodore, his bot, and answers a lot of his questions, but it's mostly wandering. He grew to a little over two metres tall in that time too, but that's not much to sink into." Alice finished her second glass of water. "I noticed I'm into the last twenty or so percent of the narrated record, so I'm coming to the end. I'm worried about the report I'll put together, whether it'll be too long or personal."

"Just keep it to the facts that you think will help fleet and to what people really might need to know about Carnie. Keep it simple," Titus said with a shrug.

"I guess, but I'm also afraid of what I'll feel like when I get to the end of the record. I mean, I already feel like I know Noah, like I've spent hours and hours with him in the same room, talking to me. What happens when he gets back, if I meet him? What if I have to interview him?"

The waiter came with two slim display slips in hand. "Would you like to look at the dessert menu?"

"No thank you," Titus said, waving him off. The waiter stopped abruptly and left.

"Are you all right?" Alice asked.

Titus wiped his mouth with his napkin and dropped it into his plate. "I think you'll be fine if you meet Noah in person, it's felt like he's been sitting with us at the table all night."

"Oh," Alice said, feeling terrible. "I'm sorry, I've been going on about it for a while."

"A couple hours. Did you notice that I ordered a salad after finishing my pasta, but you talked so much that it took you just as long to eat five crab cakes and some veg?"

"No, I'm sorry, Titus," Alice said. "My brain has been filled with this for a few days now. I'm happy you invited me out for this break."

"You're welcome," Titus said. "I'm sorry, I'm probably overreacting, but I was looking forward to this. I mean, I haven't dated for a couple years, since my wife passed away, and I was worried about what you'd think when I told you I'm a rollback."

"I didn't know," Alice said. "Rolling back doesn't matter much to me, I've restarted a few times."

"So you didn't know?" Titus asked, chuckling dryly. "I looked at your public file before I came."

"I don't really do that," Alice said. "So, sorry I didn't know much about you in advance, I thought I'd get that privilege tonight."

"Well, I rolled back forty-nine years for the Apex Program, have been married twice, and am twice a widower. I was really nervous that I'd tell you, go to the bathroom, then see an empty chair when I got back, but I'm not so worried any longer. You and Noah would make a great couple though, trust me, from the way you talk about him, I can tell." He sighed and smiled weakly. "You really are a fine woman, Alice, but I think you're a little too socially young for me." He stood and she joined him. "I really do wish you all the luck."

"We could try this again sometime," Alice said, not sure why she was trying to get him to agree to another date, she didn't want the one that was already crashing.

He gently took her hand in both of his. "Let's have a great friendship," he said with a tired smile. "Because I think anything else would end with a sad, quiet whimper. Have a good night." Titus let her hand go and started for the door.

Alice let him retreat, watching quietly with a little relief. Even though she felt bad for him, and regretted letting him down, the pull of Noah Lucas' narrated adventures were already luring her back home.

PART TWENTY-FOUR

Alice was still shaking the embarrassment and guilt off when she walked into her living room. Embarrassment because she completely burned any chance that her date could have been at least a good time, and possibly the beginning of something. She thought she was a social animal, but evidence was starting to indicate otherwise. Thankfully, there was a chance that Titus was mature enough not to spread stories of her social fumble across the fleet.

The feeling of guilt was less keen, but she hated the notion that she not only bored but deeply disappointed someone who she liked. Titus seemed like a decent man if nothing else, and she had to admit that he seemed too old for her, but as things stood she would probably never find out for sure. For all she knew, someone more mature was just the kind of companion she needed. Before the Order of Eden tore the galaxy apart with the Holocaust Virus, it wasn't uncommon for people of vastly different ages to have romantic relationships. Longevity wasn't much of a problem in some parts of the known galaxy, a person could be two hundred and look thirty five, eager to experience the new tastes and interests of people fresh to that age. No one would have given her and Titus a second glance since he was fresh from a rollback and looked about twenty years old. Regardless of how he looked, and he was fit, attractive, she felt bad about letting a nice man down when they could have had a relaxed evening trading stories.

With a sigh she said; "Low lighting, please." The dim night mode lighting activated smoothly. The main room felt too large, too empty. "Welcome back, Alice," Roomie, the stock hospitality program said cheerily.

"Oh, shut up," Alice replied under her breath. Titus was one of the nicer, more interesting people in her class. His hidden years probably explained part of that, and she wished she'd known before, not that it would have made a difference. She had the feeling that she would have rattled on about her new fascination with Noah Lucas anyway.

The worst part of their disappointing encounter was that she would probably have to work with him. Worry about awkwardness bothered her more than the embarrassment at seeming so self-centred. "I miss Lewis," she said, thinking of the artificial intelligence aboard her ship, the Clever Dream. She went to the bedroom and slipped out of her dress. "He might not know what to tell me, but he'd know how to cheer me up," she said as she tossed the green dress into a hamper.

"Off with the dating outfit, on with the 'I'm not leaving the sofa until I've finished my report' outfit," Alice said as she retrieved the comfortable, long dress from the closet. "And I'm never wearing heels again." The shoes were flung from her feet, into the back of the closet. "Even one inchers."

A static image of Ayan and her friend Lacey appeared in her mirror with a question beneath it; "We heard you were out with Titus tonight! How did it go?" The pair were looking relaxed, but a little done up as though they were having a night out or a night with visitors in.

A few rude responses crossed Alice's mind, but she let them pass. "Response to message; 'You and Dad make it look easy. Going to bed early, talk to you soon.' Now, send and mute further messages until tomorrow morning."

Alice sat on the edge of the bed. "Look up the status of the Revenge and Captain Jacob Valent. Does Haven Fleet have an expected time of arrival on them yet?"

Writing on her mirror appeared; *Only previous departure information is available.* It was a message that Alice was getting used to seeing. There was so little information available, that it was easy to suspect the worst. "This is my Dad I'm thinking about, and he has his best people with him. They'll be back." She hadn't seen him since she started training, and she felt like a completely different person with so many stories to tell. More than anything, she missed having time with him alone. Everything seemed simpler when she was with him. Even though she was biologically related to Ayan, and already began to accept her as her mother, Jacob was the one she pictured whenever she thought of family, and no one knew where he was for sure.

She flopped back onto the bed and closed her eyes for a moment. A storm of worry and unanswerable questions started to gather in the quiet. "Nope, not going to do this to myself," Alice said to herself, sitting up. "Back to the sofa! Roomie, bring up the Noah Lucas Iora File."

After ducking into the kitchen to retrieve a bag of rice cheese puffs along with a peach and orange slush drink, Alice fell onto the sofa. It was surrounded by an organized timeline of Carnie's ordeal on Iora. "Is there a narration that covers this section of time? It seems fragmented."

By looking at a range on the timeline, she enlarged it. The hover car they were using broke down over a hundred kilometres away from White Gull Spaceport. A text notification appeared with the system's response to her earlier question; *No singular narration describes the time frame you requested.* Then she realized that her house software wasn't responding through the audio system because she told it to shut up when she walked in.

"Re-enable audio responses, Roomie," Alice said.

"Thank you, do you have another request?"

"Yes. Is there enough narration in the record to describe this time frame succinctly? I have to get through this in the next two days, less if possible. I think it's affecting my mental health."

"Would you like me to begin assessing your behaviour?" Roomie asked.

"No. What's the answer to my question?"

"I can compile an accurate narration of events from Noah Lucas' narrated record and combine that with visuals from his logs."

"Okay, go ahead and do that for this time frame," Alice said, holding her hands up so they held a span of Noah's records starting with the hover car breaking down and ending months later.

"Compiling and authoring," the computer replied. "Ready."

Alice took a sip of her fruity drink and got comfortable. "Let's get started."

There was some kind of flying bot out there, looking for something to blast. Theo and I didn't notice it until it was too late, and it blasted our hover pads, leaving our car with three to try to balance on. I'm a good pilot, I know it, and all the practice I put in shows, but I don't know if I could have gotten us under cover and on the ground as fast or as well as Theo did. We really should have eaten dirt and rolled a few times with that kind of damage.

We got out of that car like it was on fire, and ended up in an upscale shopping mall. We got behind an emergency door and heard our hover car get pierced by a few dozen explosive rounds from that high flying bot. "We're walking from here," I whispered to Theo. "Do you detect anything moving in here?"

"No, but I can't sense much from behind this armoured door."

"We'll wait a few minutes before we take a look. I don't want to step up and come nose-to-nose with a flying murder machine." I tried not to move, wishing I had that rifle with target seeking bullets on me. There wasn't a sound anywhere, not even a bird in the sky, but I'd find out why later.

"It's been a few minutes," Theo said, nearly making me jump out of my skin. "Three, actually."

"Think we should wait longer?" I asked.

"I'm not sure, this is still all very new to me."

"Do you think you'd get shot if you checked alone?"

He thought for a moment, then stepped out into the open. "Dapper," Lurk croaked from my collar, where he took a snap of one of the most striking sights I've ever seen. The golden sundown light was sending shafts through the bank of windows in that hallway. Theo stood in the middle wearing his battered business suit. It looked like he was staring right up into the light coming in through the transpesteel. I realized much later that Lurk got a perfect shot of that, and it's as artful as any of those ancient paintings the masters put together back in the day.

"It scanned me and has gone," Theodore said.

"Man, you're going to get yourself killed experimenting like that," I told him as I came out from behind cover. "Be careful, all right?"

"I'm sorry, I just ran your question like a logic puzzle and knew it wouldn't shoot. It may have fired on the car more out of uncertainty – not knowing how it was being driven – than knowledge. Artificial intelligences can get strange when they're corrupted, I supposed."

"Strange. Homicidal, more like it," I said. "Thanks, man. You saved me a bunch of ducking and hiding there. I guess you should take the lead from now on."

"That would save you ammunition," Theo said.

I followed him into the mall, and the moment we opened the inner doors, I turned around and lost my lunch. The smell told me there were a lot of dead things inside. I wrapped a chunk of my sleeve around my mouth and nose then we checked it out as best as we could. There were a lot of dead bots inside, but many more dead humans. No one or nothing had come to clean up, either. It's like some of the bots tried to paint the walls with the shoppers and workers, decorating the floors with whatever was left.

I remember that like a landmark, because we kept on finding buildings just like that, over and over again. Not many bots survived in the area we were in, moving between clusters of civilized areas as we made our way to the main port, and the few that did still operate were half-fried or easy to avoid.

We didn't find any living humans, either. That pocket of civilization I found near the shore when I was running from those raiders must have been some kind of rarity, because everything else I saw for a couple weeks after made it look like Iora's human population was dead.

When the White Gull Spaceport was in sight, I was relieved, and terrified at the same time. We weren't the first to get there. We ducked behind a concrete barrier and Theodore peeked over the edge. "They are human soldiers in green uniforms."

"Can you tell where they're from?" I asked.

"No, but the small cargo shuttles they're loading have Order of Eden written on every side."

"Are they loading or unloading?" I asked, not knowing which would be worse.

"Definitely loading. In fact; I see several automated tugs affixing themselves to ships that are landed on the outer pads of the port. It looks like they are taking all the ships into space, or orbit at least, without powering them up at all."

That was the worst news. Not only was I too late, but the Order of Eden were working to trap everyone who was left alive on Iora there. I didn't even wonder why at the time, instead I pictured the same thing happening at major ports across the planet.

"Do you think this is happening elsewhere?" Theo asked.

"They're trapping us here, man," I told him. "Don't know why, don't much care, but we've gotta find a ship fast before they're all slagged or taken off world. You remember seeing anything we might try to fix on our way here?"

"A couple hover cars, perhaps, but nothing that can actually fly."

"Damn, we've gotta keep looking. Maybe we can find a small ship in a rich house, or an apartment hangar. I get the feeling these Order assholes have all the ports locked down."

PART TWENTY-FIVE

We were kilometres away from the port and thanks to some kinda mental slip, I thought that was far enough. Even under cover, rushing between thickly built structures that were made to stand up to the test of weather and time, military scanners can catch you. I should have known that.

If Order of Eden were interested in catching me and a small rogue 'bot, they would have. There is no doubt someone was watching as I put distance between me and the port for two days. That marked the beginning of the most frustrating time of my life.

Theo and I had great luck raiding shopping malls, only running into the occasional security bot here and there. They didn't recognize him as a threat, so he always led the way by a few meters, giving me ample warning. I was able to find food and ammo, but my dreams were haunted by the desecrated corpses of shoppers that stunk up the place like you couldn't imagine.

Surviving on packaged foods, depending on stolen gear and ammo wasn't the frustrating part. Moving around, raiding abandoned stores and a few homes didn't bother me much. But what we were after were ships, and we went from landing area to landing area and even risked checking a few minor ports. Five times I ran into the Order of Eden and watched from a distance as they either stole everything that could leave the atmosphere, or just slagged them in place. The other landing pads we found – you know the ones on top of those malls we kept hitting – were empty.

The malls and manufactured town centres were starting to show their age already. Weather ranging from hot sunshine to a couple of pelting hailstorms wore at their cheap facades revealing the boring, grey square construction underneath. Those fancy trims, signs, statues, and other embellishments were made of hardened foam and affixed to the sides of the buildings with glue.

Lawns were turning from green to brown in most neighbourhoods, and storm damage went unrepaired, as low quality homes with crushed roofs were avoided by squatters instead of fixed. The Order of Eden aerial bots that had me worried for a while got rare unless there was an Order shuttle nearby. I got close enough to one of them to see a bunch of survivors – probably people who paid up before the whole robot massacre started – were picked up and shuttled off into the blue yonder.

There were bigger sites too, places where the Order of

Eden had some major operations going on. There were explosions that shook the ground every once in a while. Theo said he could see large excavation ships landing in the eastern hills one day, and there was a buzz of cargo shuttles there. We decided to keep our distance, which was fine since there was a lot of continent left for us to get lost in, more than I could have explored on foot over twenty years. Oh, and as time went on, there were fewer and fewer bots around. People were becoming the problem instead.

We were taking a break under a low bridge one grey afternoon. I was having a chocolate chip muffin I saved for a while and Theo was taking five minutes to regenerate when I heard a footstep overhead. I popped the half muffin in my loose shirt collar and lowered my hand to my gun. A grizzled man wearing a couple blankets like a poncho dropped down in front of us, his pistol pointed at me.

He looked surprised when he noticed that I'd drawn my own, the blade shooter I called Needler, raised. "Give me your pack, or me and my friends will kill you for it," he said.

Looking at his scraggly hair, his yellowed teeth and shaky hands, I found myself wondering if I was in that kind of shape. I mean, I hadn't paid attention to a mirror in weeks, maybe months. Amused that I wasn't shaken by this guy or his threats, that I was more interested in my looks than that exchange brought a smile to my face. "In a minute my companion here will activate," I told him. "He's an assassin droid. Pretty good at keeping me alive. Better at making people like you dead."

"That scrawny bunch of wires? Looks more like a butler to me."

"You look more like a homeless man who found a gun to me," I told him. "That thing even work? I bet it got fried with most of the rifles around here."

"Drop your gear and your guns and walk away, boy, or I'll kill you right here." There was a new seriousness to his tone that made me pay better attention. "I'll burn your head off." He activated a switch on the weapon and I heard it begin whining. "Right off, nothing but a charred stump left, ratty-boy."

"I've got a couple extra condenser bottles, and I can leave you some food, man. I'm not going to dump all my gear."

"No deal!"

Theo's eyes opened and he started moving, drawing the guy's attention away from me for a second. I fell to my right, firing Needler. I caught him in the neck and drew a line of dozens of pierce points across his face and forehead. He got a shot off, but missed me and Theo. The rifle shot turned a spot of concrete the width of my hand to black glass.

The guy dropped twitching, his body still realizing that his brain had been chopped to pieces inside his skull as the tiny blade rounds shattered inside his head and bounced around in there. I dragged Theo with me further under the low walking bridge. "Have a good recharge?"

"Yes," Theo said, surprised. "What happened?"

"Someone trying to scare me into dropping all our stuff and walking away. You distracted him long enough for me to say 'no' in a language he understood."

"He is dead," Theo said.

"I know, looked like the only way. Can you see anyone else around? Listen for motion or something?"

"One moment," Theo said. "Turning my audio receptors up to maximum and analyzing the ambient sound."

I waited with my gun in hand and fished the second half of my muffin out of my shirt. I'd be finding crumbs for a week, but I was happy to have a few more bites as I watched the bridge.

"I can only detect one heartbeat now; yours," Theo said.

"What kind of range did you cover?"

"The wind is not particularly strong today, so I estimate you're the only person alive for at least seven hundred meters. I'll do a visual inspection of the area."

I let him poke his head out and look around while I fished through our visitor's pockets and pack. He had a couple emergency survival bars, a hand sized lamp and nine clips for his gun, which I deactivated and put into my pack. "Man, we could have been buddies, or at least traded," I said as I found eighty three platinum in loose change and a hand sized cutting torch in one of the outer pockets of his bag. "But you had to come in threatening and greedy."

"There is no one in the area, I'm certain," Theo said. "Why didn't he try to trade with us first?"

"Maybe someone else robbed him a while ago," I said. I took two small condenser bottles. They were both filled to the brim with clean water already. Fishing in his pockets was no picnic, he was filthier than me by far. "Doesn't look like he was keeping hydrated." Then I found the last clue I needed.

A small case with a variety of pills inside. I recognized some of them – blue with devil's horns impressed on them – and nodded. "Then again, he's been taking Red Ride. Addictive, makes you think you're immortal and the world is there for your amusement after a while. Speeds up all your reaction times and keeps you awake at first, but after a few days things start going wrong. Everything goes the other way towards stupidity and it slows you down. Still keeps you awake and grinding your teeth though." I looked at them for a moment and wondered if they'd be good for trading, then shook my head and tossed them down the street. "Yeah, he probably went crazy. I bet he was a couple days away from dying of dehydration."

"Dehydration?"

"You forget to take care of yourself when you're that high. His bottles are full, so that's what I'd say was about to kill him. Until he ran into me." I braved the blood on his face so I could close his staring eyes and pull the blanket on his back over his face. "Rest in peace, man." I washed my hands using one of his bottles and put both condensers into my bag.

"He was your enemy," Theo said, that curious look on his face.

"Yeah, he was, for a minute. If he wasn't high, he might have become someone we could trust, or at least trade with. If I found a bunch of pills to make this world seem rosier, instead of finding you, this could have been me."

"I understand. I wonder, though, would you ever treat the Order of Eden with such respect? You seem to hate them."

"That's different. They're a corporation picking at the

bones here. They could help, but nah, they're just feeding on this planet like a vulture on someone else's kill. From what I've seen, they may have had something to do with everything going sideways too, so yeah, I've got no sympathy for anyone wearing their colours."

"So true malice and greed without the same kind of tragic cause as the robber," Theo said. "Sober intent instead of desperation."

"Exactly," I told him. "Let's move on."

I ran into people a few times after that, and every time they ran away from us the moment they saw Theo. The allies to the Order of Eden, the guys and gals that paid for safety before everything went nuts just weren't around anymore. The people who were left were terrified of anything that could have an artificial intelligence installed, and they didn't seem to have much gear, let alone weapons or something that could help them in a fight against a bot. The first couple times I thought it was just chance; maybe those people just weren't good at surviving under the conditions on Iora. I left a little food and a spare condenser bottle since I had no trouble finding that stuff in malls and retreated.

After running into the fifth group of people who ran away from us like we were flaming devils, I started wondering what the deal was. No matter how I tried to entice them back, they just kept running. Something had scared them so bad that there was no way they'd stand still near Theo. Even after he hid, they wouldn't come out to talk to me. Every time I took a step towards that last group, they would take a bunch of running steps in the other direction. What's extra weird is that they weren't speaking a language I recognized either.

So, the Order of Eden was staying ahead of us and our quest for anything that would make it past orbit, and, no matter what we did, we ended up alone for more months than I was willing to count. The walking and the work I put in did something good for my bod though. That last growth spurt put me past two meters and I was in better shape than any carnie that I'd ever met. In the moments where I had to run and gun – another thing I was getting better at – it came in really handy. The biggest problem was finding new boots for my feet every month or two. Apparently extra-wide sizes are hard to find even when you have the whole mall to yourself. The self-adjusting systems in most shoes were fried, so I had to live with the near sizes I could find, which made for some pretty nasty blisters sometimes.

After nearly a year or so on the ground I finally fell down on my ass in the middle of a low road. I didn't want to take another step. My long hair fell into my face and I didn't sweep it away this time, just closed my eyes and scratched my blonde beard. Theo stopped and looked at me, puzzled. "Are you all right?"

"No, not really, man." He rushed to my side and started checking my vitals. I pushed his hand away and shook my head. "The problem's in my head, not much you can do. I just don't know what we're doing out here. We can't get to a ship, it feels like the Order is playing keep-away, and I know they're not out to kill us. I figure there's only one thing I haven't tried: stopping right where I am and seeing what happens when the world realizes where I'm making camp. Maybe we could start a fire, put some real signals out there."

"I don't see how setting fire to things will resolve any of our problems," Theo said, looking around. "Though that barley field looks particularly flammable if you're set on your course of action."

I hadn't even realized that we were crossing more farmland. The planet seemed to use most its land mass to farm natural ingredients, though most of the crops were failing without automated irrigation, harvesting and planting systems. "What do you think we should do? We've gotta change it up somehow."

"You are lonely," Theo said, helping me to my feet. "I can't be your only companion for such a long time span, especially since my social skills are not as sophisticated as most humans. Perhaps stopping cautiously is an option, but I would propose that we be constructive with our stationary time."

"I could take up a hobby," I said. "Whittling, maybe. There's a bunch of trees down there, I could take off a branch and start carving."

"Or perhaps you could put your mechanical skills to work. We could stop long enough to repair a proper hover vehicle. Then, instead of staying still, we could move at a much faster pace. If the Order of Eden seem to be ahead of us all the time, then perhaps we should make an effort to catch up."

"That's a little crazy, man. I think they haven't slagged us so far because we're just two harmless blips on their scanners, always at a safe distance. What if we get too close, or we get ahead and they come up behind us?"

"You wanted ideas," Theo said with a little shrug.

I thought about it for a while then started walking down the street. There was an underpass with a cluster of vehicles beneath. "Yeah, I'm so bored that I'm gonna try it. We'll fix something up and get some real speed going, maybe figure out what's going on here. I'd rather be informed and in trouble than bored out of my mind."

Theo and I checked underpasses and transit tunnels for a week before I found an armoured hover truck that looked right. It wasn't military, so the pulse damaged it enough so the crew abandoned it, but it was made to protect high valued passengers and cargo, so the side panels were nice and thick. It also had fifteen heavy duty hover pads. "Yeah, yeah, if we can find enough working parts, this'll be good." I looked inside the empty cab and nodded. "This'll be right if all the pads are okay. If not, they're just heavy duty models, so most cargo transports will have replacements."

"Hover pads don't seem to get damaged by electromagnetic pulses," Theo said. "I only see superficial damage on these."

"Yeah, hover pads have to be shielded since so much energy surrounds them when they're running, so a pulse won't do much of anything to them. I don't think it would take much to rebuild the navigational system in this truck, either. I'll add electromagnetic shielding wherever I can as I rewire it."

"Why add shielding?"

I almost said; 'I'm not the only one who can hit a button and make a pulse from that complex happen.' But instead of informing Theo that I was the one who did it, I changed what I was about to say at the last second. "If a pulse can hit the planet once, it can happen twice. Maybe every Sunday, for all we know."

"You have a point," Theo relented.

I looked past it to the hover cars clustered around and shook my head. In the middle of the intersection was a heavy maintenance bot with its lighter friends. They didn't survive the pulse I sent out way before, and were frozen in place, their cutters poised to assault drivers and the heavy treads of the largest robot placed so he was blocking half the street.

Many of the cars there were empty, telling me that my timing with the pulse probably worked, the people here escaped for the most part. The rest of the cars were occupied. The decaying drivers and passengers were left where they were, trapped inside their car tombs. "There are many stinkers here," Theo said. He was referring to the hover cars that had rotting corpses trapped inside. I coined the term, but no matter how many times I told him it was in poor taste and I regretted it, he kept using it. "Perhaps I should remove the bodies from the more intact vehicles while you make a more thorough inspection of the truck?"

I didn't have the energy to think of an alternate plan, so I sat down and nodded. "Thanks, Theo. I'm going to take a break, man." I took a packaged apple and rhubarb turnover from my bag and activated it. It self-baked in ten seconds, transforming from a flat rectangle to a thick, weighty stuffed pastry.

"It has been nearly an entire day since you had food, you should eat at least three servings over the space of forty minutes then sleep for eight and a half hours," Theo said. "You are still a growing boy."

"There's room for my pocket cot in the truck. Good idea," I said. Staying on my feet most of the day kept me wired, but my weariness caught up in a hurry. I only ate the one turnover, but I took Theo's advice and slept.

PART TWENTY-SIX

I woke up really hungry, so I ended up eating one of the few emergency meal bars I had left. They filled all the dietary requirements for eight hours, so they were precious, much better than the junk food that I tried to stick to. Normally, when I had one I tried to keep from eating for the rest of the day. Not the greatest plan, sure, but every time we had to go hunting for food in a mall, or by raiding someone's home, or corner shop, we were taking a huge risk. Where there's supplies, there could be people, or bots guarding them.

Theo let me sleep a little more than fourteen hours, and I was a pissed at first, but that faded by the time I was half way through my meal bar and all the way through a bottle of water. By the time I emerged from that hover truck's passenger cabin, I felt like all was well with the world again, or at least, like all was well with me. "Good morning, Theo. Let me sleep in, huh?"

"Yes, you were resting so peacefully, I didn't want to wake you."

"No worries," I told him. "Anything interesting happen while I was out?"

"An Order of Eden bulk transport passed overhead five hours ago. They passed out of my range without slowing down but I could tell it was a larger model. I have begun taking parts from the cars here to replace the finer systems in the hover truck. If I knew how to begin, I would have started preparing the hover truck for you. I also recovered a working communicator, an electronic tool kit and a modest selection of packaged foods." He gestured to an impressive pile in the trunk of a nearby car. There was enough food there to keep me going for a week. Added to the packaged junk we had in our packs from a mall we raided the week before, and the few things we had left from the Complex, I figured I was set for over a month. My gut craved something fresh and green, sure, and I couldn't remember what a fresh tomato or blueberry tasted like anymore, but this packaged stuff was good enough to keep me alive.

"Good job, man," I told Theo. "Let's pack everything but the parts up, and get started on trying to get this thing running," I told him, stuffing the packaged snacks into my bag. "I don't know what I'd do without you, man."

"Thank you, Noah. I mirror the sentiment, of course," he replied.

. . .

I was under the dash of that hover truck for days. The electronics kit and extra parts were speeding things up so much that I was actually whistling to myself as I replaced some of the more delicate components down there. The kit was super handy, since I could test the spare components that Theo salvaged before trying them in the car, so I knew I was only working with good bits before I wired them in. I was practically half inside the dash, twisting to get access to parts that I really should have removed sections of the car to access. Playing contortionist saved me a lot of time though, so I kept it up.

Theo kept watch, and in the week or so I was waist deep inside that hover truck, he counted nine Order of Eden cargo ships. They would pass somewhere overhead, land somewhere out of sight, then return to the skies without the cargo container they brought with them.

As more and more of them came and went, as time crept on and we stayed in the same place, my curiosity and worry grew. We'd gotten good at keeping on the move, maybe it was part of our survival strategy – an important part – and I was surprised that the cargo shuttles didn't pay any attention to us. Theo couldn't figure out what was in the sealed containers, but he knew they were insulated.

I finished working on that truck in the dead of night. I was so tired that my vision was blurry, I was fighting sleep, but I had to see if the electronics inside the cab and the generator were working. I made sure the hover pads were off, they were the loudest part of the hover truck, then I started the rest of the systems. Nothing happened.

"Boost," Lurk said, pushing a small battery across the top of the dash with his nose.

"Good idea," I told him, replacing a battery pack in an overhead panel with the charged one. I checked the controls again, then crossed my fingers and activated the truck's systems by flipping a switch I installed to bypass the security measures in the dash. Everything lit up.

"It's working?" Theo asked, practically jumping into the passenger seat.

"Yup, keeping the pads off for now though, I don't want to wake up the whole hemisphere with the sound of fifteen hover pads powering up at three in the morning. Help me run through the checklist, let's make sure this thing is in shape."

"My pleasure," Theo said.

We went through all the systems, and everything from navigation to communication was working. We kept the communications system off just in case anyone was watching for new signals, and I kept the transponder deactivated using a switch I installed as well – a stroke of genius I was maybe a little too proud of – and by the time we went through everything I was dead on my feet. I do remember finishing the checklist, but not going to bed that night.

The next day I activated the whole truck, including the hover pads, and was shocked at the thunderous sound the machine made while hovering a couple metres above the concrete. So startled, that I turned it back off as fast as I could. "Holy crap, that's loud. They're going to hear us for kilometres in every direction."

"It's actually no louder than a normal hover vehicle,

quieter than the last one we had. The hover pads are quite well made and balanced."

"Okay, maybe it just seems that way because we've been on foot for months," I told him.

"That would make sense," Theo said.

I spent a little time reducing the power levels of the hover pads until I was happier with the noise levels, but I was still worried about how conspicuous we were. I'd spent a week putting the electronics back together and adding spray-on insulation everywhere I could so the machine was more hardened against electromagnetic pulses, but the thought that we'd be easy to track even after all the work it took to make it difficult to see at a distance never crossed my mind. "If the Order are dropping soldiers or bots in those transport crates, they're going to hear us way before we can see them. No way we're surprising anyone in this rig."

"We could move this to a more secure location and park it, use it as a home instead of a conveyance."

It made sense, but I was still disappointed. "You remember the Remington Centre?" I asked.

"Your prime entertainment, dining and shopping destination. Experiences you can't order to your door, guaranteed!" Theo said, perfectly imitating the announcer voice that kept repeating the mall's slogan while we were there. It played every time you passed through a major intersection or opened an outer door, and made me jump at least twice.

"Yeah, they had bulk food and a bunch of stuff there that we had to leave behind. Maybe we should load up now that we have this thing?"

"That's a good idea. Then we could go anywhere."

"Well, except for off-world," I told him.

"Except for that."

"All right, you're driving."

After months on foot, the world seemed to speed by. We made our way down highways, through tall transit tunnels, and across fields that seemed to go on forever. All ten metres above the world whenever we could. After a while it really felt like we were flying, and that all my troubles were left on the ground.

We avoided the places Theo estimated those Order ships landed, but after a couple days we ran across one of their cargo containers by mistake, passing almost right over it before either one of us could notice. To my surprise, there were no bots, nothing was trying to put holes in my new truck, and my worry was replaced with curiosity. "I might regret this, but bring us down and about. I want to see what's in those things."

Theo reduced our height, slowed the truck to a crawl and we drove down a rough path leading to the cargo container. I had my pistol in hand, I'd named it Needler. By then I took it out as a habit, like a child who reaches for their favourite toy when they're nervous or uncertain. There was a camp fire built at the mouth of the container, but someone had doused it.

A blur ran across our path and Theo stopped before hitting it. I looked out my window, looking for it and saw a little girl picking up a small stuffed Nafalli toy, hugging its plush body to her own. Her mother, a streak of motion with blonde hair trailing behind, ran from behind the cargo container to her. "What are your scanners picking up in that cargo container?"

"Human excrement, some nutrient wrappers, but nothing else," he replied.

"How many people are here? Do you have a good reading?"

Theo activated the truck's scanners and I watched as seven green humanoid outlines appeared. "There are a total of seven people here, I detect only improvised weapons. A steel bar and two people seem to be brandishing pieces of wood. They are hiding behind the container."

They were nowhere near the woman and her girl. "Duck down, don't let them see you, and lock the doors behind me. I want to see if I can make nice." I grabbed a bunch of junk food from my pack, stuffed my pockets and left the cab. The doors locked and the windows blacked out so no one could see inside.

I put my handgun away and held up a pair of packaged pastries. "Hey, guys and gals, I'm here with food, I'm a friend."

The guys hiding behind the cargo container came out first, approaching slowly with their improvised clubs raised. They looked like hell, in disposable vacuum suits that looked like white plastic bags, and I could see that they were hungry at a glance. There's a desperation that comes with days old hunger, and it shows.

The little girl broke free of her mother's grip and ran right up to me. I didn't hesitate; there was a package of apple pie in her little hand the second she reached up. I watched as she expertly pulled one end of the package and waited as it rehydrated, inflated and heated, then stuffed as much of it into her mouth as she could.

"Get away from her," the one with the steel bar in his hands warned.

I stepped away with a smirk. "Looks like she has the right idea," I looked at him, raising my hands. "I'm really just looking to find out how you folks got here and would like to make a few new friends. If you're worried about entertainment, I've got stories you wouldn't believe, and I can juggle."

The little blonde mess a couple metres from me was still digging into her slice of pie, and the guys who were coming out from behind that crate were looking from her to me. "Head's up!" I said, tossing a preserved burrito at one of the guys not brandishing a club. It hit his chest and he caught it before it hit the ground. "My name's Noah. I know where there's food, clothing, and I've got enough condenser bottles to keep us hydrated for years." I could tell I was winning them.

I backed up to the passenger door, and the little one's mother came out of the shadows, gathering her girl up in her arms as she finished her pie. She was all smiles, with her full tummy and her favourite plushie back in her arms. "We should trust him," her mother said. "We're starving, half of us are sick. I don't see that we have much of a choice."

"I have some emergency meds that will probably clear whatever you've got up," I said. "Or I could move on."

The thin guy holding the steel bar up looked to his companion, who was digging into the burrito I tossed at him, and dropped his club. "I'm too tired to argue. We're the Pearsons."

PART TWENTY-SEVEN

Not for the first time, my best friend was my biggest problem. Theodore was sitting in the driver's seat of my truck. Perfectly hidden, sure, but as I did the rounds, meeting the Pearsons first: Donna, her husband Harry and her daughter Izzie, I dreaded the moment when I'd have to reveal Theo. The other four with them were Denny, a guy with these bulging eyes, Nate who was the shortest, Sherman with the flattest nose I've ever seen and Pete who had shining red hair. They seemed all right, but still pretty wary. Sherman kept checking out my guns, something I'd have to put an end to before long if he didn't earn a lot of trust in a hurry.

After the hand shaking was over, I opened the back door of the truck a crack and was relieved to see that the partition between the passenger cabin and the cab was up. I grabbed Theo's bag and started handing out food along with a couple full condenser bottles of water. "I just finished fixing this truck up a couple days ago, so we haven't gotten a chance to make any big supply runs. Are you the only ones who came in that container?"

"No, we were captured on the Tawny Flats. Bots came charging after us and instead of tearing us apart, they grabbed us and took us to a redistribution centre. Are we still on Shir Cana?" asked Harry.

I knew that world. It was originally a mining colony that got terraformed really well. There were some nice green cities, I got to visit Dardown, but we set up in an old mining pit well outside the city limits. I remembered a lot of middle classers, who had a surprising amount of extra plat to spend on us. "We're on Iora," I replied.

"I told you," Sherman said. "They moved everyone. It's a forced relocation."

"How many people were in there?" I asked, looking over their shoulder to the cargo crate.

"One hundred thirty-three per crate," Pete said. "I heard that was the maximum tolerance from one of the guards. We buried nine when we got here, they didn't make it."

"Are all the cargo containers filled with people?" I asked. "I mean, we've been seeing them all week."

"Yeah, there were hundreds of cargo pods like that when I got loaded," Pete said. "I kept asking where they were sending us, but the bots wouldn't say, the guards ignored me. Couldn't find out why we were all being relocated, either. I was just glad the bots we saw weren't attacking anymore."

"Iora, there aren't many natural resources here," Harry said. "Mostly agriculture and commerce services, right?"

"From what I've seen so far," I agreed. "I'm not from here either, I was forced to land. Listen, we've got a bunch of food we can spare, so let's dig in. May as well talk and eat at the same time. We were also on our way to a big mall, so there should be clothes and other supplies for you there if you want to come."

"Who's 'we?'" asked Donna. I didn't realize I'd used the word until she pointed it out. She didn't start rehydrating the brownie I passed her, and she looked worse than everyone, but her attention was laser focused on me.

"Yeah, how much do you know about the virus?" I asked.

"The one that turned our AI's bad?" she asked. "I know I lost my sister, and the galaxy's getting torn apart."

"Well, not all the bots got infected," I told her. "Some of them didn't go crazy, and they want to..."

"Every bot goes bad eventually," Donna said, tossing the brownie back at me. "Doesn't matter if it doesn't have an artificial intelligence, sometimes another bot will install one so it can get infected. Doesn't matter if it has override safeguards installed either, those can get disabled. Whatever you've got, you've got to break it into a million pieces and leave it behind. You'll be sleeping one day, and it'll find some reason to install something, and then you'll find its hand around your throat."

"Listen, I don't know what you've seen, I know I've seen horrible..." I adjusted my language for Izzie, her little eyes were focused on me. "...stuff. I have a bot that doesn't want to connect to any kind of network or install new programs, he doesn't even have a wireless receiver."

Donna picked Izzie up, she looked so thin and weak that I expected her to topple over under the toddler's weight. "No, I'm not going near a bot," she said.

"What choice do we have?" Harry pleaded. His stubble looked at least a week old. "Look at him," he said, waving his hand at me. "Whatever he's doing is working for him."

"Sure, but maybe he's a bot, we've met talkers before who tricked people," Denny said.

"That kind of paranoia is what paralyzed us, kept us here when everyone else moved on to find food," Harry replied.

"No, I'm not going with anyone who has..."

Sherman tried to grab my Heavy Hitter, the gun loaded with explosive rounds. I hadn't noticed how close he'd managed to get. I took a few steps to the side and drew my blade shooter, Needler, the Heavy Hitter was still in its holster. Sherman stared down the barrel of my handgun like he was still thinking about making a move. "I worked my ass of, walked more klicks than you could imagine getting this together," I told them. "I'm willing to share it with you if you settle down. We'll talk our problems out, my bot goes nowhere, and you'll learn to love him, trust me."

Sherman took a half step forward and I let a burst of micro-blades fly from Needler. He lost an earlobe and a few dots of blood appeared on his shoulder. "Try it again!" I told him, regretting the threat the moment I heard Izzie start crying. The wounds were superficial. Aside from his earlobe, the wounds should heal up in a couple weeks since the blades went through nothing but the thinner, meaty part of his shoulder.

They all started backing off. "There can't be many people around like him, people who would help us even though we have nothing," Pete said. His face was turning almost as red as his hair. "When is this chance gonna come around again?"

"He shot me," Sherman said, holding a hand with a superficial spatter of blood on it up.

"You went for his weapon, it's simple Darwinism," Pete shot back. "Listen, man, just wait. Wait until all this calms down."

The scene didn't match what Pete was saying. He wanted to give peace another chance, but Harry was picking up his metal bar again, Donna and Izzie were making themselves scarce and everyone else was following them. I didn't have a good feeling about Pete either. My eyes and ears were telling me that I should let him in, take him along, but my gut didn't agree. I had visions of him taking me out in my sleep and driving my truck back to this shipping container, playing the hero who beat the well supplied survivor to save his friends. "Sorry, man, the confection truck is closed," I said, hopping into the back and slamming the doors behind me. "Theo, hover up twenty metres and hold."

The truck gained altitude, and when it stopped I popped one of the doors open. They already had a couple condenser bottles, leaving me with one, which was fine, but I didn't want to leave them without food. I pulled a couple precious parts out of Theo's bag and tossed all the food inside at the container dwellers, making sure I made eye contact with

Harry before dropping a bottle of anti-toxin meds down on him. There was enough food there for about a week if they rationed it. They could make it to one of the smaller shopping centres in three or four days, so I knew I wasn't leaving them completely helpless.

I considered dropping Needler down to them so they'd have some kind of ranged defence, but slammed the back door closed instead. "Let's get out of here," I told Theo as I moved to a passenger seat.

"They didn't want to come with us?" he asked.

I was pretty sure he was pretending that he didn't hear every word, watch everything go down using the sensors in the truck and his own electronic ears. I played along. "They weren't our kind of people, man. Maybe next time."

I laid back and ran my hands down my face. I hadn't seen an aggressive bot in at least a couple weeks. The Order of Eden was transporting people by the shipping container load to the planet. These things had to be part of the same puzzle somehow.

I remembered something that made me wonder if all that wandering had made my brain soft. I had a communicator. I yanked it from the box of supplies we had stashed in the back and went to the front. "Time for answers, man," I said. "If they're letting people reach out, maybe we can get on the Stellarnet and see what's really going on."

"Those people," Theo started. He was driving the truck at a reasonable speed, keeping it in tunnels and under bridges most of the time. "They would have accepted you if I weren't here."

I knew Theo really well at that point. Most of his finer social niceties were learned from me by then, for better or worse, because we spent so much time together. His business suit attire didn't hide slumping shoulders from me. I'd never seen anything look so sad then, organic or mechanical. "Don't worry about them, man," I said, putting my hand on his shoulder. I could feel the mechanical joint moving a little under the suit's shoulder pad as he adjusted the truck's course. "I wouldn't be here if it weren't for you. When we found out that the bots didn't respond to you like they did to humans, you scouted ahead. I worried every time, the urge to follow you into those apartment buildings, malls, stores, supply depots was crazy powerful. I didn't want you to be alone in there in case things went bad, but you made sure you were the first to see every bot we came across so I could stay clear. Now the bots don't seem to be around, but there are people landing all over. It's my turn. Let me scout them out until we find some cool tribe out there that'll accept us both."

"You have a nice way of talking to people," Theo said.

"No worries, man. You're the best friend I've ever had."

"Thank you, Noah. You are my best friend too."

I turned the communicator on and snickered. "Not that you have a lot of choices," I said.

"Even if I had a galaxy to choose from, I'm certain you would be my favourite person," Theo reassured in a rush.

"I'm just kidding, man. I know we're joined at the hip no matter what."

"Another human expression," Theo said, shaking his head

a little. "That must be one of the most gruesome ones I've heard."

I was surprised to connect to a communications node in orbit. The connection wasn't that fast, but it was serviceable and there was an information network attached. My heart leapt when I realized I could start searching. The first thing I searched was; *why did AI turn on us?*

I was stunned when the network provided a few thousand answers – recorded communications, videos and statements from across several sectors – but one stood out. It was a huge information package from a ship called the Order of Eden Crimes Against Sentient Life. I started downloading it, watching the introduction as it loaded onto my device.

A hologram of a curly red-haired woman appeared. She looked at me with a dimpled smile and kind eyes. "My name is Ayan Anderson, and I'd like to say I'm a survivor who has experienced everything in this record, but I'm afraid I'm more of a descendant. As you'll discover if you begin viewing this record in chronological order, I was created using a woman named Ayan Rice as a template, and I have all her memories. This is important to mention because not many people survived the journey I'm about to take you on. By viewing this record in chronological order, you will see an honest account of the history of the people who put it together but more importantly this record will serve its true purpose. It will prove that the Order of Eden is guilty of murdering over a trillion humans and millions of their allies. They did so with the support of several large corporations, but none has offered more credit or equipment than Regent Galactic. It can be said that, without Regent Galactic and a company they purchased, Vindyne, the disaster caused by the Holocaust Virus may never have happened."

"She's an example of a lovely human female?" Theo asked.

"I'd say she's a nine or ten, yeah. It's not just in how she looks though. Maybe she'd be a seven if it were, but she's got something..." he said, watching the download meter make it past seventy percent. "Grace," he said, snapping his fingers. "She's charming too. Not everyone can just talk into a holo recorder and make it feel like one half of a private conversation."

"Like poise," Theo said. "I would like to communicate that well someday. It would be nice to be able to put people at ease. There isn't enough serenity in the galaxy from what I've seen before. I would like to give that to people."

"Sometimes you blow me away, man," I said. "I've never looked at it that way, but maybe I should have. I would have appreciated the work the carnival did more. Entertainment can make people forget all their problems for a minute. I guess that's a kind of serenity." I looked through the holographic directory as I paused Ayan's introduction. "What do you think of the pitch?"

"Pitch?"

"What she says this video is," I explained.

"Oh, I'm very interested."

"Then we keep watching?"

"Definitely."

I hit play on the introduction and watched. "I'm speaking

to you from Haven Shore," Ayan said. "It is on Tamber, a terraformed moon in the Rega Gain system, and we are working hard to protect this abandoned area of space." The point of view pulled back to reveal that she was standing on a balcony near the top of a building that looked as much organic as it did man-made. It looked like a pile of opalescent ovals carefully stacked into a massive round building. "The Rega Gain system was an out of the way terraforming project during the end of the last age. The records we uncovered indicate that the terraforming on Kambis, one of the major worlds in the system, failed when the system was abandoned when the Omnivirus infected the majority of the population in the system. We've taken up residence and are fortifying, creating homes for people who have been forced to run from a galaxy that has turned against most of us. It's not safe here, not yet, the Order could attack us any time, but we hope it will be someday. Right now democracy is returning, we have formed alliances with important forces for good in the galaxy, and our infrastructure is growing by the day, increasing the number of people we can support. Our current goal is to turn refugees into active citizens who are not only productive, but well settled and important to the evolution of our society. The development of our military is also important, we need protection and are participating in a war against the Order of Eden, but you will learn more about that later if you keep watching, or you could skip to it if you like in the menu."

The focus returned to a head-and-shoulders view of Ayan. "This isn't some kind of sales pitch for our settlement, I only wanted you to see where I ended up, so the darker parts of this account don't seem impossibly desperate. Every part of our story has an evidence and testimony section, so if you want more detail, it can be found there. Would you like to begin our story from the beginning?"

"Yes," Theo and I said at the same time.

The image of a massive space station appeared. Rings within rings affixed to bigger rings that served as habitation, production, hangars and ports. The hull looked older than anywhere I'd been. I hadn't seen anything like it. "The story begins on Freeground Station," Ayan narrated.

Theo and I spent the next week travelling, watching the history of the people I admire now. The crazy brave pilot; Minh-Chu Buu, beloved leader; Captain Valent, brilliant engineer and adventurer; Ayan, the artificial intelligence turned real girl; Alice, the champion of his circle of friends; Captain Terry Ozark 'Oz' McPatrick, and so many people they lost along the way. By the time I reached the story of the Order of Eden, we had to take a break. We were coming up on Remington Mall.

PART TWENTY-EIGHT

To my dismay, there were at least a couple dozen cargo containers on top of and around the Remington Mall. There were people everywhere, and the truck's scanners picked up three ships on their way. "Into that alley," I told Theo, who drove us expertly into an alleyway, reducing our height.

Once the pad guards under the truck touched the concrete I hit the blackout switch and the truck went dead. "Let's see what's going on," I said, leaving the truck. I took both my guns, my main pack and the new weapon I'd taken from the robber weeks before with me. I called it Slagger. It was a high energy plasma pistol, I'd never seen anything so nasty, it's wide barrel was intimidating, and with the heat dissipation fins down its length it looked even more threatening.

I still couldn't respect the weapon though. I'd been

brought up believing that any weapon that could burn through a hull was too reckless to carry around. Besides, I liked stun settings, but guns with that kind of function didn't really work after the pulse. To be honest, my favourite new toy, or weapon I guess, was a sling shot I'd made for the suppression balls Theo and I had. With that thing I could fling a ball a hundred metres and it would hit so hard that it went off on impact, filling a couple metres with gooey green web. The slingshot never left my thigh pocket, and there was room for about twenty rounds in there too.

We locked the truck behind us and got up the ladder as quick as we could. By the time we reached the top and could see the Remington Mall, the ships were landing. From the rooftop we were on a few streets over, the mall looked like it went on forever. It was several blocks wide, with landing spots across the roof and a navnet tower reaching up from the middle. There were people everywhere, coming out to see the ships land with long shipping containers marked with a stylized grain symbol. "Is it feeding time? This is new."

"There are so many people," Theo said. "Most of them are still wearing emergency vacuum suits."

I couldn't see with the detail that Theo did, the human eye doesn't come with a zoom function, but the colour of the crowds' clothing was mostly white. Those flimsy vacuum suits weren't made for long wear, it was like being dressed in cheap plastic bags. The sleek, green and white ships set down. They had pointed noses with cockpits that gave the small crew a good view of everything around. One on the roof, the other two at either of the main mall entrances on the ground. A moment later, they were ascending quickly, leaving their long cargo containers behind.

I watched as the nearest one's main and side access doors popped open and the crowd rushed the container. "Can you see what's in there?"

"Emergency rations," Theo replied. "They are fighting for the food now, a few who are dressed in normal clothing are winning. They are taking control of the food already using bats and blades from the sporting store."

The three ships didn't waste any time heading for orbit, and were gone before the commotion was over. "Looks like one group has taken control," I said. "Maybe a couple groups. Either way, we're not going to be able to loot this place again."

"That's better," Theo said. "They're handing out one bar per person. Some of the food is being taken away by the box though.

"By more guys in normal clothes?" I asked.

"Yes. No one in their emergency vacuum suit is being allowed to take their own food from the container. I would assume you're right. There is enough food there for everyone to have several days' worth, but most are being given only one emergency bar."

"So, they're dropping people off by the thousand and now they're feeding them." The next chapter in the recordings I had from Haven Shore was about the Holocaust Virus. I was hesitant to watch it. I was living it. I was in the aftermath, but I think I was afraid to find out that there was a logical reason behind it. Revisiting the horror of that first day wasn't exactly choice entertainment for me either. Even so, I'd sat through the story of the First Light, learned about Vindyne and their ruthlessness, seen the betrayal of Jonas Valent, the birth of Alice Valent, and learned about the search for Jonas and the Samson.

The story blew my mind, I didn't think it could be real at first, but there was evidence backing everything up. Records from Freeground Fleet, extra recordings of Jacob Valent bounty hunting, logs from the Samson, from the Clever Dream, and from many other ships that were directly or even barely involved. At one point, around where Jonas sacrificed himself, I just stopped questioning and believed the story this collection of info was telling me. "I think it's time we finish watching that holo series," I told Theo.

"Anything other than going to this mall seems like a good choice," he replied.

"We'll look for another mall, or an abandoned store. Maybe stay away from those ships. No need to push our luck," I said, planning out loud.

"That's a good idea. I'll drive while we continue watching the Haven Shore Record."

A few minutes later we were in the truck again, driving on with all the systems turned down low. I hadn't seen any other hover vehicles working, so I didn't want to draw attention so close to where I was sure a new gang was forming up. Any new organization would do anything to get the only working hover truck into their hands.

When we were several kilometres away I started the chapter detailing the Holocaust Virus. Ayan Anderson walked us through it, putting the pieces together for us as images of different ships, people and locations related to the events were presented.

The story, as she told it was that a virus was spread by the Order of Eden that used the emotion coding of all artificial intelligences to turn them against any human that wasn't in their database. That connected to an alien race that was covered in a previous chapter: the Edxi. They were an insect family race that saw humans as nothing more than a kind of intelligent worm, but we'd insulted their honour. A group of scientists associated with Vindyne had captured eggs and hatchlings from a brood world. Not only that, but they conducted experiments on that world before leaving.

An outcast named Zarrix followed the trail, finally commissioning the delivery of a few eggs that had been tampered with. He returned to his caste with the evidence, and they demanded retribution from the new owners of Vindyne, Regent Galactic. Long serving officers put a plan in motion that would satisfy the Edxians, who were threatening to invade the galaxy, turning heavily populated human worlds into brood planets, where their deadly offspring would feed on the population for the first thirty or so years of their lives. The diagrams and footage of Edxians sent chills up my spine. They were multi-limbed, had an interior and exterior skeleton and exo-armour that could resist most human weapons. Their tech was also scary advanced, but it became pretty clear that we didn't know nearly enough about them.

The most important thing was that we were nothing to them. They'd do what they promised as retribution and cele-brate the expansion. Those Vindyne assholes came up with a solution that was almost as bad. Billions of people believed that something horrible was about to happen, predicted by the Order of Eden's Child Prophet, and they paid a hundred thousand standard credits each to get on a list for protection. Even more pledged their lives to the service to the Order when they didn't have enough money. Regent Galactic right in the middle of everything as the owners of Vindyne, employers of the executives who devised the plan and ran the show then, extending credit to billions of people who paid their way into the Order of Eden. They became indentured and had to do whatever kind of work the Order or Regent Galactic wanted.

When about ninety percent of the populations of the few hundred worlds Regent Galactic and the Order of Eden controlled were signed up, they sent the Holocaust Virus into the universe. I was at a loss for words when Ayan's image mournfully told me that over three point three trillion human lives were lost across the galaxy and that the Holocaust Virus was still spreading. An antivirus followed weeks, sometimes months behind, but that wouldn't prevent the ongoing carnage on many worlds in time. I suspected that the bots were going nuts on other planets, but I had no idea it was so widespread.

I wanted to take a break, but I forced myself to go on. The Edxians were satisfied with the sacrifice, but saw another motivation. It was obvious to them that the Order of Eden was thinning the general population of the Milky Way in order to make turning it into a brood territory less viable. That led to the second half of the deal.

The Order of Eden had to create conditions on many worlds where a brood could be sustained. They had to make sure the population was large enough, but not well armed. The people there had to be in good enough shape to run, but not so well fed or organized to present an unsurmountable challenge to the broodlings, which were as tall as me with pincers, razor sharp edges on their inner arms, and from the rare footage included I could see they were fast.

"We have to leave this world, Noah," Theo said.

"Yeah, they're turning this place into a brood world. I'm going to start trying to contact ships, man. I don't care if it brings hell down on us. Just be ready to run if the Order tries to come for us."

"I'm always ready to run."

As the playback moved on to the next chapter, explaining how Haven Shore was settled, and how Ayan Anderson became the owner of the Rega Gain solar system for a while, I started using the communicator to look for ships in orbit that didn't belong to the Order of Eden.

It only took me a few minutes to find one – a Nordan Long Hauler called The Starlight Hauler – it was a bulk transport, one of those ships that could move a train of hundreds of cargo containers. I sucked in a breath before opening a channel. "Starlight Hauler, this is Noah, I'm a pilot who got stranded here. Looking for a ride, I'll give you everything I've got to get out of here. I even have a couple hundred plat, a universal credit line worth about four hundred, if you want real cash."

I waited for a response, but the access key on my communicator was blocked only a few seconds later. I couldn't connect to any network, and I was sure the Order saw where the communicator was. "Dammit!" I looked to Ayan's image, she was hovering over a time-lapse of the construction of the Everin Building – and said; "Bye-bye darlin', looks like this comm is trouble."

Theo brought the truck to a halt and lowered it to the ground. "How will you dispose of it?"

I pulled Slagger from my pack and got out of the truck so quickly, I almost did a face-plant on the street. I tossed the communication unit onto the ground and blasted it three times. I reduced it to a greasy black spot of melted plastic and glass. "God, I feel stupid. I can't believe I tried to reach out, what was I thinking? We have to shut everything down, lock the truck up and get out of here." I looked to the rows of buildings around us and spotted an underground shuttle park. "We'll duck in there and make our way through the tunnels under these buildings."

I have never packed my stuff so fast in my life. There wasn't much, but I didn't want to leave anything behind. We powered the truck down in a narrow alley and I pulled the processor board out from under the dash. It was one of the rarest parts, full of delicate bits that are hard to find because most of that stuff got fried in the pulse. I had to put one together from three pieces for the truck, and I insulated it like crazy after because it took four days to repair. "They'll have trouble stealing it without this," I held it up before stuffing it into my backpack.

We ran into the shuttle park, it should have had a

hundred or so hover cars and shuttles, but there were only a half dozen derelict shuttles that had been set on fire and a few hover cars. Our footsteps echoed in the eerie, dark space. I couldn't see the walls in the ring of light around us, making the place seem endless. "You know why we ditched the truck, right?" I asked Theo. I think I needed to hear someone talk after realizing that things on Iora were about to get even worse.

"After detecting our hail, the Order of Eden could have easily followed the energy from it. What I don't understand is how you know there are tunnels under these buildings."

"These places look exactly like the high rise row buildings on Segora. I had a girlfriend there, well, more like a cute make-out buddy, and we'd hide in the utility rooms. We had to use the tunnels to get there," I replied. "I'm guessing these are the same below as they are above."

"I hear a ship outside," Theo said.

I caught a glimpse of the walkway ahead, and my run turned into a frenzied sprint. "Maybe some of the heavy equipment down here, or the concrete will block their sensors."

"I'll scout ahead and find a suitable place," Theo said, doubling my pace.

"Thanks man, be careful."

PART TWENTY-NINE

The lower concourse had shops directly under the buildings, mostly convenience stuff and little grocery markets, but if you knew where to go, you'd find maintenance and equipment rooms. The shops were crap for hiding in, especially since it looked like they were mostly manned by bots who went berserk on their customers.

Some of the fine-limbed service bots and human like androids were frozen in attack poses or awkwardly splayed on the ground. I still felt pretty good when I saw bots stopped in the middle of going berserk. The pulse was my great heroic act, but there was no time to enjoy that. The bio lamp I had in my hand was pretty good at shedding light in one direction, but everything else was in shadow, and I yelped like a girl when I felt what I thought was a hand try to grab my ankle as I ran by the front of a discount clothing market. It turned out to be the fingers of a cleaning bot that was covered with a thick layer of dust. It was as still as stone, harmless, so I kicked it away and kept chasing Theo down.

"This way, there are scan resistant rooms down the west hall between buildings nine-nineteen and nine-twenty-one," he said, letting me catch up for a moment before running on. "I'll check the hall connecting to the next building just in case."

"All right," I said. "Don't go too far down." I was maybe fifteen steps down the west hall, noticing that there was a secure storage company in that direction, when I heard Theo shout.

"No! Stay away! I don't want an update!" he shouted desperately.

I backtracked and ran towards the next building. The Order must have come from both ends of the building row, and when I caught up to Theo, I still had the Slagger in my hand. He was trying to fend off a half metre wide, armoured disc bot. It was attacking him with four long, hose like manipulator arms. "Step left! I don't have a shot!"

One of them struck like a snake attack, connecting firmly with Theo's chest. I heard the high screech of a cutter and knew it was getting through one of the plugs blocking a data port. "I don't want the disease! Stop! Please stop! No! No! No!" Theo cried.

I tried to shoot the hovering bot, but hit the roof tiles instead. In a shower of sparking and burning debris, I watched Theodore go limp and fall to the tiles. The disc shaped bot turned its red and green lights on me, and I blasted it in half. I barely felt the burn on my shoulder where its laser got me, it was a minor wound, one I still keep the scar from. It was only the sighting beam, a moment later it would have cut me in half.

I made sure it was slagged, shooting it twice more before checking on Theodore. One of the arms from that Order bot were still connected to a data port in his side. I pulled it off and threw it down the hall. "Man, are you all right?"

He stood slowly, wordlessly, only the sounds of the gears in his knees and my heavy breathing filling the hall. With surprising speed he whirled and lashed out at me. I backed up quickly, getting about ten paces between he and I.

The expression on Theo's metal face shifted between sadness, joy, and something that was so malicious that it didn't look human anymore. "Non-registered human detected," he said in a voice I looked forward to hearing every morning, and came to know as a friendly one.

"If there is any chance that you can snap out of it, man, do it!" I pleaded. "You're more than your programming, buddy, come on!"

He started to run at me, and I knew I was out of time, I was out of options. I shot at his hips. He jerked and tripped, the waist of his business suit burned away to reveal damaged metal that burned red hot. "Come on, man! You're in there somewhere."

He looked at me with such hate that I took a couple more steps back. His hands slapped the tile floor as he dragged himself towards me so fast that I had to shoot him again. I caught the side of his face, but he kept coming. A third of his head was a melted mess, worse than before, I didn't mean to shoot him there, I was aiming at his arm, which I shot for again and hit on the third try.

"I'm your master!" I tried. I hated that I was, but if it could save him, I'd use it. "Stop everything you're doing, right now!"

"The Order of Eden has taken legal possession of this unit," he replied.

I knew it was over then, and shot his other arm off. "I'm sorry, Theo. I hope you don't feel any of this anymore. I hope you don't feel anything." He didn't have hands, or working legs, so I walked over to him, pulled his jacket up and held him down with my boot. "I'm not going to leave you crawling around though, not like this." I pulled the secondary power unit free from its socket and reached inside his chest cavity from the bottom. It took a moment with him squirming, he was trying to turn his head as though he could bite me to to death or something, but I managed to hit his internal kill switch, and he went limp.

I looked at what remained of him. I'm sorry, I still get choked up about this. Anyway, he was down to part of an arm, two thirds of a head, and a waist that was barely attached. Boot steps echoing behind got me moving, and I was down the west hall, running through hundreds of storage units a few moments later.

I found an open one and took a look at the lock on the door. It was sturdy, but I knew I could blast through it if I got locked in, so I closed the door and let the latch click. I leaned against the wall and slid down until I was on my ass.

Whoever came through that door would get a chest full of burning plasma, I had Slagger pointed at the door. I half-hoped they'd find me so I could kill as many Order assholes as I could, but I also hoped Theo was right, that their scanners wouldn't be able to penetrate the private storage meant for tenants in the buildings above.

I don't know how long I sat there that night, my pistol raised, but I woke up some time later, probably many hours later hungry and thirsty. I took care of that, and felt the uncertainty of my situation. I had no way of knowing if there were still Order of Eden bots or soldiers around, or if they'd given up finding a single human who had the stones to try to hail a ride off world.

I wanted to go out and get what was left of my friend more than anything. I knew he was infected with the Holocaust Virus, that he would turn on me again if I managed to fix him somehow, but I just needed to go get his core. Everything he was existed in a little chunk of memory in that armoured chest of his, and I wanted it in my backpack. Even if his personality was corrupted by the Holocaust Virus, I still couldn't stand the thought of leaving him face down in the hall until someone tried to salvage him for a part or two.

Reason won out though, partially because I knew Theo wouldn't want me to risk my neck by going after his remains. I lived in that storage container for another day. It was more boring than I could have imagined. I slept, shed a few tears, laughed at a few memories, like Theo demonstrating how he couldn't swim if he wanted to by dropping himself into a pool from a low diving board. He had to walk all the way up to the shallow section then pull himself out. He smiled the whole time, even while he tried to doggie paddle. "My synthetic skin is buoyant, but without that I have no chance of staying above water," he explained.

He had a better sense of humour than he thought he did. The whole act was to cheer me up after a couple weeks of travel on foot through this rich, sprawled out neighbourhood. I thought the yellowing lawns and faux antique houses would never end. I think he picked that up and decided to cheer me up that day. I recalled a hundred moments where I could have treated him better too, but he never made any sign that he noticed me getting short or impatient with him.

I slept through the night one more time and as I sat there eating one of the meal bars I got from that traveller who tried to stick me up, I started to plan. I would get off Iora and make it to the Rega Gain system. Those Order of Eden cargo shuttles were big enough to have a worm hole generator, and I was sure I saw the emitters in the front. It was time to get a ride.

PART THIRTY

When I was a kid I loved guns, especially handguns. The carnival was smart enough to keep weapons away from the few children who were along, even toys. We sold them to our customers, but I wasn't allowed to have one. There was an incident before I came along, but I never got the details. No one would talk about it.

That didn't mean that I wasn't taught about gun safety, or even how to care for some of the older mechanical versions in my early teens. I just wasn't allowed to have one of my own. I was taught how to shoot and got practice, too, but I was never allowed to get over-confident. I wanted my own pretty badly though, and envied everyone who walked around with a holster hanging on their hip or leg.

My time on Iora soured my love for handguns. After I had to put Theo down, every weapon I had was like a grim tool. To point the barrel of any of my guns towards an enemy was to express a hate so pure and cold that it was like me saying they weren't even people. They were obstacles, creeps that were built wrong and no longer worth the air they were breathing. It was the urge to take revenge talking, and I was listening, hearing every word loud and clear.

I emerged from the storage unit in a heavy spacer's jacket I found inside. The thing was blue and black, but had radiation and blast armour built in with an emergency coverage system that would protect me from head to toe if I got tossed into space. I liked it because it looked old, weather worn and I suspected the owner was some retired spacer with stories. I wished I could have met him, but was sure he was killed or long gone.

My quick rummage through the neighbouring storage units revealed old luggage, some garish furniture, discarded clothing and a set of sculptures of children chasing a dog that looked surprisingly eerie. There were other things, discarded stuff from people who had probably been living in the building above for a long time, but none of it was useful.

I moved through the hallways, a pair of restraint balls in my left hand and Slagger in my right. I didn't like the weapon, but it was nothing more than a tool to me at that point. It was the piece that would do the most damage if I ran into Order soldiers.

The underground halls were more like a tomb. There was no motion or sound other than what I made, and when I came to Theo's remains, I discovered that whoever saw the scene had kicked him into a corner, pulled his head off and left him there. They took what was left of the Order of Eden bot with them.

I looked Theo's head over. It was one third melted in, moving parts around the damage I'd done were fused together. The rest was fine, they'd detached his noggin at the neck using a proper spanner and wrench. It was probably faster than using a cutting tool. His speaker and a bunch of his sensors were still undamaged, so I stuck his head into the backpack he once carried. "I'm sorry, man, but I can't carry broken shit around with me," I said as I took out my electronics kit. It only took me a few minutes to disconnect what was left of his arms and legs, then his hips. What was left was the armoured core, where all his main systems were. It was a little singed, but the armour was intact. I made sure the safety switch inside was off, I didn't want him to stay awake for however long he could on his internal battery, and put him inside the backpack I gave him months before. "I don't care if you're infected. There's no way I'm giving up on you."

I put everything away and started for the exit. It took me a while to make my way there, sneaking around, making sure that I wasn't going to get jumped by Order forces. They were long gone, but they left their mark on their way out. My hover truck was a burned out mess. I was so pissed at the sight of it that I had to take a closer look. They pried one of the back doors open and dropped some kind of incendiary bomb inside. The little globe was still sitting there, in the middle of the melted seats and charred cabin. "Are you kidding me?" I asked as I grabbed a metal rod from the alley and knocked the grenade out onto the ground. I could see the trigger switch on it, and held it down with the sole of my boot while I used the tip of the rod to turn it off. "This thing isn't reusable, is it?"

I checked it, found a charging port and was astonished. "What a pack of idiots." I looked for anti-tamper devices as best as I could then used one of my spare power cells to recharge the incendiary grenade. It beeped cheerily, the switch on the top blinking green, indicating that the safety was on and it was ready to activate on a five second timer. "Well, it's a crap trade; a hover truck for a grenade, but I'll take just about anything."

I realized that I'd taken the main processor board out of the truck before I left and smiled. It would be much easier to repair another hover vehicle with that in hand. I returned to the garage beneath the residence building and started looking for the right car. I ended up checking five subterranean parking areas and ten hover cars before I found the right one. It was a hover vehicle with high altitude gliding systems. I wouldn't use the extendable wings, the controllers for those were fried and I didn't want to put the time in to fix a feature that would only make me even more visible to the Order. The rest of the systems were in all right shape, and it used a lot of standard parts. I looked at it, juggling a meal bar, my new grenade and the Slagger, for a few minutes.

"Replace the main processor board, check if auto-driving systems work, bypass if they don't, and check the main controllers," I muttered to myself. "Two days if I'm lucky, more trouble than its worth if I'm not."

With that, I loaded everything I had into the back seat and got under the dash. It was more cramped than the truck's, I ended up permanently removing the console cover, and most of the instrumentation was still fried when I was done, but it started up after only a few hours. The essentials were all in pretty good shape, I suspect because it was hardened against lightning strikes since the thing was made to glide. It was no shuttlecraft though, there was no way it would get me into orbit. I was able to steal the navigation software from the console and install it on one of the small computers I'd taken from the Complex, and I taped that along with a flexible screen onto the windshield. I slept in the car that night, dreaming that I was being chased by Order Soldiers, then by a version of Theo that had claws and glowing yellow-red eyes. I was up early. "Time to get on the road," I said to myself, or what was left of Theo in the passenger seat. I looked at that bag often. "Let's go find a ship."

The hover car started with a high pitched whine, smoothly, swiftly cruising through the large parking garage then surging out onto the cluttered street. I didn't care if the Order spotted me, that was almost the point. This car, the Wind Rider Model Five, was many times more agile than the truck. I could tell that the controller systems for the eight pads underneath needed alignment, it pulled to the left and the nose was tilted down a little on the right, but it was good enough. The lights didn't work inside or out, the wings were stuck closed under the cab, only the steering and power were running, and the controller for the environment controls were still fried, but the machine moved fast. The height adjustment was tied into the steering system, so it would move up or down, over and under obstacles as I used the control wheel, which looked like an eternity symbol.

I couldn't tell exactly how fast I was going, but it was faster than I'd moved since I landed on Iora, and I was able to get on top of a two storey building, then a three storey one, and finally up onto one of the landing pads of a mini-port from there. I drove all the way up, weaving between burned out and stripped ships until I was fifteen storeys up, looking across a bay, a part of Logan City and farmland beyond. I shut the car down and opened my last burrito. It rehydrated and cooked in my hand, ready to eat in three seconds, hot enough to seem fresh but not so hot that it burned your mouth. "We'll stay here for a bit. If we don't see any ships, we'll find another perch. Maybe go to Larness or New Detroit. Might attract some attention on our way there though, so I've gotta figure that out. I've gotta have a plan just in case Order soldiers take an interest in this heap."

I settled in and watched the sky for any sign of a drop ship, or anything else that could take me up off Iora. "We'll get there, man. We'll get back to the black and away from here."

PART THIRTY-ONE

I woke up to the sound of a sonic boom somewhere way above, my condenser bottle rolling off my chest, onto the passenger seat and to the floor. I looked up in time to see three lights in the night sky. They split and I refused to blink as I tracked each descending ship. "There, to the east, the nearest ship."

I started the car and aimed it between two buildings, the street below was littered with dead hover cars, but I was sure my rig was light enough to survive the fall. I marked my destination on the navigation system and hit the accelerator. The car dropped off the edge of the top of the mini-port building and I turned the glide power all the way up. I cringed as one of my hoverpads scraped the roof of a car on the street, but there was no significant damage, just a hell of a lot of forward momentum. I struggled to keep up with the turns as I sped through the streets over and between cars that were silent and still.

Before I knew it, I was on the freeway, turning everything but the controls and the most basic hovering systems off. Moving forward at great speed doesn't take much power if you only have to make minor course adjustments, so I thought I would reduce my energy signature. Now I'm sure it didn't matter, since I was probably the fastest moving, most energetic thing on Iora that didn't belong to the Order of Eden. I must have stuck out like a sore thumb.

I was half way to my destination when I saw the ship take off. I could make out the shape – it was another drop ship with a long, downturned cockpit nose and a curved hull used to grapple shipping containers – and I wasn't fast enough to get to it. I looked to my right, to the western most ship just in time to see its light ascend. "God dammit!"

The one in the middle was just taking off, rising above the horizon, but I was still nine kilometres out. I slowed the car and drove more casually. "I either need more luck, more speed, or to plan this better."

For two days it was the same thing. Three ships come down, I rush for the nearest one, and three ships get away. I was ready to start pulling my hair out on the third day. The chase had led me a quarter way across the continent. Then I reached Larness. I hadn't been there yet, but there was a security complex building there, domed and armoured like the Complex I landed in, and it had been cracked open on one side. A huge part of the city around it had been blasted to rubble. I'm talking kilometres of fallen buildings, city blocks that were just as flat as parking lots and craters from broken down artillery that was scattered across the landscape. I'd missed the fight though, but the aftermath was right there for me to see. People were ducking in and out of the circular building, not looting it, but using it for a shelter. There was enough room for several hundred people in the one I spent my first few months in, so I could imagine how many people might have crammed in there.

I drove down off the freeway and headed straight for a small crowd of people. Most of them scattered as I slowed to a stop, but there was this really dark guy who was tall, broad chested, but a bit heavy in the middle. He waved to me, dropped his gun into his holster and smiled. "He looks friendly," I said, drawing Needler and hiding it between my legs. I pulled up beside him and stopped, taking a package of raspberry-cherry pie from my jacket pocket. I opened my window and offered the treat. "Hey, man. Looking for some info," I called out.

The dark skinned stranger took the pie and activated it. He was surprised when it heated and hydrated. "Holy hell, this one still works! I've been eating convenience packs that are cracker dry and so hard you have to dip 'em in water. Yeah, what do you need?" He sniffed it deeply. "Anything I know, I'll tell."

"Just wondering how long it's been since you guys got a delivery of food from the Order?"

"Delivery? What, you expecting Shawarma Hut to drop something off for you?" he laughed.

"Okay, how long since this dust up finished?"

"We got through the economic building wall about a week and a half ago. No food left there now though, just people who moved in."

I looked at the side of the building with the melted, jagged crack in it and saw tarp patches here and there. There were people moving about inside as well, but I didn't see much evidence of power. Then I remembered: it was one of the buildings that had a generator that could create an electromagnetic pulse, one of the buildings that I most likely triggered remotely after I arrived. "How long since the Order dropped people off here?"

"They dropped a whole bunch of containers off," he took a bite, hiding what he was doing as best as he could from the people several metres behind him. I waited for him to finish chewing. "Bunch of containers were dropped off about a week ago. Why are you asking?" he stuffed the rest of the slice of pie into his mouth, a feat that was actually a little impressive.

"I'm tracking the drop ships," I told him. "I'm going to steal one."

"That's crazy," he laughed, his mouth still half full. "Take me with you." Then he waved his hands, finished chewing and shook his head. "Just kidding, that's too crazy. You'll get slagged when they see you coming in this," he patted the hood of my car. "Good luck, though. Hope you do it somewhere I can see; it'll be fun to watch. Speaking of watching, you're about to draw a crowd." He pointed at a group starting to get together fifty metres in front of my car, coming out of half-fallen buildings and whatever holes they were hiding in.

"You'd better get going unless you have enough food for everyone."

"Right, thanks for the info," I said, pushing my window up.

"Thanks for the pie! Good luck," he said, distancing himself from me.

As soon as my side window was back up, I drove away. I didn't drive far, just out of sight then down a street. There was an overpass with a bunch of old crates piled around, so I found I spot where I could still see the sky but I was mostly hidden and hovered in. With everything turned off, I got out to stretch, and started my watch.

Another three days passed. During that time I fixed the balance issues in my hover car so it drove straighter, repaired the locks on the doors and made a remote fob for myself using my last computer and watched the sky. I was so bored by the beginning of day three that I started knotting my hair in little braids while I sat on the roof of my car. I was starting to worry about food. I had five meal bars and three lime turnovers, the worst of the dehydrated vending machine foods. It was enough for a week and a half if I conserved.

"Hey, you still expecting a delivery, driver-man?" asked a woman who was dressed in some kind of rough brown containment suit with a fine ball gown over top. It looked like she'd been digging through the sewers on her hands and knees, and her hair was a vertical plume of brown and black. I'm not usually one to judge on appearance, but I recoiled a little. The accent she had reminded me of that idiot I'd knocked out a year ago who spoke really bad Pigeon. "Hey, driver-man, you have pie for me? You give me pie, I don't sing about your car to all the empty bellies."

I drew Needler and waved it in her direction. "I've got some bang for you," I replied.

She recoiled, eyes wide, ducking with her hands up, and I regretted drawing on her. This lady was probably as bored as I was but much hungrier. It really looked like she came round to tease me a bit and maybe get something to eat. I shoved Needler back into its holster. "Sorry, just been under a few people's boots, you know? I'm a little jumpy."

"No worry, no care," she replied, easing a little but starting to move on. "Just movin' on, gettin' on," she said.

I tossed her one of my lime pies and she snatched it out of the air. "Keep my spot secret, yeah? Sorry about the scare."

"Yeah, can't talk while eating, fly-man," she said, running off.

I had a feeling everyone would know exactly where I was by nightfall. With a quiet curse, I got in the driver's seat, started the car up and headed for a mall I remembered seeing on the outskirts of town. It had turned into another settlement, with so many people that some of them slept in makeshift tents on the roof. I momentarily imagined a brood ship touching down, the eggs hatching. The hatchlings would have no problem feeding on the hundreds there. I moved on, pushing those thoughts away. I hit a few convenience stores, not finding much until I blasted the bars on the last one open with Slagger. There were people only a couple blocks over, the sound of my car and the flash of light would definitely draw them closer, so I stuffed my backpacks with the meal bars, then grabbed armfuls of unopened boxes from the medical and snack shelves.

I looked at my haul after a few trips between the car and the store and shook my head. There was enough food there for two months if I rationed, probably three. There were medications, emergency recovery systems, burn kits and more medical stuff than I'd ever need. "Well, New Years is coming early, I guess."

I drove off as I spotted a crowd running towards either my car or the store. Pulling my window down, I shouted; "Store's open, guys! There's a year's worth of food and other crap in there. Sharing is caring!"

My old spot was out of the question, so I found another one under a fallen sensor tower not far from the clearing. "All right, everything's gotta fit in one backpack," I said. In the back seat I carefully chose medical supplies for burns and vacuum exposure, enough meal bars to get me through a month, and a few choice treats. With Theo's remains in the bottom of the bag not everything fit, so I ended up loading the remainder in my pockets. It wasn't so bad that it hindered my movement, but if I lost a piece of clothing, I would be saying goodbye to some of my food and supplies. I tried powering on a hoverboard I snagged for fun, and wasn't surprised when it didn't work. "Damn, always wanted one of those. I'd probably break my neck anyway."

I could imagine Theo cautioning me, asking why humans liked the thrill of speed without protection so much, and I laughed. "I don't know, but I can't stop chasing the rush."

"You find someone new?" asked the dark fellow I met when I drifted into the area days before.

"Nah, just talking to myself," I told him. "Here." I tossed him a meal bar. "I just hit a store a few blocks away.

"I heard," he said. "Thanks. I'm Andy. Any idea when that food delivery you talked about is coming?"

"Man, I wish I knew. I've only seen one, and it was hundreds of klicks away. Why?" I looked at what remained in my back seat. There was a backpack and the rest of the supplies I'd stolen, enough to feed someone for over a month at least, and enough medical supplies to open a small clinic.

"I made the mistake of telling a few people about that when you first came. I wasn't serious, of course; told them I thought you were crazy. They're clinging to it like it was universal truth anyway: food is coming, the stranger in the hovercar said so."

"I'm sorry, man, I don't know much more than anyone. I'm stuck here like you guys."

"Not really like us," he said, holding up the meal bar for a moment before stuffing it into his pocket. I was a little surprised he wasn't going to eat it right away. "Especially with a working car."

"Barely working," I said. "Had to scavenge and work for it." I reached into the back seat and grabbed a few more meal bars for myself, enough for a week, and then I backed up and smiled at him crookedly. "People are starving, yeah?"

"They're trying to ration what they've got in the building

I'm holed up in. I'm with a few friends who came late and didn't get a spot in the Commerce Complex. So, yeah, my people are empty."

"That's who you're saving that bar for?" I asked.

"I'll drop it in the pot later. We melt and mix everything together in a soup we make every day. Something an old guy started in the building. Tastes like random chemicals and garbage, but it keeps us alive," he said. "Just barely better than starving."

I crooked my finger at him and gestured to the back seat of the car. "Think this'll help?" I asked.

He came over slowly, like he didn't know what to expect. "You're teasing me, man, that's just wrong all over," he said, surprised at the corner store bounty.

"Listen, I've got a spare backpack. Fill it up and get this stuff to your people. Any chance they'd want to come with me when I steal a ship?"

"Naw, they all think you're crazy like I do, but I'll take what you're offering. You should hide your ride and come back with me, get a proper thanks. They're good people. So you want to give me all this, no strings?"

"No strings. I took too much for myself," I said, grinning.

"I'm gonna start calling you Robin Hood," he said, grabbing the empty backpack and getting into the back seat. My backpack with Theo and my supplies was already hanging off my shoulder.

I couldn't stand there, watching him load up without trying to warn him. "Listen, there's something coming, you'd never believe me if I told you what, but everyone here is going to die," I told him. "The Order is going to wipe everything out."

"But you say they'll be delivering food," he replied, stuffing handfuls of snacks and meal bars into the bag. "Which is it? Forced resettlement, or murder?"

"I said I saw food delivered once, not that it's going to happen regularly or for everyone. Besides, it's not really the Order who are going to kill everyone here, but who they're trying to protect themselves from. It's a bug race that's threatening the galaxy, and the Order put the virus out there to make the Milky Way seem less appealing for hatching broods, but they saw through the Order's plan. Now they're making brood worlds with lots of humans who are disarmed for the broods to feed on. I don't know how many people you're helping now, but if they'll fit on the ship I steal, they've gotta get on board and get out of here."

He finished stuffing the bag, closed the top flap, took a box of medical supplies under one arm and withdrew from the car. He wasn't smiling. "I don't know what you're trying to do here, but you're all over the place. I mean, look at you; I can see you have two guns, probably have more. You have a hover car running, and no problem getting supplies. Why haven't the Order taken you out? You say these bugs are coming and we're not supposed to be armed, but you are the contradiction."

"I'm just one guy," I explained. "Probably not worth going after."

"All right, maybe you spent a little too long on your own, it's messed with your head. Hide your car, and come with me.

We'll settle you in and maybe some time with people will get your head straight."

"I didn't come up with this myself, I found it on the Stellarnet, posted by the British Alliance from the Rega Gain system. Ayan, a commander in Haven Shore, this place they're building there that's safe, where there's food and good people, narrated the whole thing. There was proof going back ten years."

"Can I see it?"

"I tried to use the comm to call out, and the Order blocked all transmissions, started tracking it so I had to blast it."

"All right," it was clear he didn't believe me. Andy patted me on the shoulder and Theo's head fell out of the large pouch on the outside of my bag. He looked at it, part melted and inert, then back at me. "That's the friend you were talking to when I came up on you?"

"He wasn't infected until a few days ago, I had to slag him," I explained lamely. "But the core is still good, so maybe I can cure him."

"I'm telling you this for your own good, because you're helping me and my friends. You should find a safe place to sort all this out. I don't know what you're on, maybe it is just loneliness, but whatever it is, you're imagining things. I don't know why we were relocated here, I think it was so they could use our home worlds for resources without having to deal with the citizens, who knows? What I can tell you is that I found a few good people since I first met ya, and thanks to you we've got enough supplies so we don't have to beg and trade favours for our daily calories. You'll be welcome with my people, maybe even be a hero. Come with us when we get enough stuff together to move on."

"What's the difference between that and getting on a ship then blasting out of here?"

"The difference is that the Order is going to blast you so bad that you'll be nothing but a grease spot, or if you do get into one of their ships and take off, they'll vaporize you once you leave orbit. So, if you're not going to come with me, I'll thank you for the supplies, and wish you luck. Really, thank you so much." He extended his hand and I shook it.

I watched as he retreated into the shadows of the tall, half fallen city. Sometime after he had gone, I took Theo's head and made sure it was securely sealed in my bag's outer pouch.

PART THIRTY-TWO

A small group of people found me a few streets over from the blasted clearing in front of the Commerce building, and I was thankful that Andy only took a bag full, leaving about twenty-four bars and a small selection of loose snacks behind. I wished he believed me for obvious reasons, sure, but also because he seemed like a good friend to have.

When a couple kids approached my car, I made sure they each left with a turnover in their belly and another in their pockets. "It's a secret, this car," an older fellow said as he approached with a younger man and woman. He looked older than most people I'd seen, but was spry, steady on his feet. "We're from that old building there," he pointed. The structure looked intact; an old red bricked apartment building. It was the same one Andy took his bag of goodies into the night before. "Most of us know where you are, but we're keeping it from those greedy bastards in the Commerce Centre."

I got ready to give him and his friends meal bars and a packet of emergency nanobots, but he waved his hand. "No need to bribe us, son," he said. "I just thought you might want to hide your car and come inside tonight. It's starting to get cold, and I noticed you don't run your machine at night. Can't be too warm."

He was right, it was starting to get cold. "I have to stay near my car," I said with a shrug. "I'm going to steal a ship next time they come here. I bet they'll land in the clearing, so I've gotta stay close."

"Delivering food, fattening us up for the bug invasion," the old man said, nodding, smiling a little. "We heard. Most people won't go near you, they think you're crazy."

"I can't help what I believe," I said. "Are you sure you don't want this?" I said, waving the boxed nano treatment and the six bars. "Crazy's not contagious."

He accepted my offering. "Thank you," he said. "And when you've lived as long as I have, you see that crazy is plenty contagious. When do you think they're coming?"

"The Edxians?" I asked.

He recoiled a little. "The Order, the food."

"I don't know," I told him. "But there's a building with hundreds of people inside," I nodded in the direction of the Commerce Building. "There's a clearing right next to it, and I bet when they come, they'll drop right there. When I saw it happen at the Remington Mall, soldiers didn't stick around to see everyone got fed, either. It was first come, first serve until a bunch of thugs took charge."

"You've seen a lot on this planet, haven't you, son?"

"Guess I have," I replied. "Seems like I've been here forever."

"Lost some good people?" he asked quietly, compassion in his eyes.

I swallowed hard. "A good friend, yeah."

"When you get tired of watching the skies, you come to us. Fifth floor. Ask for me, ask for Orillio."

"You could always come with me," I offered.

"Best of luck," he said, waving as he turned away. He and his companions walked to the building in no great hurry, and I have to admit that I was tempted to ditch the car and catch up. I was finally meeting people who seemed nice, who seemed like they wanted to cooperate. I was doing better than everyone I saw, as though I was born to the wandering, looting life while they were newly marooned. They were, that was the truth, and I was hoping that there was another round of ships coming. Dropping off people or food, it didn't matter. I started wishing on the stars for Order ships, going through my plan to take one every few hours.

Like most nights, I fell asleep in the driver's seat. The sound of thrusters passing overhead woke me, and for a moment I thought I was dreaming. I looked up and saw an Order of Eden drop ship flying so low that I could read the slogan on the side of the large cargo container. *'Bringing Life Saving Sustenance To Those In Need,'* it said. I laughed and started my hover car.

It roared to life and I was off, chasing the ship down the street to the clearing. I got there just in time to see it drop the large food container off, decouple from it and lift into the sky at great speed while the doors on the container popped open. I was within ten metres without a ghost's chance of getting to the rear hatch of the ship. "God dammit! They're too fast!" I shouted, pounding the wheel.

Then I realized that I'd beat everyone to the cargo container. In fact, people were just starting to realize it was there, they weren't even running for it yet. The cargo doors yawned open, maybe five metres from my passenger door. I realized I could grab a few boxes with enough emergency rations for ten people for a year inside before anyone even knew what was happening. I could go to that apartment building, do something really important for them, buy my way into their group. If I filled my back seat, we could eat for a couple years if the group didn't grow too large.

A streak of light crossed in front of my windshield as my hand reached for the door handle. Another ship was on its way, from the low altitude I guessed it would descend some-where nearby. "That's not far away," I told Theo. I looked at the cargo container, still open, still right there. I rushed out of the car, grabbed a box of three hundred sixty emergency meal bars and shoved it into the back seat. "New plan: We take less food than we could, and drive like hell. If I miss the next ship, I won't have to regret passing up good clean food. If I make it off this dirt ball, I'll leave the car and the food for some lucky guy."

A giant plume of black dust surrounded my car as I hit

the accelerator and headed for the streets past the battle-flattened patch of land. It felt like my heart was in my throat. I expected failure, there was no way I'd catch a cargo ship if I had to travel for more than a few seconds to get to it, but I was so eager to try that my car took a few dings and dents as I rushed through the streets as fast as I'd ever gone. "We learn most from trying, not from sitting around, hoping shit gets better, right, man?"

I imagined Theo commenting on how clever my little expression was and laughed. "Of course it's clever, I live on clever, clever keeps me entertained and fed."

Through narrow, and broad streets, over hills and down sudden drops, I pushed the car to its limit, and when I spotted the landed ship with two crewmen outside, I grinned maniacally. They were struggling with one of the clamps on the crate they were supposed to drop. The doors on the crate were already wide open, and people were already starting to move towards the public park they'd used as their landing spot. "Surprise, assholes!" I howled as I pointed the front of my car at the pair of lightly armoured Order soldiers and slowed down just enough so I wouldn't kill myself and rammed into the side of the cargo container. One of the soldiers was caught in the middle of my bumper, crushed so bad that his helmet came off, the middle of his suit burst and part of him was spread across my hood.

The collision felt like an iron fisted punch that hit me everywhere at once, but my adrenaline was pumping so hard that the driver's seat was open, and I was out of the car with Needler in my right hand and a few suppression bombs in my left. I pinched a suppression bomb and tossed it at the Order soldier who managed to jump out of the way of my bumper. He was pinned to the grass by a thick web of suppression fluid, a perfect shot. I pulled Needler's trigger briefly, rattling thirty or so rounds into his torso. His armour protected him from a lot of it, but not all. I could see spots of blood spreading from tears in his light green uniform before I turned my attention to the most important part of my plan.

The rear hatch was opening, only a metre and a half above the ground. A man in a dark green pilot's suit was poking his head out. "What the hell was that, Regibald?"

I turned on him and squeezed my trigger, catching him before he could close the door and filling him with tiny pinholes. I knew what my weapon did to people. It filled them with micro shrapnel that shredded their insides, and at that time I celebrated it. To me, there was nothing worse than an Order of Eden soldier, or pilot, or even sympathizer. They were responsible for killing my entire family, marooning me on Iora, and then destroying my only friend.

The pilot fell through the door onto the grass and I leapt onto him. "Give me the control chip! The security key! Whatever the fuck you unlock this thing with! Now!" I pressed the hot barrel of my weapon to his cheek.

He reached into the collar of his uniform and pulled a tiny golden chip on a chain out. "It's just a job, man, I'm just a bus driver," he said before coughing and sending a spatter of blood onto my coat.

With a yank the chain came off his neck, and I rushed the rear hatch of the ship. It was small inside, with four seats for crew that folded away so bunks could be pulled out, and a couple heavy lockers for equipment and precious cargo. There was a slim medical alcove, an emergency stasis pod across from it, and then the door to the cockpit. It opened, and I squeezed my trigger not a second later. The face of the co-pilot's helmet was open, and most of my needle rounds hit their mark, filling his head with rounds. He was dead before his helmet bounced off the deck with what was left of his noggin inside.

The rear hatch slammed with a firm pull on the handle, and I rushed the cockpit. The co-pilot was surprisingly light, so it was easy to pull him out of the front cabin and into the rear. I was sitting at the controls in a heartbeat. I dropped my bag into the co-pilot's seat, the idea that Theo was in there was comforting.

PART THIRTY-THREE

I began lifting off, an alarm indicating that one of the grabbers on the underside of my ill-gotten ship was still jammed in the closed position, meaning that I was awkwardly stuck to the container filled with food. I didn't want to leave the people below without, so I looked for a solution while I jiggled the controls, hoping that the crate would break free. It didn't.

Then I spotted a statue in the middle of the park made of gleaming metal. It was rose coloured in the early morning light, a woman clothed in a single piece of cloth wrapped around her as though it was windblown, pointing a bow and arrow straight up. "That'll work!" I said.

I'll understand if you don't believe this next bit, but I tell you it's all honest, true to the last word. With reflexes and visualization skills I didn't know I had, I lifted the cargo container up, moved forward, and planted it onto that statue, spearing the thing with the metal woman and her bow. When I tried to pull up again, the container came free of that one stuck clamp with a creak, and the ship lurched into the sky.

I looked at the rear scanners in time to see my handiwork: the cargo container was perfectly planted with the tip of the arrow poking through the middle of the top. I don't have pictures, but I'm telling you that's what it looked like. People were already running through the park towards the Order soldiers I put down, two of whom were still moving They were after my car, and the cargo container too. It would be a good day down there, and I didn't expect there would be many after that. There were hundreds of them, and I wondered how many were believers in my unintentional prophecy; that the Order would come with food, and I'd steal a ship.

I looked away from the screen and examined the information projected across the windshield in front of me. "Okay, everything looks pretty obvious here," I said. "Way more modern than I'm used to, but the controls are pretty normal." I located the damper controls, the local navigation panel, the interstellar navigation panel, and the system status displays.

"Where are the navnet and combat scanners?" I asked, looking in every direction but behind me and right in front of me. After a few seconds I realized that they were projected in the middle of my view if I looked straight ahead and nodded. "Okay, good." To my surprise there were markers indicating nine cargo ships in the sky. That could be a problem if any of them decided to intercept me. I was always told that the best way to win a fight – even a dogfight – was to avoid getting into one if you could. I pushed the thrusters hard and watched the altimeter reading climb fast, the whine of gravitational dampers filling my ears. "Burnout, we go flat," Lurk warned from the inside pocket of my jacket.

"Good point, we don't want to burn the dampers out," I replied, slowing my ascent a little. "This thing probably has a different set of rules when you're flying without cargo."

I was in space a few moments later, and my scanners marked two destroyers and a carrier along with ten smaller ships. They were a hemisphere away. I set the autopilot on a path to orbit between the hulls of large derelict ships that littered the near space around the planet, aiming for a clump of debris that was so large it must have been a space station, then switched seats. "You're going to have to go on the floor, buddy," I told Theo as I moved his bag out of the co-pilot's spot.

I tried to use the interstellar navigation panel, and it asked of my credentials. I held up the golden command chip, it scanned it, then a superior sounding male voice said; "Bioscan mismatch. Please ensure that the correct crew member is attempting to use this terminal with the correct command chip in their possession. Error one-one-four-zero-four."

I tried again and got the same result. "Oh, God, the chip's matched to the pilot," I cried aloud.

I hurriedly opened the cockpit door and searched the co-pilot for his command chip. "Tell me you've got one, the jump system is in front of your seat, you've gotta have a command chip!" After searching through the gore of his neck and reaching into the neck of his shirt, I found it. "Okay, back in your seat, man," I said as I half picked him up, half dragged him back into the co-pilot's seat and tried to access the navigational panel.

"Life sign failure. Error-one-nine-six-zero-one," the computer said.

"Of course the computer can tell if he's dead!" I said, throwing up my hands. I pushed on his chest, compressing it over and over, trying to force a beat into his heart and cringed at the same time as blood started pumping through the holes in his neck and face. After a few pumps, seeing that the blood was moving, I took one of his hands and tried to access the interstellar navigational panel. It activated, and I sat in the thin co-pilot's lap awkwardly. Hey, he wasn't just skinny, he was dead, and I had trouble keeping him from slumping out of his seat. I didn't have time to get the corpse out of the way though, so I muddled through. "You are injured, Petty Officer Arsenault, seek medical attention immediately," the computer said. "Error six-zero-one-four."

"No shit," I laughed as I hurriedly looked up the Rega Gain system. It came up, and I ordered the computer to start plotting a course and generating a wormhole. As soon as I saw that it was working, I returned to the pilot's seat. My hands were bloody, somehow the back of my neck was wet, and I expected everything to go wrong any second.

"Cargo Shuttle Seventeen," came a voice through the cockpit communication system. I spotted a holographic recorder between the seats and grabbed a meal bar from my pocket, busted it open and crammed half of it into all the crevices and tiny receiver rods. There was no way they could see what was in the cockpit with it clogged up like that. "I see here that we are not receiving any data from your service crewmen, or the pilot. We also received an error code: Six-zero-one-four for the co-pilot. Report immediately." His words were urgent, but he sounded way too calm, too collected for me to believe he was really concerned.

After a moment of looking at the tactical scanner, I could see that the transmission was coming from the carrier, The Rectifier II. I froze. The computer was still making calculations for the wormhole jump, so I didn't even know where the jump point would be, and the drive was only charged to fifty-three percent.

"Shuttle Seventeen, come in. Report immediately," the stern sounding officer said.

Even through the gunk of the meal bar covering the holographic recorder, I could see a light turn on. Hopefully they saw nothing but black. "This is the pilot," I replied. "The computer had some kinda mismatch error with my ident and the command chip you gave me, so everything's going haywire."

"We can tell there is one person alive in the cockpit who doesn't match our records, we can't see inside the compartment, and that your co-pilot is six-zero-one-four. Can you confirm?"

The jump drive was seventy-nine precent charged and going up quickly. "That's the genetic mix-up. I'm in the right shuttle, showed up for the right shift, but the computer just gives me this mismatch error. As for the six-zero-one-four, can you remind me what that is? Please respond, Rectumfier," I didn't realize that I'd mis-spoken the ship's name until it was already too late, and I covered my mouth in surprise, trying not to laugh.

"We're sending a ship over to assist you. Please enter the space indicated and follow the new course."

The shuttle lurched towards the new course and I began to panic. "We're fine, just putting in an honest day's work for an honest day's pay, you know?" I said. "No need to take control."

"Who are you? If you've hijacked that ship, we will go easy on you if you cooperate and allow the automatic flight systems to do their job. Otherwise, we will use lethal force."

The tactical display showed three fighters and a larger, shuttle sized ship starting in my direction. It said I had two minutes and forty-two seconds before they were in range to fire. "Good to know," I said without thinking.

"Pardon me?" asked the voice over the communicator. He was starting to get testy.

I frantically looked around the control panels for an override, anything, and failed to find one. I muted the communicator, and that didn't help. I tried to shut it down, but they were in control of that too. "What else do you need to remote control another ship?" I asked. "How do I stop them from getting signals to the cockpit?"

"Are you asking me?" the officer from the Rectumfier, or Rectifier II – sorry – asked.

"Sure! What's your answer?" I asked. "You have ten seconds on the clock! Answer correctly and you win a lovely

Nafalli plushie! Not the tree tribe kind either, but the cuddlier burrowers. Some people call them 'space pandas!' Not that we've seen a panda anywhere but in anime and historical vids!" The moment I stopped babbling I realized that I had to cut the main line to the antenna.

"You are not helping yourself," the officer replied. "This is not a game. You are in violation of several antiterrorism and piracy laws."

The navigational system beeped, it finished calculating my jump, but whoever had taken control of the wormhole system had stopped it from charging, so it was stuck at eighty four percent. "I'm sorry, Rectumfier," I did it on purpose that time, "I'll be out of the cockpit for a minute." I said, rushing to the rear of the craft and climbing up the cargo netting.

"Did you say; Rectumfier?" the Officer asked.

I almost slipped, I was laughing so hard. I remembered where I saw the antennae sticking up after seeing so many of those shuttles from a distance, and found the box where they were connected in the ceiling. "Buh-bye Rectumfier, time to leave!" I said, ripping the cables from their terminals. I couldn't help but notice the shoddy workmanship and crappy materials they used to put the ship together. It looked great on the outside, a bit like a long-beaked bird with downturned wings, but it was all thin wiring and flimsy plating on the inside.

Back in the cockpit, the ship was under my control again, and I directed it back towards my launch point, turning the thrust up to maximum. One nice thing about haulers is that they become some of the fastest ships when they're not dragging a load around because they have huge thrusters. Those fighters were still catching up though, and it would take a few more seconds to finish charging my jump drive.

I found the holographic display for the single turret gun, and shook my head as I realized that I'd pulled the wires connecting that to the cockpit along with the antenna connections. "I hope I didn't pull anything I really need out."

Several pings sounded behind me, the fighters were opening fire and hitting their target - me. I turned the ship into a quick dive under the hull of a dead colony ship and wove between the hulks drifting around it. I kept to the larger masses, knowing that they would be surrounded by small and medium sized rubble. A few small pieces of metal clanked against the hull, but nothing that the navigational sensors warned me about. "Doesn't this thing have shields?" I asked.

The panel controlling the energy shielding blinked overhead and I saw that they charged from the main generator, the same as the jump drive. "Well, that's cheap," I muttered. "I can either charge up the jump drive and hope to leave, or activate shields and try to out fly these bastards."

I looked to the jump drive display and saw it was ninety-eight percent. "Time to go, then."

I broke from cover and headed for the jump point, weaving like a maniac. It worked for a while, and I watched rounds pass by as those fighters tried to blast me, there had to have been hundreds of shots. That kind of luck can only last so long though, and as I activated the wormhole generator, I heard a whole bunch of hits behind me. The cabin behind the cockpit lost containment, and I could feel the air leaving the ship.

The cockpit door closed automatically, and I made it into the wormhole, but not before a couple shots almost made it to the thick cockpit door, leaving bulges in the metal. The cockpit was still sealed though, and I didn't have to turn my emergency containment suit on.

I worried that the weakened metal would burst, leaving me in a containment suit the rest of the way, unable to eat. I wondered if those fighters damaged anything important behind me, but I didn't have the nerve to suit up and check. I also worried that I would get shot to pieces the moment I arrived in the Rega Gain system because I was in an Order of Eden ship. Really, I worried about everything, talking to my silent companion, Theo, the whole way.

PART THIRTY-FOUR

Without an antenna, there was no way for me to broadcast, and I didn't have the nerve to go back and try to fix it. There was something about that unreliable compartment that made me nervous. I didn't have a working transponder, either, so no one would be able to tell who or what I was unless they got close enough to eyeball my ship. I didn't know if this would work for or against me.

I finally arrived in the Rega Gain system and started flying towards Tamber. As I got closer, I could see the gem of a world, blue, green and brown, hanging out by Kambis, a darker, larger brother. Using secondary sensors, I was able to stay away from most ships. There were all kinds of identifiers from independent ships in orbit there. Cargo haulers, transports, and all kinds of personal craft were in attendance. It was as if the Holocaust Virus never happened. "Man, if we're lucky, I might be able to mix right in here," I said as I figured out how to get to Haven Shore from orbit. "I see it, locking it in."

I joined a stream of ships headed in that general direction. I couldn't register with navnet, so I was sure an alarm was going off somewhere in the control centre, someone was trying to get a message to me. "Sorry, can't hear you. Coming from a world that's got all its circuits burned out. My fault, I know, but that's the way it is," I said to the imagined flight control officer.

I was white-knuckled on the stick, there was every chance that I could screw things up and cause a huge collision. I stayed close to a few mid-sized ships, really close, trying to merge my signal with their shadow, and I'm sure I succeeded because I didn't see fighters coming for me or the skies clearing.

Finally, I was over my approach window, and I dove for the atmosphere. The shields held up fine, and I knew I only had a short amount of time to land before something blew me out of the sky. In retrospect, it would have been a lot smarter to drift into orbit, turn my systems off and wait for rescue. If I knew then what I know now, that's exactly what I would have done, but my head wasn't exactly clear back then. My tactical display showed a huge circle around Haven Shore and a lot of the sea beyond. They had a defensive shield! "That changes my plans a little." I planned to land on a small, nearby island, too far away to threaten the main island but close enough so someone might come and pick me up.

Three fighters came towards me, fast and agile with a

really slim profile and four pod engines. They had me dead to rights, and they knew it. They flew so close that I could feel the hull of my ship shudder, hear their screaming thrusters. I spotted a small piece of land below and made a decision. "Well, I can't tell you I come in peace, so hopefully the bullet holes and scorch marks tell my story for me." I cut the thrusters and let the ship fall.

"Crashing," Lurk croaked as he buried himself in the collar of my shirt.

"You're such a pessimist," I said. "I just want to land before they decide to blow us out of the sky. That means quick, and there's no velocity like terminal velocity. We'll be fine." Hearing the plan out loud made me laugh and roll my eyes. "Unless there was too much damage to one of our thrusters, then we'll pinwheel for a second or two before impact and die."

I watched as the altimeter crossed the thousand metre threshold and said; "Here goes!" I activated the thrusters and sighed as they fired evenly, reducing the speed of the cargo shuttle just in time for a nice, easy touch down.

I got out of the pilot's seat and had to fight with the cockpit door for a few minutes before it opened. The sounds of those fighters landing filled my ears. "Here they come," I laughed giddily. I fell through a hole in the cabin floor on my first step, landing with a thud on the fine white sand beneath the ship.

I sat up, coughing through a face full of the white stuff, unable to open my eyes.

"Hold it right there!" shouted a stern female voice. It was

deep, from a large woman, for sure, with a great deal of authority.

I held up my hands and tried not to cough. I still couldn't open my eyes. "I come in peace, just me and my pet lizard. Oh, and a completely broken, deactivated bot." I coughed a couple times then tried to scrape the sand off my tongue with my teeth. "Did I just fall through the deck of my ship?"

"Hold on," said a male voice. "Here's some water, keep your eyes closed." He said before squirting water from a bottle, clearing my eyes and the rest. I opened them to see a smallish guy and a giant woman. They were both in heavy combat armour. "I'm Sergeant Remmy Sands, Haven Shore Rangers. I'm guessing you're not an Order of Eden Admiral?"

"I wouldn't even believe he's an Order pilot," said the giant woman who had her rifle pointed at me.

"Hell no, man. I'm a former defence pilot, used to work for a travelling carnival. I got stuck on Iora and man do I have a story for you," I told him. I was so happy to be there, that it took me a moment to realize that whole panels from the underside and port side of the ship had been shot through. It didn't look like the ship would take off again.

The large woman laughed and nodded. "A carnie? Now, that I believe."

"You wouldn't be looking for pilots, would you?" I asked.

"Let's get you processed," Sergeant Sands said. "I need you to carefully give Dottie there all your weapons. Don't make any sudden moves."

"On the sand there," the giant woman said. She must

have been two and a half metres tall, and I thought I was tall at a little over two.

I dropped one pouch of suppression balls, then the other, then Needler, and then my Heavy Hitter, and finally Slagger. For reasons I cannot comprehend, Lurk jumped out onto the sand and I scooped him back up. "You are not a weapon, you are a memory lizard," I told him. "Sorry," I held him up. "Just a toy, really. He's got a few petabytes worth of memory and I keep all my personal stuff in him. I could pass him on to the Rangers or whatever, I downloaded some pretty cool stuff from a commercial building a while ago."

"Scanner verifies," Remmy said. "It's a toy. No problem. There's an old bot chassis in your bag that could be trouble though."

"I hear you guys have a cure for the Holocaust Virus. It got in him a few weeks ago, I'd like to get him cleared and rebuilt if I could. I'll pay, I've got some plat."

"The shops are backed up, but I'm sure you can get him fixed when they have time. It'll cost some luxury credits, but if you're a decent pilot, I'm sure you'll get a chance to earn some," Remmy replied, helping me to my feet. I watched the giant woman, who was actually quite attractive, I don't mind saying, gather my guns into a sack she expanded from her belt as the little guy went on. "You have any objections to a painless brain scan?"

"You might be shocked at what you find," I told him. "Or at least a little freaked out."

"We won't be recording, or looking deep. We just ask a few questions and watch for indicators that you're a spy from the Order. If you don't want to agree to it, then processing will take longer, but you could eventually make it to Haven Shore. The military are going to start demanding them though, so if you want to fly anything, you may as well."

"Then I don't mind, scan away, just expect the unusual and unpleasant," I replied. "No Order sympathy though."

"I have a feeling I know which fighter wing will want you," Dotty said with a smirk.

"Don't get his hopes up," Remmy replied.

The narration stopped, and a series of records surrounded Alice. She hadn't realized that it was nearly midnight. There were the results of his body and brain scans, which showed some malnutrition but no indication that he was a spy for the order. He only spent five nights in the intake facility on the island. During that time he studied, finished the qualifier tests to become a civilian pilot, the basic combat qualifier, and then earned access to the military entrance tests. He finished those on day four, and then entered a dogfight simulation using a brain-bud he bought with one hundred and sixty five platinum that he converted to luxury credits.

The direct to brain simulation allowed him to fly against members of Haven Fleet, then still called Triton Fleet, and every other player who wasn't an official pilot. He got Commander Minh-Chu Buu's attention, the leader of Samurai Squadron by the end of the first day when he hunted down and obliterated his girlfriend and gifted pilot, Ashley

Lamport in a simulated asteroid arena. He was also the last man standing for that round.

The next day he was in the barracks, and within another week he was a newbie in Samurai Squadron. They were desperate for pilots, and finding someone like him was a boon. Minh-Chu wasn't easy on him though. Physical training, difficult simulations and drills were a constant for two weeks before he got to sit in the cockpit of an Uriel fighter. It was quick training, but Minh-Chu Buu's report said; "Most of the work is already done with this one. He is in excellent physical and passable mental condition. Some more militarization is in order, but as a pilot he understands discipline, the importance of following orders, the chain of command, and has the skills to fly with us. I'll continue to develop him, and he'll be an excellent member of our fleet."

He was given the callsign; 'Carnie' and accepted into Samurai Squadron, the fighter wing of the Revenge, which had left for the Iron Head nebula on an important mission some time ago with her father in command.

Even though she was satisfied with the information she dug up on Noah Lucas' fate, one question bothered Alice. "What happened to Theo?"

PART THIRTY-FIVE

"I could find no record of a robot named Theodore anywhere in storage, servicing or acquisition records. Would you like to try another search?" Roomie asked.

"Gah!" Alice barked, throwing her hands up. She hadn't been able to find him either. A chime from the door, the gentle tinkling of small bells, told her that someone was waiting outside.

She looked at herself; she was in her loose, stretchy dress and it was pulled a little out of shape. There was a soy sauce stain on its collar from the chicken ramen she had for a snack. Two empty bags of Rice Poppers were beside her on the sofa and three empty Fruit Blaster bottles littered the coffee table in front of it. "Just a minute!" she called, alarmed.

Her dress from the night before was discarded onto a chair along with the delicate undergarments she'd worn with it. She grabbed them on her way to her bedroom and came out a minute later in vacsuit, pulling her hair into a short ponytail. The door chimed again. "Just a few seconds!" she shouted as she pulled her empty bottles and bags together in her arms, ran them to the kitchen counter and dumped them there. "Come in!" she called.

The door opened automatically and Iruuk loped inside. "I couldn't sleep and saw that your light was on. Are you all right? You look like you've been running."

"Just a little frustrated," she said. "Trying to find a lost robot."

"Oh?" he asked, his caramel coloured fur ears pointing straight up. "The same ones you found while you were with the Rangers?"

"No, a different robot, this one is a part of that classified project I'm finishing up. I got the report put together, and there are some strategic points that could help Fleet, but this is more of a personal, completionist thing. There might be a bot still infected with the Holocaust Virus somewhere on the island. Inactive, but still there."

"Then we have to hunt it down and destroy it," Iruuk said.

"Or cure it?" Alice offered. "We could load the antivirus and cleaning program onto a chip and fix it."

"Oh, that would work too. Want me to help you find it?"

"Sure, your clearance is high enough," Alice said. "His name is Theodore, and the last images of him looked like this." She brought up images of his partially melted head and battered chest.

"Are you sure you shouldn't bring him to recycling when you find him? There's not much left."

"I'm doing it as a favour for the subject of the report," Alice said quietly. "So, no."

"More and more interesting. Was he the last to have the machine?

"Theodore," Alice corrected. "Yes. Noah Lucas had him."

"Does Noah own property? Where is he now?"

"He's with the Samurai Squadron on the Revenge," Alice said. "I didn't find an apartment. He's in line to be assigned one here."

Iruuk brought the files for Noah 'Carnie' Lucas up and looked through his residency records. "From intake, to the barracks, then to the Revenge. The bags he checked into his bunk aren't large enough to carry Theodore's chest. His head, maybe."

"Security would have detected it if he brought it aboard the Revenge. They would have had to turn it on and inspect him," Alice added.

"None of that happened," Iruuk said. "What about Noah's money?"

"What do you mean?"

"Where did he spend it?"

"His luxury grant went to..." Alice trailed off as she looked through the expenditure records. "God, I hope he doesn't get pissed about us going through all this..." she said.

"Is it part of your mission? Do you need it for your report?"

"Well, Mom, er, Admiral Anderson told me to follow this

as far as I wanted, to do whatever I had to, and Theo is a big part of the report, so I guess so."

"Then we'll investigate now and apologize later," Iruuk said. "There it is! He spent luxury credits on several of Haven Shore's restaurants, a couple lounges, and one dance club. It looks like he visited the Alberton's Variety Club more than anywhere else – I hear there are a bunch of singers and comedians there. I've never seen it, you?"

"No, this is the first I've heard of it," Alice replied, looking at the images of the club's interior. There were tables with red tablecloths and a stage made for live entertainment.

"Oh, and he had platinum," Iruuk went on. "So, there was a brain bud he bought, then he gave some to Haven Fleet, Bunker Nine."

"What's that?" Alice asked, looking it up. An image of a heavily shielded bunker filled the holographic field in front of them. It had been cleaned up and restored. "There's a storage facility in there," she said. "He must have a locker."

"It's open, let's go!" Iruuk said, starting for the door.

"Wait!" Alice said, downloading the software package she'd need to cure the Holocaust Virus into her command and control unit and making sure she had a spare chip installed. There were five available, each the size of the tip of her little finger but able to store half a petabyte of data. "Okay, we're good."

Iruuk pointed to the small safe beside the door. "Sidearms?"

"I don't think we'll need firepower, but just in case," she

said, taking her sidearm and shoving it into the holster attached to her upper thigh.

The bunker was on the edge of an area of flat stone that was too windy and barren for the jungle to conquer. Framing for two large Haven Shore residence buildings was almost finished, they looked like thin girders reaching up from the earth like thin fingers. The faux wood walkways that led them down to the jungle floor swayed a little as they made their way.

"I don't see it, but we should be close to the bunker," Iruuk said.

They could see haven shore in the distance from where they were through the trees, they were close to emerging from the jungle. Just as they thought they'd break through into the clear air, the next walkway they took led them back in, and then the grey and black bunker came into sight. Two smaller entrances had been cut into the large armoured sliding doors, and they pushed through.

The floor within was made of dark, polished metal, and the walls were redecorated with brown stone panels. There was a holographic map detailing the purpose of each subfloor in front of them. Most of the space was dedicated to storage, and what wasn't off limits was offered to civilians who paid monthly or annual fees.

A tall, thin woman approached them immediately. Two bots wheeled behind her. They had long folding arms, rounded heads with a blue eye in the middle and balanced on one wheel. "Welcome to Bunker Nine, can I help you, Sir, Ma'am?"

"I'm investigating someone and need access to a storage unit," Alice said, showing her the unit number on her command and control unit.

"Can you tell me the nature of the investigation? I'm the curator here, I may be able to help."

"I'm afraid that's classified level seven," Alice said.

"I'll have to check the protocols for access," the Curator said, retreating to a windowed office. "One moment."

They waited as the Curator looked through holo displays that neither of them could see, and several minutes passed. Iruuk started looking something up on his own comm unit and nodded. "We're officers, investigating a classified matter," he said. "Regulations say we don't need her permission as long as we only open what pertains to our mission."

"Right, let's see if we can find directions," Alice said, raising her arm unit and checking the locker number against the holographic map.

"I already looked the location of the locker up," Iruuk said, leading the way. "This is fun, I'm glad I came."

"So am I," Alice agreed. The Curator was still doing something in her office, her back turned to them. "I have a feeling this lady's going to trip a breaker though."

They took the elevator down to sub-level twenty-one. "I wonder what this place was before?"

That was something Alice knew. "It was a safe storage space for equipment and supplies used to terraform Tamber. I checked another bunker just like this for the Rangers. I didn't know this one was here, but it's identical. Well, except for the new walls and flooring in the lobby."

"I wonder where they went, the terraformers?" Iruuk asked.

"Well, the terraforming of Kambis was their real goal, and that failed when the Omnivirus spread to this system, killing most of the people here. The couple million people who were living on Tamber until the Holocaust Virus hit were descendants of them, the workers who never left."

"That's a lot of workers."

"Yeah, but a very small population for an earth sized terraformed moon. The Carthans wanted to take over, to populate it, but they ended up facing war at home, so they couldn't afford it."

They came out into a dim space with thousands of lockers in a row. One of the curator bots that looked exactly like the ones above blocked them from leaving the elevator. "Move, please," Alice said.

It remained in place.

Iruuk shrugged and roared so loudly that Alice jumped. The bot moved aside. "Thank you, little machine," he said to it as they passed, patting it on the head.

It took them several minutes to find the locker, but eventually they came upon the half-height storage cabinet that Noah Lucas rented. "Feels like I'm opening a grave," Alice said as she used her Officer software to override the security code. It popped open and Alice was filled with a strange selection of emotions.

There it was: Noah's backpack, along with the jacket he

was wearing when he stole the cargo ship. It had been cleaned, but she recognized it right away. There were four locked cases at the bottom of the locker. He'd written Lurk, Heavy Hitter, Slagger, and Needler on them in orange grease pencil, indicating which lockbox had which item. It was as though she'd uncovered sacred artefacts that connected her to Noah's story.

"I don't see a bot," Iruuk said.

Alice picked up the box that was marked 'Lurk' first and handed it to Iruuk. "This goes directly to Fleet Intelligence tomorrow morning. The files stashed inside will earn Noah a lot of bonus luxury credits."

"What's a Lurk?" Iruuk asked, shaking the box beside his ear.

"Careful. Lurk was Noah's toy lizard. He managed to connect to a secure system and get some encrypted data that could be important. Synthetics aren't allowed on my dad's ship, so he left him here."

"Oh, they can be distracting. I always wanted a synthetic dog, but I was never allowed to have one."

Alice carefully took the backpack from the locker and opened it. From the front pouch she retrieved Theo's head, then the electrical tool kit from the side pouch, and finally the main body from the largest part of the bag. "We found him," she said.

"Well, the important bits, I guess. Do you know how to fix him?"

"Noah showed me," Alice said, putting Theo's chest back in the bag. "Let's go."

Iruuk carried the head while Alice slung the bag over her shoulder and secured the locker. They were met on the top floor by the Curator and her bots. Iruuk, seeing that the bots' eyes had turned red, held Theo's charred head up and pointed at it, looking at the droids blocking their way with a gleeful grin. "I like playing with robots."

They moved aside, leaving the Curator alone. Her arms were crossed. "You can't intimidate me, I've reported you to my supervisor."

"Does he answer directly to Haven Fleet?" Alice asked.

"I, uh," the Curator said. "That doesn't matter."

"If you just let us go, I'll make sure I mention you in my report to the Admiralty. I'll tell them how helpful you were, and how important your guidance was. Here's my clearance," Alice said, holding up her command and control unit up so it projected a hologram that assigned her to research a file that was classified. It had a file number and a date of issue along with clearance to investigate, but there were no specifics. She withdrew it before the Curator could finish reading. "Good enough?"

"I suppose, sorry for the misunderstanding," the Curator said.

"No problem," Alice said as they rushed past.

"Did you get her name?" Iruuk asked as they retreated through the outer doors.

"No, did you?"

"No. It's going to be hard to mention her helpfulness, I suppose."

"I guess so," Alice replied with a smile.

. . .

They were back at her apartment soon after, printing parts so they could re-join Theo's head with his torso properly. The cleanup work on the connector didn't take as long as she thought. For power she pulled a recharging cable from the wall and plugged it into Theo's battery port.

Within an hour they had his head back on, and he was ready to activate. Alice held her breath as she slipped the data chip into one of his chest ports and turned him on. There were a few twitches on the robot's face, then utter stillness for several seconds.

His good eye opened. "I'm back?" Theo asked. He looked to Iruuk, who was watching him expectantly and recoiled a little in surprise. "Well, you're new."

"Hi Theo, I'm an officer with Haven Fleet. My name is Alice," she said, trying to hide her excitement, unable to suppress a grin.

He looked at her, and the working side of his face seemed surprised. "Haven Fleet, as in Haven Shore?" he asked. "You look so much like Ayan, the woman from the presentation."

"Thank you, she's my mother," Alice said. "How do you feel?"

"My legs and arms are absent, along with much of my stabilization systems. I'm not going to be much use to anyone like this, you know. The Order of Eden control commands have been overridden, and all murderous tendencies are gone. What a relief. The data input record says you cured me, is that true?"

"I did," Alice said. "What's the last thing you remember?"

He gasped, momentarily overcome with shock, then worry. "I tried to kill Noah! Is he all right?"

"He's fine. I think he had to leave you behind because the queue for the robot repair shop is pretty long."

"Six weeks, three days," Iruuk said. "That's an improvement."

"Where is he? He was my master, you know."

"I know, and I'm not planning on changing that. He became a pilot with Samurai Squadron. He's on an important mission with my father."

"Oh, he loved flying," Theo said, sounding pleased. "I'm sorry I'm not with him, but he must be very happy there."

"I think he is," Alice said. Iruuk was performing a deep scan on Theo, holding his comm unit closer to the robot's chest. Alice couldn't believe that Theodore the robot was on her sofa. It was as though something she dreamt stepped into the real world.

"Alice, there is a data chip affixed to my chest plate, do you know what it is?" Theo asked, doing his best to look down.

She noticed it then, tucked under a piece of tape. Alice pulled it off and read the scrawl across it. *Play me when you're fixed.*

"I think that's Noah's writing," Theo said.

"Want me to play it?" she asked.

"Yes, please."

Alice held it up. "Roomie, run a safety scan on this then play it back if it's safe."

"Scanning," Roomie said. "Playing."

An image of Carnie appeared in front of them. He was in his black Samurai Squadron uniform: a lightly armoured black vacsuit that covered him from neck to toe and a heavy black bomber jacket. "Hey, man. If you're awake and clear-headed, that means I found someone to fix you. I tried to find a shop or an independent tech who knew what they were doing right until I left the system, but everything was back-logged. Some of 'em don't even take bribes, not that I had the plat to really get someone to put you ahead of the other bots getting fixed up. Anyway, you're awake now, and I hope you're surrounded by people you can trust. If not, get away, and show anyone from Fleet this message or give them my service number. Tell them you belong to me and they'll take care of you. Man, I hope you wake up surrounded by good people though."

Noah cleared his throat and ran his hand over his finely braided blonde hair. "We had one hell of an adventure together, didn't we? I managed to find a new family in Samurai Squadron, a bunch of fliers that are going to kick some Order ass. As much as I hate leaving you behind, I know you'd want me to follow this, to get out there and help people. This is the best way I can figure on how to do that, and when I get back you'll be the first guy I go looking for. Don't wait for me at my locker, though. Go hang with good people from Fleet, find some way to help, I'm sure they can find a job you'll like in Haven Shore, and if they don't, just tell them I'm your master and wander off, go see a lady named Persephone in the Alberton Club, she'll set you up.

Don't take less than nine plat an hour, though, you're worth it, especially if you get new skin and a nice suit. I'll be on the Revenge, so watch the arrival board for it." Noah sighed and shook his head. "I can't tell ya how much I miss you, man. You got me through a whole trip across hell, and I can't wait to see you back on your feet. To whoever fixed him up:" the hologram looked directly at Alice. "If you're trying to steal him, I'll find you, and I'll have military support, so reconsider. If you're doing it out of the kindness of your heart or for a few credits, I'll definitely pay you well when I get back. I'll have some luxury credits to throw around."

His image looked back to Theo then. "All right, that's all the time I've got, so good luck, man, and I'll see you as soon as I can." The hologram faded.

Alice looked to Theo, who seemed almost too still. "How do you feel?"

"I miss him," Theodore replied. "But something strange has happened. I am free," Theo said. "The directive to serve one master has been overwritten with a new loyalty program, so I am free, and it seems like Noah wants me to be." He looked down then back up at Alice, then Iruuk. "Well, I'm as free as anyone can be without arms or legs."

Iruuk burst into laughter, slipping from the sofa to the floor. Alice didn't find it quite as funny, but laughed a little and said; "I want to have you repaired," she said. "So when Noah gets back home you're there to..."

Iruuk's laughter stopped suddenly and he looked at his command and control unit.

"Everything okay?" Alice asked.

Iruuk looked at her with alarm. "Alice, something important has come up."

"Did something come up on the scan?" Alice asked, patting Theo's chest plate. Theo's head turned towards Iruuk with a jerk.

"Oh, him? The virus is gone, his file integrity is good, and all his internal systems are functional." Iruuk took a deep breath before continuing. "It's the Triton. They've arrived with Freeground Alpha and a fleet of Nafalli ships, but the Revenge has been marked as missing in action."

"What? Noah is on the Revenge," Theo said, looking to Alice, back to Iruuk and then back to Alice. "We have to find him."

"We will," Alice said. "That is, if they don't get here before we have a chance to. That's my father's ship."

The adventure continues in Spinward Fringe Broadcast 11: Revenge.

For more information, please visit:
www.patreon.com/randolphlalonde
or
www.randolphlalonde.com

THE SPINWARD FRINGE SERIES

(In chronological order)

ALSO BY RANDOLPH LALONDE

Highshield

Brightwill

Dark Arts

www.ingramcontent.com/pod-product-compliance
Lightning Source LLC
Chambersburg PA
CBHW070845260626
47170CB00007B/2503